THE SOUTHERN LAWYER

PETER O'MAHONEY

After more than twenty years away from the law, Joe Hennessy is forced back into the courtroom...

The Southern Lawyer: An Epic Legal Thriller
Joe Hennessy Legal Thrillers Book 1

Peter O'Mahoney

Copyright © 2022
Published by Roam Free Publishing.
peteromahoney.com

1st edition.
All rights reserved. No part of this publication may be reproduced, stored in a retrieval system, or transmitted, in any form or by any means without the prior permission in writing of the publisher. This is a work of fiction. Any resemblance to any person, living or dead, is purely coincidental.

Cover design by Belu.
https://belu.design
All rights reserved.

ALSO BY PETER O'MAHONEY

In the Tex Hunter series:

**POWER AND JUSTICE
FAITH AND JUSTICE
CORRUPT JUSTICE
DEADLY JUSTICE
SAVING JUSTICE
NATURAL JUSTICE
FREEDOM AND JUSTICE
LOSING JUSTICE**

*****

In the Jack Valentine Series:

**GATES OF POWER
THE HOSTAGE
THE SHOOTER
THE THIEF
THE WITNESS**

THE SOUTHERN LAWYER

JOE HENNESSY LEGAL THRILLER BOOK 1

PETER O'MAHONEY

CHAPTER 1

CRIMINAL DEFENSE attorney Joe Hennessy was in danger.

He knew it the second he stepped back into the city of Charleston, South Carolina. After an absence of twenty years, he knew his return would be fraught with risks, threats, and violence. He knew his name would cause many long-forgotten grudges to stir, his secrets would create nerves for the wrong people, and his presence would cause great unease amongst the corrupt. He wasn't there to cause trouble, he wasn't there to stir up the past, but trouble always had a way of finding him.

Hennessy looked at his watch—11:05pm. He couldn't sleep. The heat had gotten to him again. He wiped his brow with the back of his hand, wiping away a thin layer of sweat, fighting through the jungle-like humidity. As he neared the edge of Hampton Park, walking along the dirt path, he noticed the shadow of a man fifty yards away. Hennessy looked over his shoulder and around the area—a black sedan had stopped nearby. Its headlights were off.

His wife often told him his greatest flaw was that he didn't know when to fight, when to forget, or, more importantly, when to run. He never knew when to run. It wasn't in his nature. He turned off the path and walked across the grassy area, directly towards the parked sedan. The other man turned, walking faster towards Hennessy.

Hennessy could see the man clearer now—six-foot, shaved head, with the shoulders of a linebacker. He was wearing a jacket. It was too hot for a jacket.

"Can I help you?" Hennessy called out. "Do you need help?"

"Joe Hennessy." The man's voice was deep. "There's someone that wants to talk to you." The man continued towards Hennessy, slowing once he was within ten feet. He stopped and looked up at the lawyer's towering figure. "He's waiting for you in the car."

"Tell your friend that I'm busy," Hennessy stepped past the man, brushing his shoulder into him.

The man reached out and grabbed Hennessy's arm, gripping it tightly. The grip caused Hennessy to turn, and, on instinct, he threw a solid left hook into the man's ribs. The man doubled over, falling to his knees, holding his side and exhaling in large gasps.

The back door of the nearby sedan swung open, and another man stepped out. Henry Cruise. Hennessy sighed. Cruise had aged since Hennessy had last seen him, but that look, that unmistakable glare, was still present. He was balder now, heavier, and his stomach protruded out. He was dressed in black trousers with a crisp white shirt, along with his trademark suspenders.

"I should've known that Joe Hennessy wouldn't have been threatened," Cruise called out and then looked at the man on the ground. "Get up, Dave."

The first man rose to his feet, rubbing his side, before he pulled his jacket back to expose his waist. He was carrying a handgun, a Taurus G2c Compact.

Cruise stepped back inside the sedan. Dave removed the weapon from his belt, holding it in front of him, and indicated towards the car. Hennessy groaned and then walked towards the open door of the sedan. He looked around his surroundings, perhaps for the final time, and stepped inside. He left the door open, but Dave pushed it shut from the outside.

"I never thought I'd see you in Charleston again," Cruise said. He'd moved across the back seat to the other side of the car, allowing enough room for Hennessy to sit down. "I thought you were done with the law for good. There were a lot of people who were happy when you left the prosecutor's office."

"Henry Cruise." Hennessy leaned back on the beige-colored seat. The leather seats were spotless, but the heavy smell of cigar smoke was unmistakable. "You've aged."

"Haven't we all?" Cruise scoffed. "How long has it been? Ten, fifteen years?"

"Twenty."

"Twenty years? Really? Where did that time go?" Cruise smiled. "I was surprised to hear you've come back to the law. And more than that, you've jumped the fence and switched to the dark side. The thing is," Cruise rubbed his fingers together, "my current defense lawyer has had a heart attack and I need a new one. And as I hear it, you need the money to save Luca's Vineyard." Cruise took a cigar from the box next to him and clipped the end of it off. He pressed a button on the door and put the window down, and then lit the cigar, taking a long drag before blowing the smoke outside. "It's good that you named that place after your son."

"Don't talk about my son," Hennessy responded.

"After twenty years, you're still touchy about it? Ok," Cruise said. "Been back to church, Joe?"

Hennessy shook his head.

"That's a problem." Cruise studied the end of his cigar. "We don't like non-religious folk around here. You can't trust them."

"I can't trust you and you go to church every Sunday."

"Now that's the Joe Hennessy I remember. Never short of a sharp comeback," Cruise smiled before he sucked back on his cigar again. Cruise's once firm jawline had disappeared under a layer of fat, and his pale skin was now spotted by moles. His eyebrows were messy, his lips were cracked, and his forehead was covered in beads of sweat. "I need you to take on my case, Joe. I know you, and if you're still the same caliber of lawyer you were twenty years ago, then I need your expertise."

"I'm busy."

"With the murder case you took on? I hear the Taylor family doesn't have much money to their name. I'd be surprised if they had enough to cover your expenses." Cruise scoffed. "I'm talking money, Joe. Real money. A fifty-thousand-dollar retainer. And I know that's the only reason you came back to Charleston. I know that and you know that. You're only here to earn enough money to keep the banks off your back. A few poor seasons in the vineyard, I hear. That's got to hurt the hip pocket, especially if you've come back here."

"You're involved in a side of the world that I haven't seen for a very long time," Hennessy responded. "And this isn't exactly the famous

Charleston hospitality I remember. You approach me in the dark, force me to sit with you in a sedan, and blow smoke in my face. Not the type of friendly introduction I'm used to."

"Fine." Cruise grunted. "Fifty thousand as a retainer and an extra fifteen thousand if you win."

Hennessy drew a breath, sat up straighter, and looked out the window.

"I thought so. Money always talks," Cruise smiled. "I'll see you tomorrow—2pm at the Five Corners Art Gallery. We can discuss the details of how you're going to take over my case." Cruise indicated to Hennessy's door with his cigar. "And try not to beat up any more of my guys before then."

Hennessy held his stare on Cruise, and then reached for the door. He opened it and stepped out of the sedan without saying another word. Dave had remained waiting on the sidewalk, his gun back under his jacket. He glared at Hennessy before he walked around to the driver's door of the sedan.

Under the bright South Carolina night, under the smells of springtime in Charleston, the sedan pulled out from the curb and drove around the corner.

Hennessy knew going into business with Cruise would be a bad idea, he knew he was inviting danger into his world, but Cruise was right about one thing—the only reason he came back to the law was to save his vineyard.

CHAPTER 2

IN A city that had built its reputation as a place that accepted all faiths, Joe Hennessy was struggling with his own. He hadn't stepped foot inside a church in twenty years, ever since he carried the casket of his ten-year-old son out of one of their front doors. How could he have faith when so much was taken from him? He was angry for so long, filled with so much fury, drowning in a sea of grief. For years, the depths of grief had summoned and beckoned, inviting him to step into it, seeking to lure him into its grasp and drag him into the vacuum of agony. He'd been in the midst of grief many times before—in the blackness, gasping for air, struggling to breathe, fighting against the nothingness—only to wake in pools of sweat. In the depths of his dark anguish twenty years earlier, he walked away from the church, turned away from his faith, but as he aged, as the end came nearer, he began to question his beliefs again.

Hennessy walked deep in thought, hands tucked into his pockets, taking in the morning sunshine as it spread across Colonial Lake. A tidal oasis on the Charleston peninsula, Colonial Lake was a locals' hangout—tucked away from the tourist hotspots, it was frequented by residents who enjoyed jogging, rollerblading, or walking around its splendor. The trees were mature, the walkways wide, and deep in spring, the flowers were stunning. The scents provided constant pleasure for the nose, hits of jasmine mixed with the soft smells of pink wisterias. Groups of ducks were dotted along the edge of the lake, birds were chirping, and in the quiet morning, the ambiance was serene.

"Henry Cruise?" Wendy Hennessy walked beside him, looking up at the man she'd been married to for more than three decades. "I remember the name. You don't forget the sort of things he was messed up in—money laundering, bribery, corrupt deals. The rumors were endless. You even tried to prosecute him once for money laundering. Are you sure you want to work for a guy that approaches you in the dark?"

"Intimidation matters to men like Cruise. Although he's almost 70, he still thinks he wields the power he once did. He's an angry man, and intimidation was always essential to his business," Hennessy said. "It's fifty thousand, plus an extra fifteen if we win. I know it's a bad situation, but we need the money, Wendy. I'll have expenses for this case, but we can put down fifteen, maybe twenty-thousand, and get the bank off our back for a while. That'll give us a chance to get through another growing season, and maybe, if the weather stays good, we can have a great year on the vineyard, and I can forget about living in Charleston again."

"But is the money worth it? You're stepping into a dangerous world, Joe. This wasn't what we had in mind when we decided you'd come back here. We discussed working on small cases—nothing too dangerous and nothing too deadly. And you don't know this world as well as you used to. A lot of things have changed in twenty years."

Wendy Hennessy had come from a great South

Carolina family, one that had been in the area for hundreds of years. She had great respect for the history of her state, from the Native Americans that inhabited the area, to when her forefathers first arrived in 1795, all the way through to raising her own children in Upstate South Carolina. She was staying at the vineyard while her husband worked in Charleston, although she enjoyed driving down occasionally to see her husband, shop, and drink coffee with old friends. She'd driven the two hours and forty-five minutes earlier that morning, leaving home at 5am so she could enjoy a full day on the Peninsula.

"I'm not losing Luca's Vineyard, Wendy. I already lost my son once. I'm not going to lose the only thing left that is keeping his memory alive." Hennessy stopped and looked across the lake. "I know you're worried, but the only reason I'm back here is to earn money. Defending people like Henry Cruise is the quickest way for us to get the bank off our back."

Two boys and two girls, no older than ten, giggled and laughed as they rollerbladed past them. Hennessy watched the children, and his mind drifted back to his son. Wendy reached up and rubbed his shoulder, worried for the man she'd adored for more than thirty years.

"Are you sure you're not taking on too much? You've already got one murder trial on the books, and then you've got a client with a DUI and another charged with breaking and entering. Taking on this one sounds like it will overload you."

"There's always more than one case," he said. "I can manage it. I've got a good assistant, and I'm here to work."

"It's ok if we lose the vineyard," Wendy's tone was

soft. "We can sell it, pay off the bank, and start somewhere new. We could rent a house until Casey finishes school, and then maybe buy a travel-trailer and tour the country. We don't need to keep the vineyard."

Hennessy looked to the ground and shook his head. "I can't lose Luca's Vineyard. I just... I can't."

Hennessy began to walk again, and Wendy strode faster to keep up.

"I was stumped before," Wendy tried to lighten the mood. "I was trying to remember how to spell 'cesarean,' so I looked it up in the dictionary. I was looking under the letter 's,' but then I remembered it was in the C-section."

Hennessy shook his head, a small smile escaping from his lips.

"Oh, you don't think that's funny?" she smirked. "Well, did you hear about the actor that fell through the floorboards yesterday? He's ok. He was just going through a stage."

Hennessy tried to suppress his grin, but his dimples showed and gave him away.

"At least you can still smile," Wendy laughed. "Although I have noticed your hair is starting to go grayer on the sides. But I must say, I like the salt-and-pepper look. It makes you look distinguished."

"Distinguished or just old?" Joe smiled. "How's the vineyard coping without me?"

"Oh, it's falling apart. I don't know how we can survive without you."

"There's no need for sarcasm. I know that you're more than capable of running the entire operation. I've never met a smarter, or more capable, woman, but you could at least make me feel like I was somewhat valuable to the place."

"Of course," she tucked her hand into his arm. "We miss you up there—Casey, especially. We know you need to be down here to earn money, but Casey's sixteen now. She likes having your large presence around to scare away the boys and, trust me, they're all looking at her now. She's growing up to be a very beautiful woman."

Hennessy stopped walking as he watched a patrol car pass the end of the road. The patrol car eased around the corner before continuing to monitor the area. Wendy watched her husband before turning the focus back to work. "How's the murder case with Zoe Taylor coming along?"

"Slowly." Hennessy shook his head. "We're lucky there's not a lot of solid evidence. They've indicted her for the murder of her ex-boyfriend. She claims she didn't stab him, but there are witnesses that say they saw her running from the scene, there's blood on her clothes, and she was heard threatening to stab him the day before."

Joe and Wendy continued walking and talking, chatting about the heat, the humidity, and the recent storm. Wendy talked about the drive down from the vineyard in Upstate South Carolina. Joe talked about the beauty of Charleston in spring. As they walked, they reminisced about their past lives in the city. The long dinners, the nights out at bars, the mornings spent recovering by the river. They smiled as they talked about their son. His early days, his school years, his weekend football games. They remembered his smile. His laugh. His great jokes. They remembered his drawings, the ones they put on the fridge, and they remembered his athletic trophies.

After they finished the lap of Colonial Lake, they walked along Broad St. in silence, each of them fighting their own feelings of grief. After not saying a word for two blocks, they stopped outside the Five Corners Art Gallery.

Wendy glanced up at the building. The Federal-style building had a symmetrical rectangular facade, four bays, paneled balustrades, a double-storied central block, and an entrance with unadorned windows. The building had been painted a clean white, with a small, discreet sign above the door. Built by a wealthy merchant in the early 1800s, the neoclassical building stood out, even in an architectural heaven like the Charleston Peninsula.

"I didn't think you'd come back to Charleston and then get into art," Wendy commented as she peered through one of the windows.

"Hey, I'm cultured." Joe looked around the doors and then nodded towards the window of the gallery. There was no sign of anyone inside, or any lights on, and there was a closed sign hanging on the door. "Henry Cruise owns this place. This is where the police raid happened and where they found five small stolen paintings, but Cruise claims he was set up."

"That's a likely story. What was found?"

"Five Stephen Scully paintings were taken in the raid. They were part of a series. The cops are saying that Cruise stole them and planned to sell them privately. Three of the paintings were stolen in the 1980s, and two were stolen the week before the raid. It was the first time in forty years that all five of the series were in the same place at the same time."

She whistled. "Stephen Scully's are worth a small fortune. Actually, remove the 'small'. You think he did it?"

"I don't think it matters."

"Be careful, Joe," Wendy looked at him with a tender glance. "As long as guys like Henry Cruise are alive, they're dangerous. People think that they've faded away into obscurity, but just because they've lost a bit of muscle doesn't mean anything. Men like that who are still trying to cling onto power can be the most dangerous of all."

"I know what I'm getting myself in for," Joe ran his hand along the edge of the building, studying the walls, looking for any cracks. "Just doing a little investigating before I meet with Cruise later today."

"Don't you have an investigator for that?"

"I hired Damien Bates for Zoe Taylor's murder trial, but I don't trust that man at all. Unfortunately, he's the only investigator I can afford at the moment. He's working on Zoe's case, but I don't think I want him on this one. I might look around and see who else is available."

Joe led them around the edge of the building. There was a small driveway between it and the neighboring house. There was some graffiti—art to a different generation—and a number of puddles. He noticed a lack of surveillance cameras near the back entrance to the gallery, but noted there was a steel-door with a deadbolt and keypad at the end of the driveway. He studied the door and then tried to open it. It was locked. He slammed his shoulder against it. It didn't move.

"Not easy to break in," he said as he stepped back. "It'd have to be a professional job if it was a setup."

"If it was a setup," Wendy said as they followed the building back to the edge of the street, back to

Broad St.

Joe looked up and down the street—the morning tourists were beginning to venture out, gathering in groups, ready to snap a picture at a moment's notice. Joe liked the tourists—they brought with them smiles, a calm sense of freedom, and a jovial nature. They were always there, a part of the Charleston landscape as much as the architecture, ready to enjoy the famous Southern hospitality.

"Joe?" Wendy tugged his shirt sleeve. "Is that man staring at us?"

"I see him." Joe placed his hand on the small of Wendy's back and moved in front of her. "Go back to the apartment."

"Who is he?"

"I'm not sure, but I saw him earlier, maybe fifteen minutes ago." Hennessy's jaw clenched. "You need to go back to the apartment. I'll meet you back there."

"Where are you going?"

"I'm going to talk to him."

"You're going to talk to a man that's been following us? Why am I not surprised?" She stomped her heel, just a little bit. "If you're going, I'm coming with you."

He raised his eyebrows, ready to argue, but he saw the look in his wife's eyes. He knew that look. The one that meant, 'No matter how this goes, I win the argument.'

Joe turned and began to walk towards the man standing a block away. He stared the man down, at least 6 feet but stocky with a muscled chest, wearing a short-sleeve white button-up, black pants, and dark shades over his eyes.

As Joe and Wendy approached, the man turned

and jogged across the street away from them. He grabbed the front door handle of a black Range Rover and climbed in, slamming the door hard behind him. The car sped off, pulling out in front of the traffic. Horns honked, and one red sedan came to a screeching halt. The Range Rover didn't slow down.

"I told you, Joe," Wendy said as they watched the car disappear around the corner. "Working for Henry Cruise is going to get dangerous."

CHAPTER 3

JASON NORRIS surveyed the bar as his eyes adjusted to the dim lighting. It was always dark inside Monty's, even in the middle of a sunny afternoon. Located in North Charleston, the bar was a world away from the picture-perfect tourist streets of the Peninsula. It was where the lonely and broken-hearted gathered, escaping their lives under the spell of beer and bourbon. Half the red neon lights that hung on the side wall were blown out, the concrete floor was always sticky, and the tables were either scratched, dented, or broken.

Norris muttered his order to the bartender, then took his beer and moved to a booth at the side of the room. The booth looked like it hadn't been cleaned since the week before, and the smell of stale beer and burgers was strong. He flicked a stale chip off the table. A late 70s track by the band Blue Oyster Cult played on the jukebox—Don't Fear the Reaper. The melancholic rock song brought back memories of his long summers as a kid in the Lowcountry. Memories of an innocent time. Memories of the last time that he was close to his family.

Norris nursed his beer and nodded towards another lonely soul sitting hunched over at the far end of the bar. He couldn't remember the man's name, but many years ago, they'd shared a jail cell. Not someone that he was proud of knowing, but the nod between them was an acknowledgment that they had something in common—a past filled with crime, violence, and perhaps, regrets.

As he looked around the bar, Norris caught a glimpse of himself in the dingy mirror behind the bar. His dark hair was thinning. The lines around his green eyes were getting deeper, the jowls a little droopier. His skin had dried out from years of alcohol abuse. He was carrying more weight than ever before. His shoulders were slumped. The tattoos on his arms and knuckles were starting to fade.

"Don't fear the reaper," the song called out in the background. He grimaced at the thought. His time was coming. He could feel it in his bones. He was becoming more tired and more rundown. Puffing more when he jogged to cross the road. His knees were hurting. His eyesight was failing. His back pain was constant. As the days rolled past, as the months turned into years, he'd started to think about what came next, what came after his death, and whether it was worth fighting for. Sometimes, when he was alone in the world, when he only had himself for company, he could feel the heartbeat of something bigger, something more magnificent than his own minute presence, as if the depth of the world was calling out to him, calling him back to a place where his faith once led him, to a place where the glory and connection to his soul were unmistakable.

He squinted as daylight flooded into the bar from the open door. He glanced up and saw a tall figure in the doorway; a man, late fifties, who appeared like a foreign traveler who had wandered into an unknown land by mistake.

"Samuel," Norris called out. "Over here."

The man took an unsteady step into the bar and then relaxed, just a little, when he spotted Norris. "It's good to see you're still alive, Jason. It's been a while since we've heard from you."

"Still alive and kicking," Norris smiled. "Don't they make you wear a collar?"

"You've got the wrong religion."

"They're all the same to me." They shook hands. There was a stark contrast between their hands—one with scarred knuckles and tattoos, and the other's looked like it had been moisturized every morning. Norris nodded towards the bar. "Beer?"

"No alcohol for me," Samuel shook his head. "They got sweet tea?"

"Beer against your religion, is it?" Jason said with a scoff. Then, "Sorry, sorry. I didn't mean that. I take it back."

"That's ok, Jason. No offense taken."

Samuel Norris unbuttoned the top button of his light blue shirt and rolled up his sleeves. He was out of place, a holy man in foreign territory. He was a 'clean-skin'—someone with no tattoos, no scars, and no visible wounds. His clothes were spotless, his hair was neat, and his face was clean-shaven. He looked around, waved to the man at the end of the bar who was staring at him, and then ordered a sweet tea from the bartender. The bartender's eyes widened in surprise. He offered Samuel a Coke instead, and Samuel agreed. He returned to the booth with a can of Coke and a glass of ice.

"Sorry, Samuel," Norris said as his brother sat down. "I didn't ask you here to poke fun. I asked you here for your…" Norris' throat tightened. What had he asked his little brother there for? Advice? Help?

Forgiveness, maybe? He gripped the glass of beer with his strong fingers. "I guess I wanted some tips, coming from your religion, and I figured you were the best person to ask, being my brother and a pastor."

"It was your religion too, once."

"As a kid," Norris took another sip of his beer. It was now lukewarm. He felt as though he deserved it that way. "When Mom used to force us to say our Sunday prayers."

"You're still a part of the church."

Norris gritted his teeth. On a technicality, maybe. He hadn't seen his brother in more than five years, but somehow, the conversation started where it always ended—his lost faith. He often argued that Monty's Bar was his church—the place where he spent many years worshipping the great presence of alcohol, desperately trying to forget his past filled with violence.

"Nobody has heard from you in years, Jason." Samuel poured his Coke into the glass and took a small sip. "We all thought you were dead, buried somewhere around the country. Aunt Sally was asking about you last month. She asked if I knew where you were buried, so that she could at least drive past and say goodbye."

Aunt Sally, their mother's sister, was the one surviving older relative the brothers had left. When they were younger men, in their twenties, they made an effort to travel each Thanksgiving to her home near Lake Marion. She hadn't had children of her own, nor married, and the brothers were her only family.

"Glad to hear she's still alive."

Samuel smiled. "She's still got the canoes, and the

rope near the lake is still hanging there."

It was a well-worn, yet well-received, anecdote—one that the brothers could always return to. It was a memory they could take refuge in, like a comfortable home. Samuel couldn't suppress the laugh as he said the word 'rope,' and Jason smiled, leaning his head back a little as he remembered that summer day almost fifty years earlier. They'd gotten back to Aunt Sally's before church, and Jason had dared his little brother to swing on the rope and jump into the lake fully clothed. Samuel had taken up the dare but landed in the middle of the muddy shallows, covered head to toe in wet, stinking mud.

Jason grinned at the memory. "You thought it was so funny, and you were so proud that you'd fulfilled the dare. Fully clothed and all. Mom lost it... over your ruined Sunday best."

Samuel laughed, then nodded. They'd had to miss the service that day, but Aunt Sally made them fresh lemonade and hotdogs anyway. "I was trying to impress my big brother."

Jason let the silence fall between them for a moment. He looked at his younger brother and said, "Well, you succeeded."

"Come on." Samuel shook his head and rolled his eyes. His voice turned a little somber as he stared into his tall glass of Coke. "You've never respected what I do."

"That ain't true." Jason shook his head. "You're a pastor. A good religious boy. You made our mother proud right up to her final days... me, on the other hand, I was too busy breaking into homes to even say goodbye." Jason turned away and looked around the dark bar. "There are things that keep me up at night, you know, and I'm not just talking about Mom and her final breath. Other stuff. Lots of things. I'm almost sixty now. Well past the halfway mark of life. In fact, I'm pretty close to the end of it all." He paused and looked into his beer, avoiding eye contact with his brother. "But I've been wondering if it's too late to turn around now and go back to the beginning."

The jukebox went silent. Jason reached into his pocket for a couple of quarters, but he had no change.

"Here," Samuel said, passing a quarter to Jason. Jason grabbed his beer and walked over to the jukebox. Samuel followed him.

"Your pick," Jason said.

Samuel blinked at the jukebox a few times. "Give me a little bit of Boston."

Shaking his head, Jason selected a track by the soft rock band. "Peace of Mind. There ya go."

Samuel nodded along to the track and stood there with one hand on the jukebox as the jaunty guitar kicked in and the bright vocals followed. "I've got to admit, Jason, this is a world I don't see very often," he looked around the bar. "It's a behind-the-scenes look into the underworld."

"Stick with me, and I'll show you a whole lot of things you've never seen before."

Samuel nodded. "And if you stick with me, I can show you the opposite to this type of world."

Jason shot his older brother a meaningful look.

"What is it you wanted advice about?" Samuel asked. "Don't get me wrong; it's great to connect again. I've always worried about you, but you said you wanted advice?"

"I'm getting out of the game."

Samuel raised his eyebrows. "You're not working for Henry Cruise anymore?"

"No, I'm out," Jason drew a long breath. "And I want to do some work to try and change the things I've done in the past. Maybe even get into heaven and see Mom after I die. But… I just don't know where to even begin."

"Coming to a church service would be a great start."

"I just… I just feel it might be too late for that."

"It's not too late to make amends. It's never too late."

Jason shook his head and looked back down into his beer.

"The Lord will forgive you, Jason, for whatever you've done," Samuel reached across and rested a hand on his brother's shoulder. "But you have to ask for it, and you have to work on making a difference. Forgiveness doesn't come without sacrifice."

Jason looked up. "I don't know if I'm worthy of forgiveness."

"Of course you are. Anyone is, if you ask for it. But you have to truly want it."

"I've done some bad things, little bro, things that would make your stomach churn. But this last one, well, it was too much. It was the straw that broke the camel's back," he shrugged. "I want to see Mom in heaven, and I want to do the right thing, but I know I don't have long left to do it."

The jukebox played out till the end of the song. The two brothers stood there, silently bobbing along to a moment in time that reflected the past. Maybe it wasn't too late to go back to the start.

But if Jason Norris was ever going to find his way home, if he was going to find his faith again, it was going to take more than just a few prayers of forgiveness.

It was going to take one long Hail Mary.

CHAPTER 4

SOME PEOPLE were born into a life of crime, some were forced into it to survive, and some chose to watch the world burn, and for Henry Cruise, it was all three. Even amongst the crowds of corrupt businessmen he floated in, he stood out more than the rest, always notable in how immoral he would dare to be. From what defense attorney Joe Hennessy had heard, Cruise had managed to escape the clutches of the law through decades of wheeling and dealing, selling out everyone and anyone to survive.

Hennessy wiped his brow as he walked along the historic Broad Street toward the Five Corners Art Gallery. The afternoon was hot, the sun sweltering the streets with a sultry, humid bath that was usually associated with summer. Hennessy tried to stay in the shade as he walked, but it was making little difference. The fifteen-minute walk from his office to the gallery took him through the lower end of Downtown Charleston, highlighting a day in the life of the city—old sports cars parked outside large colonial-style homes, gardeners busy trimming bushes, and locals gathered on porches, talking loudly about the oppressive heatwave.

Since being watched the last time he'd visited the art gallery, Hennessy had taken extra care to ensure that he wasn't being tailed or followed. He'd walked a different route, but he was no spy—just a vineyard owner who'd returned to the law after a twenty-year absence. He knew that eyes—the wrong kind of eyes—were going to be on him during this case. He just had to keep out of the line of fire long enough to get paid.

He approached the Five Corners Art Gallery door. The sign still read 'Closed.' After his knocks went unanswered, Hennessy pressed a doorbell, and soon, the door was opened by a grim-looking Cruise. "Glad to see you're here."

There was no handshake, or a formal greeting, just a nod of acknowledgment. Cruise stepped aside and signaled for Hennessy to enter. The main area of the ground floor in the two-level building had been hollowed out to leave one large exhibition space for the modern paintings. The ceilings were high, the walls a stark white, and the remaining pillars were left as exposed brick. The paintings hanging up were modern—punches of color on large canvasses, the paint swished one way and then the other, trying to portray something that Hennessy couldn't understand. Still, he liked the colors. Cruise led Hennessy through the art gallery, which smelled sterile and clean, almost like a new car, to the back office. It was there that the distinct waft of cigar smoke began to tickle his nose.

The office was spacious—a large mahogany table sat near the window, a leather couch was on the left of the room, and a floor-to-ceiling bookshelf to the right. The smell of cigar smoke was now unmistakable. Cruise picked up the remote control for the air-conditioner, punched two buttons, and then stared at the box as it whirled into action.

"The gallery is temperature-controlled, but not out

here," he groaned. "This office almost becomes a sauna when it's hot."

"Saunas are good for the soul." Hennessy sat down in the leather chair opposite the desk. "Do you make a habit of trying to intimidate people in the middle of the night?"

"Intimidation is an important part of what I do." Cruise sat down in the tall black chair, leaned back, and then spread his arms and legs wide. He grinned a little. "People have to be aware of what I can do before I deal with them. I might be getting old now, but I want people to remember that I can dispose of them at a moment's notice."

"I have no interest in your games," Hennessy's tone was firm. "If I'm going to work for you, then you treat me with respect, and you leave your little schoolyard tactics for someone else. If I take this job, then we're on the same team, and I expect to be treated with respect."

"I knew I'd like you, Joe," Cruise smiled. "A no-nonsense sort of guy."

"And the retainer needs to be paid in full before I begin."

"Of course." Cruise clasped his hands and leaned on the table. "A month ago, there was a police raid on this art gallery. They found five stolen artworks leaning against the wall in the storeroom." Cruise shook his head and clicked his tongue. "Some artist, all pastels and pomp. Small paintings. No bigger than a picture frame, but apparently, they're worth a million each. I never saw them before in my life."

"Tell me about the artist."

"A man named Stephen Scully. I read about him after they arrested me—he painted in the 40s and 50s and was apparently the foundation for a lot of Postmodernism Art. I didn't know who he was, and when they showed me the pictures, I laughed outloud. How could those paintings be worth a million each? Ridiculous," Cruise shook his head. "The artist died in '85, but a lot of art collectors really value his work and think he'll be worth fifty times that in the future.

Hennessy raised his eyebrows. "If you didn't know about the paintings, then how did they end up in your gallery?"

"They were planted. The raid was just a ruse to frame me. Someone wanted me behind bars, and they figured the gallery was my weak point. I heard people were coming for me, so I had everything else covered. Guards, surveillance footage, and twenty-four-seven coverage at my home, vacation house, and my restaurant." Cruise sighed, shook his head, and leaned back in his chair. "But this was my ex-wife's gallery. Five years ago, she wanted it, and I bought it for her. When we were divorcing, I knew how much she wanted to keep it, so I fought her for it. And I won."

"How honorable."

"Divorce makes a man do crazy things, and I should know—I've had four," Cruise chuckled. "But I'd only had full ownership of the gallery for five days before this happened. Someone broke into the side door via the driveway and planted the artworks on the morning before the raid. And then as soon as I walk into the gallery that morning—bang," he clapped his hands together. "The police charge in and arrest me. Do you think I'd be dumb enough to keep stolen artwork in my own gallery? Come on. I'd sell them before I even got my hands on them."

"I looked at the driveway this morning. There are video cameras and a steel door with a strong deadbolt. If that's their entry point, then there was no damage. And why didn't the surveillance footage pick it up?"

"Don't you get it? My ex-wife is in on it. She gave them access. I didn't change the locks or the codes to the building. She turned the stupid cameras off five days prior, her last day here, and she still had access to the keys and alarm codes."

"You think your ex-wife set you up?"

"I don't think she's smart enough to do it, but she was definitely in on it." Cruise stood and indicated for Hennessy to follow him. "She was as dumb as a log, but very pretty. Great body. And she was a gold-digger. Always after more money."

Cruise walked out of the office, past the main gallery, and through a smaller door into the storeroom, where twenty paintings lay up against the wall. The storeroom was also temperature controlled, with large paintings covered in brown wrapping. It smelled of mothballs and stale paper.

"All legitimately acquired," Cruise pointed to the twenty-five paintings laying against the wall. "At least, legitimately acquired through the divorce."

"The defense is simple," Hennessy moved to study the back door more closely. He bent down and studied the lock, which appeared undamaged. "We'll argue that the paintings were here before you took full ownership of the gallery. We can paint your ex-wife as responsible."

"That's what I thought," Cruise grunted. "But two of the five paintings were reported stolen from a New York apartment on the day I took ownership. This

35

was all planned. My ex-wife was fighting and fighting to keep the gallery, and then suddenly, one day, she changed her mind, and the divorce was finalized. Someone got to her, probably offered her a lot of money, and then set me up."

"If it wasn't her, then who set you up?"

"That's the problem," Cruise leaned his shoulder against the wall next to a stack of paintings. "I don't know. If I can figure that out, then this case is over. My last lawyer, Tim Donnelly, said that he had no proof of anyone else being involved. He was pushing for me to take a deal, but then he had a heart attack. He's still in the hospital, and they say it'll take him months to recover. His secretary has agreed to send you all his files."

Hennessy walked around the perimeter of the storeroom, looking for any other sign or clue of damage. There was no scuffing on the walls. Nothing broken. Nothing out of place.

"Did you launder money through the art gallery?"

"Ha," Cruise scoffed. "Straight to the hard-hitting questions. I like that, Joe. Never afraid to hit hard, and never back away from the tough issues."

"You didn't answer the question."

"Ok. Sure," Cruise shrugged. "There may have been times when the art gallery's books were smudged. My ex-wife wouldn't know that, though. She left all the accounting up to me."

"That complicates things," Hennessy said. "If it's a setup, someone had to do the setting up. And if I'm going to launch a defense for you, then I'm going to need to know who did the setting up, or at least have some kind of alternative theory for how the artworks got into your office. The members of the jury aren't going to believe that a ghost set you up. You're going to have to give me something, especially if you're sticking to the story of being framed." Hennessy glanced up at the futile security cameras. "I need a lead, somewhere to start."

Henry Cruise bowed his head a little and sucked in a long, slow breath. "Y'all heard of Richard Longhouse?"

"Heard of him? I used to work with him. Once upon a time, we were both young lawyers in the prosecutor's office."

"Different career paths, eh? You go and make wine, and he goes on to become one of the most corrupt politicians this state has ever seen," Cruise said. "You should talk to Longhouse if you want the answers to the questions you keep asking."

"I'm not sure I'd be welcomed in his office. There's no chance that he'd accept a meeting with me," Hennessy shook his head. "I tried to take him down once. I knew he was doing shady deals when we were prosecutors, and I tried to prove it, but nothing happened. I figured he paid off the right people."

"Money does a lot of talking in powerful circles." Cruise walked out of the room, through the main gallery, and towards the front door. Hennessy followed. "Just talk to Longhouse. Go and see him at his home. He won't refuse you then. No good Southern man would refuse a man at his door. Besides, he owes me a number of favors, and it looks like it's time to cash them in. He's got connections all over this town. Deep connections." Cruise turned to face Hennessy. "But be careful with the questions you ask him because people have been known to disappear if they ask the wrong ones."

CHAPTER 5

FOLLOWING ASHLEY River Rd. twenty-five minutes from Downtown Charleston, Joe Hennessy drove through the alleys of tall established trees. Following the edge of the nearby river, the road still followed the same path it did when it was first authorized in 1691, with Colonial homes of a past era hidden behind iron gates and brick walls, some older than the Civil War. The grand homesteads were sought-after real estate—a world away from the busy streets of the city but still within easy driving distance.

"Why have iron gates if you're just going to leave them open?" Hennessy whispered to himself as he turned off the tree-lined street into one of the residences.

The gravel crunched under the tires as his truck hummed further up the drive. The grass was neatly clipped, the bushes trimmed, and there was a tire-swing hanging off one of the oak trees. When he came to the end of the long driveway, he parked next to a new Range Rover, spotless and clean. He stepped out of his truck, gazing up at the large Colonial-style house. The home sat on a sweeping acre of grassy lawns, former plantation lands, and had extensive views of the river nearby. The entrance to the home was stately, elegant, with two large pillars framing an impressive door. This house could be a tourist attraction, Hennessy thought. He walked to the front door and pressed the buzzer.

"Joe Hennessy. Here to see Richard Longhouse."

Hennessy pulled his hand away from the buzzer and placed his hand in his pocket as he stood at the gate to the colonial home. Someone on the other end was talking, but the sound from the speaker was distorted like a bad drive-thru service. He made out the word, "Who?" somewhere amongst the static.

"Joe Hennessy. I've been sent by Henry Cruise."

There was another muffled sound before he heard some shuffling behind the front door. The tall and heavy door slowly creaked open.

"Joe Hennessy," the man said. "My old friend."

Richard Longhouse smiled as he opened the door. It wasn't a welcoming smile—the grin was laced with distrust, unease, and fakeness. Longhouse was in his fifties, but his olive skin was tanned deep by the southern sun. He was tall and thin, well-groomed with a thick mustache. He was dressed in a short-sleeved crisp white shirt and blue chino shorts, and his hair was dyed brown in an attempt to cover the inevitable grays.

"Joe, Joe, Joe. My old friend. You're a lot taller than I remember. You've put on a bit of muscle too," Longhouse chuckled a bit. "I heard a rumor that you were back in Charleston, now practicing defense law. And by the looks of it, the rumors are true—you need the money to save your vineyard."

Hennessy raised his eyebrows. "How would you know that?"

"Don't act surprised, Joe. You must remember how things work around here. Everyone knows everyone's business. You talk. I talk. We all talk the talk. It's the Southern way." Longhouse squinted his eyes at Hennessy as if he was a fly that he wanted to swat away. "Why don't you come inside?"

Hennessy stepped through the impressive foyer, complete with a chandelier and spiral staircase to the back. He didn't linger, following Longhouse into the nearby office. Brown was the color of choice. The large table in the middle of the room was brown. The wood-paneled walls were brown. The leather chairs were brown, as was the bookshelf to the left of the room. The carpet was brown. The door was brown. The only relief from the brownness was a tall window at the back of the room, which looked over the luscious green lawns.

"Would you like a sweet tea?" Longhouse asked. "Or something stronger?"

"Tea is fine," Hennessy sat down on the leather armchair. The musty smell of leather was strong in the office.

Longhouse walked out of the office and returned moments later with a jug and two glasses. He poured the two glasses and handed one to Hennessy.

"I was hoping you and I would never cross paths again," Longhouse sighed and sat down in the other armchair. "The last time we talked, you tried to take me down. You accused me of fraud and taking money to approve an estate development. And honestly, you almost did it. You almost made my world crumble."

"I did," Hennessy said. "And I saw you do things that wouldn't look good for your hopes of becoming Governor."

Longhouse clucked his tongue again. A scent of sandalwood and vanilla shot out of an air freshener nearby. Along one of the walls, there were pictures and accolades—a framed degree in business, a master's in political science. On the far wall there was a photo of Longhouse with his arm around the current Governor and another one of him at dinner with former President George W. Bush. Or at least, Longhouse was in the background of George W.'s table.

"I'm a South Carolina Senator now, Joe. You can't just come in here and threaten me," Longhouse leaned forward. "Is it blackmail that you're after? I hear you need money, but I didn't ever think you were the type to resort to blackmail. You were always the good guy, standing up there with unshakable integrity and honor."

"I haven't come to make threats. I'm here to talk to you about Henry Cruise." Hennessy shot a glance over at Longhouse and saw the politician's lips twitch. "He's in some legal trouble. He told me you could help."

"Cruise said that I would help that son of a…" Longhouse didn't finish his sentence. He shook his head in amusement. "That guy has some nerve. But I'll admit that I've been to his restaurant a few times this year, but each time, it's almost come to blows. I can barely stand to be in the same room as him."

Hennessy furrowed his brow in confusion. "I take it the two of you aren't close anymore, then?"

"I can't stand the guy." Longhouse's voice was firm and dismissive. "He's dirtier than the pluff mud. I've got no connections to him anymore. None at all. And if I want to run for Governor, I need to stay far away from him."

"Cruise used to pull a lot of strings."

"The key term is 'used to.' He's an old man, and he's well past his prime. He's lost most of his power.

Nobody is scared of him. He's a has-been. An old mobster trying to hang on to the past. But I guess it's like that old saying—fear the man who has nothing to lose," Longhouse shrugged. "What's your interest here?"

"He's asked me to defend him."

"Right. Tim Donnelly had a heart attack, and that meant Cruise needed a new lawyer. And he chose you?" Longhouse pointed his skinny finger towards Hennessy. "Lucky guy, aren't you? But I'll give you one piece of advice for free—don't let yourself be a piece in his chess game. If you do, you'll end up getting burned. Or worse."

"What do you know about the raid on his art gallery?"

"Only what I've read in the papers."

"Really?" Hennessy raised his eyebrows. "You want me to believe that a man as connected as you are has heard nothing about a police raid on your associate's property?"

They locked eyes, neither man refusing to budge until Longhouse smiled and leaned back in his chair. "That's what I said, isn't it?"

"So you won't help him?"

"No chance."

"Then it seems I've been sent on a wild goose chase." Hennessy stood up and placed the glass of sweet tea on the table. "I'll see myself out."

Hennessy walked out of the room and into the large foyer, and Longhouse trailed him the entire way. Hennessy got to the front door, opened it, and stepped into the bright sunshine.

"Joe," Longhouse said as he leaned against the open front door. "Charleston has changed in the twenty years since you've been here. Be careful where you poke your nose."

CHAPTER 6

PRIVATE INVESTIGATOR Barry Lockett glanced over another line of data on his laptop, his eyes drifting from his computer screen towards the nearby mouth of the Ashley River. He loved working in the outdoors. He found being inside an office too much was suffocating. He would much rather take his laptop and sit on a park bench than work inside four walls, slowly being driven insane by boredom. For him, living meant being outdoors, seeing the sun, taking in its rays. It meant getting dirty, feeling the warm breeze on his face, and smelling the freshness of the ocean. He had no time for modern offices, with all their new equipment, clean seats, and fake niceness.

He sat on a bench in the White Point Gardens at the tip of the Charleston Peninsula, looking out to the mouths of the Ashley and Cooper Rivers as they emptied into the Atlantic Ocean. The park was covered in massive oak trees draped in Spanish moss, the sort of trees that photographers dragged newly married couples in front of for memorable wedding photos. It was busy in the park—tourists rode bikes past on the lakeside path, teenagers were kicking a soccer ball on the grass nearby, and a family was having a domestic dispute behind him. The perfect Charleston view, he thought.

Lockett wiped his thick forearm across his brow,

turned up the music on his earphones, and continued reading another line of data. As he worked, an older red pickup truck caught his eye. He watched as the old truck pulled into the parking lot near the park bench.

A man stepped out, wearing a shirt and tie with dress pants, and loosened his tie before removing it completely and throwing it back in the car. The man jogged across the street, briefcase in hand, and looked around.

"Barry Lockett?" the man asked as he approached.

"And you must be Joe Hennessy," Lockett said as he stood. The two tall men shook solidly and with respect, looking at each other eye to eye. "I didn't expect a defense lawyer to be driving a truck like that. Most lawyers around here drive new expensive cars to show off their excess wealth."

"I own a vineyard Upstate, and little clean city sedans aren't much good up there," Hennessy said, staring out at the river that was shimmering in the sunshine. "Nice spot. It's a pity your laptop interrupts the view."

"It's where I like to work," Lockett turned around. "Can't keep me indoors for too long. I go crazy if I'm locked up inside."

"And is that an accent I hear?"

"Australian," Lockett confirmed. "But Charleston's home now. I married a Charleston girl, fifteen years ago this month. Met her on a beach in Sydney and fell for her hard. She was on vacation, and I couldn't take my eyes off her. We stayed for a year in Oz, but she was close to her family, so she convinced me to move out here." He spread his arms wide to focus on the view. "And it's not a bad place, this South Carolina. Good weather, good people, and good food. Can't go wrong with that."

Barry Lockett's broad Australian accent was clear. He was mid-forties, with tattooed arms, scars on his knuckles, and a playful grin to match. He was tall, tanned, and tenacious.

"Do you miss Australia?" Hennessy dusted the park bench with his hand, placed his briefcase on the table, and then sat down. "I hear it's a pretty good place."

"Of course," Lockett sat back down and closed his laptop. "That place is heaven on Earth. The beaches…" he drifted off for a moment, "Mate, nothing beats the beaches of Australia. Long, pristine, untouched, and empty, with perfect wave after perfect wave rolling in. You could surf all day long and never see another person. But I've got kids now, and they've got their own American accent. I still get back to Australia every now and then, but Charleston's home." He looked out at the river in front of him. "Did you know that both these rivers are named after the same person? The Ashley River on one side and the Cooper River on the other were named after Anthony Ashley Cooper, an Englishman who never set foot in this country," Lockett said. "You've got to be pretty influential to get two rivers named after you."

"That's something I didn't know," Hennessy nodded in surprise. "Thanks for meeting with me. And you're right—it's nice to get outdoors. I've been hunched over paper files for the past five weeks and barely seen any sun."

"You said on the phone that you're on the lookout for a new investigator?" Lockett asked. "You need someone to help you out?"

"I've currently got a guy looking into a murder case for me, but I need someone else to help with another case."

"Who have you currently got?"

"Damien Bates."

"Ouch." Lockett sat back a little. "Not a well-respected name in my circles."

"You've heard of him?"

"Heard of him?" Lockett laughed. "Mate, I've had a few run-ins with that fella. He's foul, untrustworthy, and will never miss a chance to make a quick buck. I broke his jaw once, maybe ten years ago. He slapped my wife on the bottom, and I let him know that it wasn't appropriate behavior. The guy couldn't talk for a month, but I didn't hear anyone complain about that," he laughed. "But seriously, that man is a dirty, dirty dog."

"That was my first impression as well, but he's a lot cheaper than you."

"You get what you pay for."

"So true," Hennessy sighed. "I've taken a job that pays decent money, so I'm willing to hire a better investigator. Like I said on the phone, I'm defending Henry Cruise. I'm sure you've heard of him."

Lockett nodded in recognition of the name. Cruise's dominance of the underworld of South Carolina was decades long, and his reputation still packed a punch, even if his powers had dimmed. Cruise's name still garnered a reaction when it was spoken within earshot of anyone in the legal or law enforcement professions.

"I had a run-in with him once. I wasn't hurt. But the investigator that worked for him..." He shot

Hennessy a meaningful look. "He wasn't so lucky. Men like Henry Cruise aren't happy when you lose, let me tell you that. Cruise has a reputation built on exacting revenge on anyone that crosses him."

"You're not the first person to warn me off this case."

"I'm not even warning you, I'm telling you—if you get involved with Cruise, you'd better hope you win the case. Bare minimum," Lockett shook his head. "But winning doesn't guarantee your safety either."

"I've already decided to defend him, and I'm looking for someone to work as my investigator on it," Hennessy said. "If you're interested, I'm happy to pay the fees as we discussed on the phone. If you're scared of getting involved with Cruise, I'll ask someone else, no hard feelings."

"Scared? Mate, I grew up in a country where the spiders on the toilet seat could kill you. Nothing could scare me out here."

"Sounds dangerous."

"But what's life without a little bit of danger, eh?" Lockett grinned. "And I was thinking about my death last week. I decided that when I go, I want to be buried in the middle of nowhere in a spring-loaded coffin filled with confetti, so that in the future, some archeologist is going to have one crazy day at work."

"That's one way to go." Hennessy laughed before he clicked open his briefcase, took out a file, and handed it to Lockett. "If you do well with this case, I'll have more work for you. These are copies of the files that Cruise's last lawyer compiled. I need you to look through them and tell me if anything stands out to you. Anything odd or strange. I'd also like to know all the information that you know about Cruise as well."

"I'm on it, mate," Lockett said. He reached across and took the files. "I'll have my preliminary assessment for you tomorrow afternoon."

"Great." Hennessy stood and offered his hand to shake again. "I look forward to working with you."

Lockett shook hands with his new employer. "But a word of warning—working for Cruise may get dangerous."

"That's good," Hennessy smiled. "Because you're right—what's life without a little bit of danger?"

CHAPTER 7

JOE HENNESSY'S law office seemed miles away from the tourist-filled streets of Charleston, a serene sanctuary amongst the chaos of one of the country's favorite tourist destinations. That's how he preferred his office—a tranquil retreat, a place to spend time calmly thinking, a haven from the courts.

Located on Church St. in Downtown Charleston, his office was on the second floor of a plain brick building. The walls were soundproofed, the windows double-glazed, and only the hum of the air-conditioner could be heard above the silence. The view from the second-floor window was partially blocked by a large oak tree, which also sheltered the office from the rays of the burning sun. He rented the office for cheap from an old associate, who'd mentioned that the office had been empty for years.

Joe Hennessy rolled his sleeves up to his elbows, wiped his brow, and opened the file on his desk, trying to keep his focus on the person sitting in front of him.

Zoe Taylor was twenty-one, educated, and working as a manager for a tourist bus company. Five weeks after her birthday, she was charged with murdering her ex-boyfriend—convicted felon Andre Powers. Zoe didn't fit the typical murderer's profile—she spoke well, she dressed well, and was an otherwise law-abiding citizen. No school suspensions.

No run-ins with the law. Not even a parking ticket to her name. Her family was nice. Her home was nice. Her job was nice. Everything in her world was nice.

Everything except Andre Powers.

Andre was twenty-eight, unemployed, and had been to prison numerous times. Muscular, heavily tattooed, and piercing eyes. The ultimate bad boy for a nice girl like Zoe Taylor.

Zoe Taylor's case was Hennessy's first job after his return to the law. He'd known Frank Taylor, a hardware store owner and Zoe's father, during his previous time in Charleston, and he agreed to take on the case for a reduced fee. Hennessy needed the exposure that a murder case could bring, and the Taylor family needed the best lawyer their limited funds could afford.

Hennessy had five other files sitting on the side of his desk, almost screaming at him to look them over. They were minor cases—two DUIs, a breaking and entering charge, an assault case, and a fraud charge. He was busy, but he liked it that way. It kept his mind away from the vineyard and how much he missed his family. He missed his wife's hugs at night, he missed his daughter's stories of school, and he missed the comfort of his own home.

As much as he tried to focus on Zoe Taylor's case, as much as he tried to complete the other files, the interactions with Cruise kept creeping back into his head. What if Cruise was guilty? Could he justify helping him get back on the street? Of course, he had to. That was his job, a part of the ethical preparation of a defense lawyer. Guilt, or the lack of it, didn't factor into his planning, but it was always a nagging thought in his mind, always there to distract him at the wrong times.

When he was a prosecutor, he always felt like he was on the right side of the law. He was the hero. The man putting the criminals away. He was brainwashed to believe that the world was black and white, and that the criminal game only had good guys and bad guys. But as he grew older, as he began to understand the world around him, he realized that society was a lot more complicated than he'd been taught. Good people did bad things, and bad people often did great things.

"So what do we know now?" Frank Taylor brought Hennessy's focus back to the present. He was seated in front of the desk, flanked by his daughter. They both looked paler than before. More broken. Sadder. "Can't we just push this through the courts and get it over with?"

"Dad, please," Zoe pleaded with her father. "Let Mr. Hennessy explain what's happening."

"Zoe, you'll be pleased to know that we're getting to the point where the State is beginning to offer better deals." Hennessy turned a page in the thick file on his desk, attempting to draw his attention back to the two people in his office. "But the evidence against you is strong. You were seen running from the car, your fingerprints are on the car where Andre was murdered, and you were seen fighting with him the day before."

"But still no murder weapon?" Frank pressed. "How can they convict her if they don't have a murder weapon? Surely this has to be downgraded to second-degree murder?"

"Although some states differentiate between degrees of murder, South Carolina does not. Instead,

Section 16-3-10 of the South Carolina Code of Laws states that murder is simply defined as the killing of any person with malice aforethought, either express or implied. Generally, murder charges mean the prosecution believes the accused had the specific or general intent to commit murder," Hennessy confirmed. "And even though they don't have the murder weapon, it doesn't mean that a jury won't be able to convict Zoe. Many murder suspects are convicted without a murder weapon."

"And still no wallet?"

"That's correct. Andre's wallet is still missing from the scene of the crime."

"Well, this has to be a mugging gone wrong then," Frank grunted and stood, rubbing his brow and pacing the back of the room. He was experiencing every father's worst nightmare—he was helpless. He had no control as he watched his daughter fight a losing battle against a system that seemed determined to convict her. "How can the police charge Zoe with murder when it's so obvious that it's a mugging gone wrong?"

Hennessy waited. He wasn't sure if Frank was asking direct questions or if he was just letting off steam.

"Do you think I'll go to prison?" There was pleading in Zoe's eyes as she looked at her lawyer. She ran her hand over her jeans and then fixed her sweater, desperate to disperse some of the nervous energy coursing through her. "Do you think they've got enough to convict me without a murder weapon?"

"I like to be honest with my clients," Hennessy leaned forward and clasped his hands on the table.

"And right now, I would say it comes down to the make-up of the jury. We're really looking at a fifty/fifty case. They've got blood on your sweater, they've got a witness that says they heard you threaten Andre the day before, and on the recording of your call to 911, you sound very calm."

"I was in shock. I don't even remember making the call."

"Of course, but this is about how a jury will see it," Hennessy continued. "What helps us is that there is no murder weapon, nobody saw the crime being committed, and you have no history of violence. South Carolina murder charges mean that the prosecution has to establish clear malice."

"All this lawyer talk." Frank shook his head as he spoke, leaning against the back wall of the office. "Can't we just take it to a jury and finish it now? I'm sick of having this murder charge hanging over our heads. She's innocent. She didn't kill her ex-boyfriend. What part of that is hard to understand?"

"And people are starting to think I'm actually guilty," Zoe added. She brushed her hand over her brown hair and then rubbed her ankle. "This ankle monitor doesn't help. People thought I was innocent, but as soon as they see the ankle monitor, they think I'm guilty. All my friends believed my arrest was a mistake, but now that it's been five weeks, people aren't returning my calls. They're not responding to my messages. My friends are starting to look at me differently. Work has told me to take a 'vacation' until the trial is over. I'm feeling… numb. I didn't do this."

"I understand your frustration, but if we took it to court now, then it's still possible, based on the evidence, that you'll be found guilty. The prosecution needs a win around here. That shouldn't matter, but it does. This case is gathering attention, and the Circuit Solicitor has been instructed to get a win. There's an election coming up next year, and they need convictions to boost the numbers in their annual report."

Zoe bit her lip, trying to hold back the tears. Not only was she fighting the grief of losing her ex-boyfriend, someone she once loved, but she was fighting against a system that wanted to see her convicted.

After Hennessy had convinced the judge that his client was not a flight risk, nor a threat to the community, she was released on bond. Her bond said, 'Will reside in the state of South Carolina pending trial. Will wear an electronic monitor (ankle monitor). House Arrest with only doctor, court, attorney, and church visits. No Contact With Victim's family.' Her one escape out of the house was attending church daily. She hadn't been to church for more than a year before her arrest, but if it meant walking out the doors of her home, if only for a few moments of freedom, then that was what she was going to do.

Zoe and Andre had dated for a year before Zoe ended the relationship. He was her first real love, and she was smitten by his confidence, but after a year, she realized that the relationship wasn't going anywhere. Andre just wanted someone to be with, and Zoe wanted more. She ended it a month before his death, but they kept finding a way back into each other's arms.

On the day before the murder, Zoe and Andre were seen arguing at a diner. Zoe admitted that she slapped him and also admitted that she said she wanted to stab him. That didn't look good, and when she made the 911 call on the morning of the murder, her voice sounded remarkably calm. Still in shock, she spoke with a measured tone, calmly explaining that she had found her ex-boyfriend dead in his car when she went to apologize to him.

"I didn't do it. I didn't kill him," Zoe said. "That's why we have this justice system, right? To protect the innocent. I had nothing to do with it. How could I stab Andre?"

"Yes, Zoe." Her father patted her shoulder as he stood next to her, not entirely convinced by her statement. "We'll be ok. Mr. Hennessy is going to sort it out. He's going to make all this go away."

"I found his body in his car and then ran away. Who wouldn't run away after seeing all those stab wounds and all that blood?" She sat with a straight back, legs close together, an unyielding gaze in her eyes. "I was scared, and I went into shock. Who wouldn't go into shock after seeing what I saw?"

"I don't care how you get her off, or why you get her off, but I need you to make sure there's no record of this crime," Frank's voice was firm. "Not now, not ever."

"I didn't do it," Zoe continued. "That should be enough. I'll go on the stand and say that."

"It doesn't matter what you say," Frank hushed her. "What matters is what Mr. Hennessy can do in court."

Hennessy didn't respond to the family dispute.

He knew that as a criminal lawyer, there would always be more than one case, always more than one job on hand, and it was always a juggling act. Hennessy had to be skilled at managing cases, at switching his focus between clients, courts, and procedures. Without Jacinta Templeton, his new assistant, his working world would be a mess. That morning, when she placed Zoe Taylor's file on his desk, she informed him that he didn't have the time, or the capacity, to take on another case. He was at his limit. He knew she was right, but the Cruise case was something he couldn't let go. It was an opportunity too good to pass up. But, for now, he had to focus.

"The prosecution has indicated that if there's evidence that Andre was abusing you, they will consider a deal for manslaughter," Hennessy said. "If that were the case, as your lawyer, I would advise that we fight for self-defense. I'm going to ask you a direct question, and I would like you to consider your answer before responding," Hennessy paused. "Was Andre abusing you, and did you ever have to fight him off in self-defense?"

"No. I'm not lying to get off these charges. I want to tell the truth," Zoe's answer was direct. "Andre was always good to me. He might've been in trouble with the law, but he never laid a finger on me. He never harmed a hair on my head. I was his angel."

Hennessy closed the folder and leaned his elbows on the desk. "Most criminal cases don't make it to trial. Most cases are dealt with long before they make it into the courtroom. We're going to go slow with the case, and I'm going to lodge a number of motions to push the case out, because if we take it to court now, you might lose. I'm going to negotiate with the prosecution many times over the coming month to see if we can get this to go away without a record. The longer it goes on, the more strength we have in our case. We're due to go to court again soon, but I'll lodge numerous stalling tactics, and the prosecution is going to be forced to present a better deal."

"What if she did do it?" Frank lowered his tone.

Zoe turned and glared at him, almost cutting him in two with her stare.

"That doesn't make a difference to our defense," Hennessy said. "My job is to get you the best outcome for this case."

"I didn't do it." She shook her head again, not taking her eyes off her father. "I didn't kill him. How many times do you want me to say that?"

"Yes, honey," Frank said. "Of course."

"The last hearing that you attended was the Grand Jury, which was a very important part of the process, and now we'll move through to filing pre-trial motions," Hennessy continued. "I imagine that the prosecution has more evidence to present over the coming month. That will come out in the discovery process, and my assistant, Jacinta, will keep you updated on any further developments. You're welcome to call her at any time for an update. If there are no further updates on the motions, then our next court appearance will be in five weeks, where we'll begin the trial. If anything changes, I'll let you know."

"Thank you, Mr. Hennessy," Zoe stood. "Your confidence is very reassuring."

"Yes, thank you," Frank rubbed his brow again. "The one positive out of this is that my daughter doesn't have to deal with that criminal anymore."

"What do you mean by that?" Hennessy stood.

"Just…" Frank looked away. "Andre wasn't good for my Zoe. She deserved the best, and he wasn't it."

Frank turned and hurried out the office door,

leaving it open for his daughter to follow.

Zoe looked to the door, back to Hennessy, and then back to the door. She offered Hennessy a half-smile before she followed her father.

Hennessy watched her leave, an uneasy feeling hanging in the room.

CHAPTER 8

HENNESSY WALKED into the meeting room in his office with three ice-cold soda cans.

He threw one to Barry Lockett and placed the second in front of Jacinta. He popped the lid of the third, took one long cold gulp, and then exhaled. There was nothing like the cool fizz of a soda on a sweltering day.

The air-conditioner in the meeting room was working overtime, trying to cool the large space. The boardroom was long and wide, with a dark wooden table in the middle and five office chairs around the outside. There was a new whiteboard at the end of the room, next to the tall window that looked out to the street, and a large painting of the South Carolina sunset from Folly Beach on the far wall. Hennessy loved that painting. It was one of his favorite spots in the world.

Jacinta had organized Henry Cruise's casework into separate folders, arranged on the boardroom table in a methodical pattern. There were police reports in one pile, photos of the scene in another, and evidence documents in another. Each pile was organized with precision, a post-it note placed on top of each one with a description of the contents. Although the world had moved on to electronic tablets for seemingly everything, Hennessy still preferred his notes on paper.

Barry Lockett lounged on the chair closest to the window, sitting with a sense of calm that escaped Hennessy most days.

"Thanks for getting back to me so quickly," Hennessy said. "It's good to know that I've got someone I can rely on, not someone like Damien Bates, who seems to be high on drugs every time I see him."

"I was just thinking the other day that the saying 'Just say no to drugs,' is a bit redundant," Lockett smiled. "Because if you're talking to your drugs, you've probably already said yes."

Hennessy laughed. "So, what have you found on the Cruise case?"

"I read through the case files you gave me, and a couple of things stuck out. For instance, why is someone like Henry Cruise dealing with stolen artworks? And if he was dealing in stolen artworks worth millions of dollars, why would he unload them through his own gallery? He's much more likely to unload the stolen art elsewhere." Lockett removed a paper file from his messenger bag and placed it on the table. "So I made a few phone calls this morning. Talked to the right people. Listened to their advice. Reached out to a few others. Tried to find any evidence that someone planted those artworks."

"Y'all don't sound confident," Jacinta Templeton said as she took a sip of her soda through a paper straw that was already growing soggy.

Jacinta was thirty-five, with a husband who worked in banking and a five-year-old son at home with her mother. She agreed to work four days a week as an assistant for Hennessy, as long as he promised her flexible working arrangements. Hennessy was hesitant at first, but she was the best applicant for the position by a country mile. And since he hired her, she'd proven herself time and time again. She was no slacker. Hard work was part of her DNA.

"If it was a setup, then they've done a good job." Lockett shrugged and flicked his finger on top of the soda. He wiped the outside of the can on his black t-shirt and then popped it open. "They've kept it quiet, and if someone knows anything, then they're not talking. 'If' it was a setup, then whoever's behind it is very influential."

"That's what I thought as well. If it was a setup, then whoever was behind it is very powerful, or the other option is that Cruise is lying to us, and he did purchase the stolen artworks," Hennessy sat down. "Regardless, our job is to create the best defense for Cruise. Win, lose, or get the case thrown out, it doesn't matter. We're getting paid to do a job, and that's what we'll do."

"From what I've seen so far, it's looking like this case might be difficult to win."

"At least tell me you've got something that we can start with." Hennessy took another gulp of his drink. "From the files I've received from the last lawyer, he was clearly positioning them for a deal. He didn't think Cruise had any chance of beating the charges, so I need something new. I need a scrap of evidence. A hint. A sniff. Something. All we've got so far is Cruise's word that someone set him up, but he's about as trustworthy as a paper boat in the Atlantic Ocean."

"I've got two things," Lockett said. "One—there are rumors in the art world that all of Stephen Scully's paintings are about to be devalued."

"Why?" Jacinta asked.

"At this point, they're just rumors, but it's said that there's evidence he sexually abused young boys in the past. Stephen Scully was at the height of his painting career in the 50s, and he moved into an apartment inside his old all-boys boarding school. They offered him a studio to work from because they enjoyed the publicity his artwork gave the school. There were a number of rumors floating around for decades, but it's all about to be exposed in a new book by five of the abused children, who are now all in their eighties. They've been approved by a publisher, and the book is due for release next year."

"Stephen Scully died in 1985," Jacinta read from the bio in front of her. "And yes, it says here that he spent ten years living in a studio at the back of an all-boys school."

"That book would plummet the value of every Stephen Scully painting. The paintings would go from being worth millions of dollars to nothing overnight," Hennessy said.

"And if they were reported as stolen," Lockett drummed his fingers on the table. "That's an insurance payout worth millions."

"But that's only two of the paintings," Jacinta said. "What about the other three?"

"My contact said that the three paintings had been originally stolen in the 80s and kept in a private collection by a wealthy owner for decades."

"And again, the owner of the three other stolen paintings would want to off-load them before the allegations were published. Nobody would want to keep those paintings, whether it was in a private collection or not," Hennessy turned to Jacinta. "I need to talk to the authors of that book."

"On it, boss. I'll get you their details by the morning."

"Thank you," Hennessy turned back to Lockett. "And what's the second piece of information you've got?"

"A person." Lockett nodded and then reached into a manilla folder and pulled a photograph out. It was attached to a slip of paper with some notes. "This is Jason Norris. He might be our starting point. A former associate of Cruise's, but the word is that he's looking to get out of the game. He's late-fifties, and it looks like he's had a late-life crisis and wants to go straight. And if he's looking to get out of the game, then he's going to need help. You don't just walk away from working for Cruise without paying a price."

"What are you suggesting?"

"That we talk to Cruise and say that if he helps Jason Norris get out of the game, Norris will provide an honest testimony about where the paintings came from. Norris can explain to the police how Cruise had nothing to do with the paintings."

"That's all well and good, but there's a problem," Jacinta said while taking notes on her laptop. "What if Jason Norris doesn't know where the paintings came from?"

"I think Barry was using the term 'honest testimony' quite loosely," Hennessy stated. "And that's not the way I want to play. I won't cross that line, not for anyone, but especially not for a guy like Henry Cruise. But if Jason Norris does know something, anything, that can help us, I'm sure I can convince Cruise to help him out. Let's get him in here and talk to him."

"There's just one problem—if we know that he's looking to get out of the game…" Lockett's voice trailed off.

"Then everyone else knows it as well. His testimony is going to go to the highest bidder." Hennessy placed the photo down. "Which means we need to get to him before anyone else does."

CHAPTER 9

NIGHT HAD fallen by the time Jason Norris stumbled out of Monty's bar in North Charleston. He was bleary-eyed, wobbly on his feet, and ready for a place to crash. He'd been sober for a week, struggling each night to fight off the desire for a beer. He vowed to try and stay sober, but after he went to church that afternoon, it all became too much for him. He walked out of the church and drove twenty-five minutes to his home, but instead of going inside, he walked straight to the nearest bar. He'd gotten to the bar at about five and had only been inside for long enough to order a beer when he got a text from his brother, asking him to join him at his Aunt Sally's that Sunday. A family BBQ, followed, no doubt, by a homily. His first instinct had been to ignore the text and put his phone face down, but he had picked it up and replied.

"I'll be there."

A session of heavy drinking had followed the text message, with Norris desperate to avoid the feelings growing inside of him. He pushed the feelings down with beer after beer. Whiskey after whiskey. Shot after shot. The emotions were overwhelming, the sensations confronting, and he didn't know any other way to handle them.

At 10.50pm, he stumbled out of the bar with the promise he had made to Samuel pressed in the back of his head. He had meant it. The following Sunday, he'd be at Aunt Sally's. He'd grill a couple of burgers for the nieces and nephews. Force a smile. Have a laugh. He planned to turn up freshly shaven and with scrubbed fingernails, just like his mother always wanted.

He stumbled into the humid night. He liked the smell of the night in North Charleston. There was a comfort to the polluted stink from the nearby paper mill, a feeling that he was home. He liked the cigarette smoke that lingered in the air. The smell of gasoline as he passed the service station.

He walked a little bit slower so that he didn't trip. Took it all in. There were two options to get home. A longer, but more well-lit way, and a shortcut through a dark street. He didn't have the energy to walk the long way. He turned into the narrow street that had no lighting and smelled like urine, trash, and dog food, all rolled into one. Halfway down the street, a dark sedan passed him. It stopped under the dark shadow of an oak tree. Two men exited. Norris struggled to keep his vision straight. He could see the shadows of the two men standing at the other end of the street. They were waiting for him. He kept his head down, hoping to pass them by without any aggravation. If they tried to take his wallet, he was ready.

He was always ready for a fight.

As he walked closer to the men, he saw that they were in their 20s. One was blondish; the other one had light-brown hair with flecks of ginger. They were wearing black suits, but not expensive ones, mid-range that didn't quite fit right, but which covered up their reasonably large frames. Cops? He wondered. Even more reason to dodge them.

They stepped forward as he approached, and he realized it was too late to turn back and take the other route. They were not going to let him pass. His back stiffened, and he sobered up as if someone had punched him in the face.

"Jason Norris?" The ginger-flecked one asked. The two men shared a glance like they already knew the answer.

Their smirking faces made him want to revert to his old ways; back to the way he used to deal with faces like these. Things that involved fists, knuckles, backs of pistols.

"What if I am?" He continued forward, head down.

The blonde one stepped towards him and held out his hand to stop Norris. Norris stopped and looked up at them. There were scars on both their faces. Despite their youth, they looked well-versed in violence. "You got anything to confess, Jason?"

The words caught Norris off guard. Confess. Had they followed him to church earlier that day?

"I've got nothing to say," Norris stepped forward again, but the first guy pushed him back. The second man pointed to the gun that was now visible at his waist.

"We're not here to make trouble," the blonde one said. "But our boss wants you to do something."

"And who's your boss?"

"That doesn't matter." The blonde stepped closer. "What matters is that our boss wants Henry Cruise to go down. Cruise has got a court case against him, and the rumor is that you want to get out of the game."

Norris stepped back, his mouth open. "How would you know that?"

"People talk, and bad news travels fast." The two men looked at each other and nodded. "Our boss can help you get out of the game. He wants to set you up in Florida. He can get you a rental house, a job, and a new name. You can disappear from South Carolina forever and start fresh."

Norris stepped forward, looking for a way to walk past them, but as he tried to shoulder his way past the blonde one, he found the younger man was stronger than he thought. Or maybe the truth was that Norris just didn't possess the firepower he once had. The blond guy pushed Norris hard. He rocked back and forth for a second before regaining his balance.

"Cruise has a trial coming up," the blond man closed in. "You worked for him closely. Any jury will believe what you tell them, so our boss needs you to testify against him. Our boss will give you the details, and all you need to do is go to court and repeat it, word for word."

Norris sucked in a tight breath like he'd been punched in the gut. Testifying against Henry Cruise was a way of signing his own death certificate. Even the thought of doing so produced a pounding in the back of his skull.

"Your identity would be protected." The blonde one softened, just a little. "We can get you through to the trial, and then you disappear."

"What would I need to say?"

They looked at each other before the hammer hit. "You need to tell the police that you saw Henry Cruise purchase stolen artworks on several occasions."

"Stolen artworks?" Norris' eyebrows shot up. He'd seen his former boss threaten people at knifepoint.

70

Order contract killings. Make sure people disappeared. Launder money by the millions. But stealing art? That was a stretch.

"He's looking at ten years in prison if he gets convicted. This is big enough to take Cruise off the streets forever."

"So he was set up?" Norris' eye twitched, and he shook his head. "Being a witness against Henry Cruise is a death sentence at the best of times. But a setup like this? He'll kill me before I even get to the trial."

"I don't think you understand, Norris." The man brought his face to within an inch of Norris'. "If you don't testify, it'll also be a death sentence."

As Jason Norris stood in the darkness, under the threat of violence, the realization hit him hard—he was the perfect man to send to the gallows. A washed-up, former felon with little to lose. Norris gripped his fist, his knuckles turning white. He didn't have much, but he still had something to lose. It wasn't his life. It was something greater. Something his mother and Aunt Sally had talked about. Something that Samuel said he still possessed, deep down, hidden under all that pain and regret—a soul.

"If he protects me." Norris was between a rock and a hard place, and he had to make a choice. "Tell your boss I'll do it."

CHAPTER 10

JOE HENNESSY walked into the grocery store closest to his apartment and waved to the owner, a black man in his seventies, who'd owned the store for more than fifty years. It was a small store where people had to squeeze past each other in the aisles, but it was filled with a sense of community. Hennessy grabbed a hearty rib-eye from the deli counter and a fresh bunch of broccoli to cook for dinner, looking forward to smothering them both in smokey mesquite sauce. Buying his items, he chatted to the owner, catching up on recent incidents around the community. There was a shooting nearby, the owner said. Crime was getting worse. He'd installed cameras outside the building and put an extra lock on the door. Good time to be a defense lawyer, Hennessy joked, and the owner laughed heartily, more than the joke deserved.

As he stepped out of the store, Hennessy noticed the black Range Rover SUV waiting near the entrance to his apartment building. He'd noticed it earlier that week, following him as he went to work, and then following him as he went to the gym at night.

Never one to run from danger, Hennessy drew a long breath and stepped towards the vehicle. He walked up beside the car, leaned his tall frame down, and tapped on the driver's window.

"Joe Hennessy," the man said as he rolled down

the window. "I see that you've noticed the car."

"Who are you?" Hennessy brought his face close enough to smell the man's minty breath. "And why have you been following me?"

The man was solid, clean-cut, with weathered skin and a square jaw. He was dressed in a suit, without a tie, and moved slowly and with purpose. "Why don't you get in the car, and we can discuss that."

"I don't get in cars with strangers. My mom taught me that when I was five years old."

"I'm not a stranger. I'm a friend."

Hennessy scoffed. "Of whom? Certainly not one of mine."

"My name's Roger East. I'm a friend of some influential people, and I could be a friend of yours as well."

Hennessy stood and glanced up and down the street before he looked at the security camera of the nearby building. He didn't want to stop to talk—he was looking forward to relaxing with a beer—but maybe the man could provide the break he was after. He walked around the back of the SUV, opened the passenger door, and stepped inside the car, his knees squashing up against the dash. The car was tidy. Not a piece of trash, nor a speck of dust. Not a receipt, nor anything out of place. It smelled like a new car that had only just rolled out of the showroom.

"So you're representing Henry Cruise?" East started the engine and signaled as he pulled out of the parking spot. "How'd you get so lucky?"

"I'm a lucky man. Things tend to fall into my lap." Hennessy looked out at the road. "Where are we going?"

"Just around the block. It's best to keep moving. It

helps any wandering eyes from seeing us together."

"And why is that a problem?"

"You seem like a good man with good morals, Joe Hennessy," East ignored the question. "Two kids, a lovely wife. I hear your youngest daughter, Casey, is in high school up in Greenville. Is she thinking about going to Clemson, or will she join your other daughter, Ellie, in New York? Ellie's studying at NYU to become a lawyer like her father, right?"

Hennessy didn't respond.

"And, of course, I know the reason you left Charleston twenty years ago." East turned the corner to go around the block, following the slow-moving traffic. "After your son was murdered, it must've been so hard to know that you were working in the Circuit Solicitor's office, and you couldn't find out who killed him. You spent a year here before moving out to the vineyard."

Hennessy struggled to hold his rage inside, but he knew East was testing him, pushing him to see where his breaking point was.

"How was that?" East continued as he stopped at an intersection. "Not being able to convict someone for callously murdering your son must've been horrifying. That must still eat you alive at night. Do you have nightmares? Or at least, uncontrolled bouts of rage? I'm no psychologist, but I know that would almost break most men."

"Are you telling me that you had something to do with it?" Hennessy's jaw clenched tight.

"Not me, but you must've thought that maybe your job as a prosecutor, a man determined to bring down the corrupt, might've played a role in his death?"

"You can either start talking about why you've been following me, or I can put your head through that window."

East smiled. "There it is. The breaking point."

Hennessy glared at him. "Start talking."

East smiled for a few more moments while he drove around the next corner, passing a horse and cart, and then coughed, the smile disappearing from his face. "I know that you're a former prosecutor, and you don't want scum like Henry Cruise walking the streets of Charleston."

"If he's innocent, then he doesn't deserve to go down for this crime."

East raised a patchy salt and pepper eyebrow. "That simple, is it?"

"It is."

"I know you haven't been around for the last two decades, but Henry Cruise is a very nasty human being. He's had his hand in a lot of crime here over the past few decades. Drug deals, beatings, murders. You name it, he's been involved. It's time to get him off the streets." East nodded and pursed his lips a little. "There's a briefcase next to your feet. Open it."

Hennessy reached down to the black briefcase and clicked open the hinges. He pulled the top up slightly.

"That's a lot of cash," Hennessy whispered.

"Fifty thousand."

Hennessy closed the briefcase and clicked the hinges shut.

"It's a donation," East continued. "To ensure that Cruise's case is wrapped up without any further trouble."

Hennessy narrowed his eyes. "By 'wrapped up', you mean lost?"

"The prosecution is about to put a deal on the table for five years in prison, and you should strongly encourage Cruise to take it."

"He won't take it."

"He will when he realizes that two of his old employees are about to step forward and testify against him." East didn't take his eyes off the road as he turned another corner. "They're going to step forward this week and testify that they saw Cruise deal in stolen artworks on a regular basis. That's the killer blow for this case. Cruise is done. He's cooked. It's time for you to take the money and say goodbye to the case."

"No."

"No?" East threw his head back and chuckled a little bit. "Come on. Are you serious? Cruise has a decades-long history of dodging charges and slipping through the cracks in the system. This is just karma finally catching up with him. Who are we to stop that?"

"What Henry Cruise has or has not done in the past is irrelevant right now. He still deserves a fair trial, as does anyone else in this country." Hennessy placed the briefcase back at his feet. "And my values cannot be bought off. Not for 50k, nor any amount."

"Think about it, Joe. I know you need the money to save the vineyard named after your dead son. I know that's the only reason you took the case. I know that's why you came back to Charleston." East turned back onto the street they started on. "Just take the money and forget about Cruise. Focus on your next case. Don't complicate things."

"Is that what you offered Timothy Donnelly?"

"Cruise's former lawyer? Well, now, Donnelly was

a lot of things, but a stupid man wasn't one of them. He was encouraging Cruise to take the deal."

Hennessy didn't respond as East pulled the car over to the curb.

"Take the money, Joe." East stopped the car and turned to his passenger. He leaned across and tapped his hand on the briefcase. "Make it easy for everyone."

"I don't think Henry Cruise would like to hear that you're trying to strong-arm his defense attorney, do you?"

"If a word of this meeting gets back to Henry Cruise, you might find that a fire will rip through your precious vineyard."

Hennessy sat up straighter.

"I'm not going to force you to take the money, but I'm telling you that this meeting is secret. Only you and I know what's been said here, and if this rumor gets around, there'll only be two people to blame—you or me. And if you start talking, you'll find a lot of trouble coming your way."

Hennessy didn't respond as he opened the door and stepped out of the SUV. He leaned back down and said, "I don't appreciate the offer. I don't know who you're working for, but let your boss know that I'm not corrupt, and I don't play those types of games."

East paused for a moment before he added. "There's a storm coming, Joe. The old power-players are getting replaced. Be careful which side you choose to be on when the storm arrives."

CHAPTER 11

THE BOATHOUSE at Breach Inlet in the Isle of Palms had vintage wooden boats hanging from the rafters, a rooftop deck, and a beachside charm that was unmatched. Opened in the 90s on the site of an old bait shop, the Southern cooking and breezy views made it a favorite for locals and tourists. The local seafood always tasted as fresh as the ocean, sourced from local farmers, fishermen, clammers, and shrimpers from around the coast.

Henry Cruise sat on the Waterfront Deck, eating a butter-poached lobster tail with a side of stone-ground grits. Hennessy approached the table as Cruise stuffed another piece of lobster into his mouth. He indicated for Hennessy to sit. Before he sat, Hennessy moved his chair back to avoid any splashes of excess butter.

"How's the murder case with Zoe Taylor coming along?" Cruise licked his fingers and leaned back in his chair, running his thumbs on the inside of his suspenders. He took a large breath and stared out at the water. "I hear that it's starting to get a bit of attention."

"Zoe Taylor's case is none of your business, and I don't discuss my other cases with my clients, unless you've got something to tell me about it."

"Nothing to say, but I'm interested. A pretty white girl stabs her black ex-boyfriend? You can't avoid a case like that. That's got half the state talking, and some people in the media are saying that this case will prove there's no bias in the legal system. That the system will convict a white girl of killing a black man." Cruise licked the fingers on his other hand and then wiped them on his napkin. "Just give me a hint about how it's going. Does it look like she'll win it?"

"Like I said, I don't discuss my other cases." Hennessy shook his head.

"Alright," Cruise sniffed loudly. "But before you tell me why you so desperately needed to meet, I need to talk about my ex-wife."

"Go on," Hennessy replied.

"Can I stop Maire from testifying? Don't I have rights under Spousal Privilege to stop her from disclosing anything I said during our marriage?"

"Unfortunately not. While spousal privilege in South Carolina is statutory and allows a spouse to testify, it prohibits 'requiring' them to disclose communications made by their spouse. In South Carolina, the witness is the only one who can assert the privilege. The defendant cannot say, 'I assert spousal privilege; therefore, my spouse cannot testify.' The witness holds the privilege, and it's their choice whether to assert it or not."

"Are you sure about that?" Cruise questioned.

"Yes," Hennessy was firm. "The South Carolina Supreme Court held in State v. Motes that a defendant could not assert spousal privilege when his wife voluntarily testified. The privilege was sought to be exercised by the defendant's husband, however, the fact that the wife voluntarily testified is not questioned in that case. You have no control over her testimony."

Cruise groaned loudly and reached for his red wine. He brought it to his nose, smelled it, and then took a long sip. "So, what is it you so desperately needed to talk with me about?"

"We have two new problems," Hennessy leaned forward. "The first is a man named Roger East."

Cruise paused as he went to take another drink, the glass halfway to his mouth. He thought for a moment and then placed the glass back down. "Roger East? He approached you?"

"That's right. He talked to me yesterday and asked me how this case was going."

"Did he ask you to drop it?"

"He asked me if it looked like we were going to win." Hennessy didn't reveal the whole truth. "What do you know about him?"

"He's connected to a lot of people. He's the go-to guy for getting deals done but doesn't really have a mind of his own." Cruise sat back and stared out at the view again. A sailing yacht moved past the restaurant, a beautiful day to be out on the water. "East sells his services to the highest bidder. If he wants to know how the case is going, then someone has asked him to keep track of it. That's a problem. That means people want to see me sink."

The waitress came to the table and offered Cruise another glass of wine, which he happily accepted. Hennessy refused.

"I'll talk to some people. See who East is connected to at the moment," Cruise brushed the large white napkin over his mouth, looking out to the sea as the yacht disappeared from view. "What's the second problem?"

"Two new witnesses came forward last night. Both

witnesses are former employees of yours."

Cruise's fist clenched into a ball as he looked out to the horizon. He stared at the horizon for a long moment before he turned back to his lawyer. "Have you got names?"

"Michael Morrison's testimony says that he saw you discussing buying the stolen paintings. He says that he overheard you on the phone discussing selling these Stephen Scully paintings for five million dollars," Hennessy said. "But we should be able to get his testimony thrown out before it even makes it to trial. Even at first glance, I can see holes in it. There are a number of inconsistencies, and any judge is going to have to throw it out. That's the first testimony. The second is more of a problem."

"Name of the witness?"

"Jason Norris."

"Norris?" Cruise raised his eyebrows. "What's he saying?"

"He's saying that he saw you, first-hand, buy a number of stolen paintings in the past. He told the police that he had witnessed the transactions. There are no holes in his story, and everything seems to line up. We'll have to tear the testimony apart, but at this point, it looks convincing."

Cruise's fist clenched tighter. "That lying, two-timing low-life."

Hennessy thought about the money he was offered to lose the case and imagined that Norris would've been presented with a similar offer, although for a lot less money. It would've been enough for Norris to retire from the criminal game.

"Two days ago, I heard that Jason Norris was looking to get out of the criminal world, and we were going to approach him with an offer to testify for you. Word is that he wanted to make some money and then retire," Hennessy said. "But it looks like someone else got to him first."

"I'll deal with him," Cruise grunted.

"He's gone underground. Norris has someone helping him, and he's not going to show his head until the trial. My investigator has tried to contact him. His phone is off, his home is empty, and his car is in the shop. He's gone off the grid, and we're going to have a hard time finding him. And the prosecution has requested that any deposition is conducted via email or video link."

"I know Jason Norris, and I know his weak spots. I know how to smoke him out. It won't take me long to get him to pop his head up," Cruise squinted as he looked out at the water again. He considered his next move before turning back to Hennessy. "Can you deal with Morrison's testimony?"

"I can," Hennessy said. "I'll file a motion to have it suppressed. That shouldn't be a problem. What are you going to say to Jason Norris?"

"I'll be friendly." Cruise leaned forward on the table. He lowered his tone. "I'll talk to him nicely and ask him not to testify."

CHAPTER 12

"IS THIS really the place?"

Jason Norris cleared his throat and muttered to himself as he pushed through the polished glass doors of The Civic Lantern. He wasn't used to drinking in such comfort. He wasn't used to doing much in the expensive part of town. This time, he felt like the foreign visitor stumbling into hostile territory.

The overhead chandeliers from the bar were blinding. The patrons of the Civic Lantern were on the older side, and wore mostly flowery, light garments and pieces of large jewelry that almost swallowed them, even the men. Flutes were on tables, and the air was crisp and clean. The nighttime crowd had dressed their best—too much make-up, way too much perfume, and way too many fake smiles. Norris gulped and fought the instinct to back out.

Norris had found his best shirt—a white one—and his best black slacks. He polished his shoes and shaved his stubble. He felt uncomfortable, but he wanted to present a good image. An image of a man cleaned up and trying to make amends for his violent past.

After giving a statement to the police, he was supposed to be hiding in the city of Columbia, two hours away by bus, in a small basement apartment rented by the Charleston PD. He was told not to leave town, keep a low profile, and not to log onto the internet, but Norris had received an unexpected text message the night before.

"Hi Dad. It's been a long time. Do you want to meet up for a drink?"

It was the first time he'd heard from James in five years. At first, he was wary, but then he settled on the fact that the universe, or faith, was working for him. He was starting to atone for his past, and the way he treated his kids and their mother was something he needed to deal with.

He sat at the bar, and an attendant, a woman in her late 20s with shoulder-length dark hair, pale skin, and thin limbs who looked like she probably modeled on the side, approached him and asked what she could get him to drink.

"A Budweiser, if you've got it."

She looked a little hesitant, and Norris noticed her eyebrows twitched in judgment. She turned and fetched him a bottle from a fridge underneath the bar—none on tap—and returned to the table with a waning smile. He glanced over to his right towards the door, wondering where James was. A tubby man wearing a black button-up, who had been staring at him, looked away, but not quickly enough. As Jason moved his eyes around the room, he noticed five other people repeating the same move.

"Hey…" He looked at the attendant. "Server?"

She spun around and returned to him. "Everything all right with the lager?"

"It's perfect," he lowered his voice. "Look, call me paranoid, but I kind of get the feeling that everyone in this bar is staring at me. Is there something I should know?"

"Most people who come here know each other.

You're a new face," she said. "I wouldn't take it personally."

Norris shifted in his too-small bar seat and gripped the beer bottle. He turned his head around and saw grave, subdued faces in several directions. There was a nervous static in the air.

"And what's with all the hostility?"

The server didn't answer.

"Come on," Norris continued. "It seems like everyone inside this bar is in on some kind of secret joke, and I'm missing the punchline."

She seemed to take pity on him. She moved a little closer to him and spoke. "Are you Jason Norris?"

Jason furrowed his brow. "Yes. How did you know my name?"

"Because Henry Cruise has booked a table for you."

The comment struck him like a punch in the face. A buzzing spread from the back of his neck towards his temples, but he remained calm on the outside. Norris took another careful sip of his beer and swallowed it, feeling the cool bubbling liquid slide down his throat.

There was no message from his son, James. It was a setup. A dirty one. A cheap shot to the groin. They'd used his weak spot and exploited it. He fought off the numbing disappointment and glanced around the bar. He was a sitting duck.

It's just a warning, he told himself. It's just Cruise flexing his muscles. He wants me to know that he's still powerful.

He took another sip of the lager that suddenly tasted bitter and regretted his decision to go to the police. To testify, falsely, that he'd seen Henry Cruise purchasing stolen artworks. On the balance of right and wrong, Norris knew his former boss deserved to be locked up, but at what cost? Was it up to him to clinch the deal?

He placed his half-empty beer on the bar, stood, and walked towards the door. Shoving his hands into his jacket pockets, he pushed his shoulder against the door to make it swing open and stepped out onto the street.

As soon as the door swung shut behind him, he checked the street—there was a man sitting in a car opposite the bar entrance, another man talking on the phone, and another walking towards the bar. He looked around. There was an alley half-a-block ahead. If he could make it there, he could try to run.

He kept his head down and walked towards the alley.

He heard the bar door open and close behind him. He didn't look back.

He was closer to the alley now.

He slowed as he walked towards the corner, keeping the rest of the street in his peripheral vision.

The man from the car stepped out.

Norris continued walking.

He stepped around the corner into the shelter of darkness.

But then he saw a man step out from the shadow of the alley. "Hello, Jason."

CHAPTER 13

Five Weeks Later

JOE HENNESSY was wearing his sharpest suit. Before he returned to law, he hadn't bought a suit in more than ten years. He just didn't need one on the vineyard. His daily clothes were boots, jeans, and a flannel shirt. A beanie if it was cold. A tank top if it was hot. The collars of the business shirts felt like they were choking him now, and he struggled with wearing a jacket in the heat, but presentation counted. He needed to look his sharpest for his next meeting with the opposition in court.

The 9th District Circuit Solicitor's office building was filled with history and charm, and Aaron Garrett greeted Hennessy at the receptionist's desk. He was a young black man, still a little wet behind the ears. Hennessy had done his research—Garrett had cut his teeth prosecuting vandalism and reckless driving cases, and had only just stepped up to the big leagues. He recently scored a big win in a kidnapping case—a good case that spread his smiling face all over the media. That success might make him a little overconfident, Joe thought as they shook hands. His grip on the handshake was firm, something that Hennessy respected. Garrett was just over thirty years of age, and the rumor was that his hard work ethic, charming smile, and quick wit made him a certainty for a run in politics.

Garrett led Hennessy through the halls to his office, with his name proudly displayed on the frosted glass door. The office was spacious and modern, complete with a furniture set that looked like it had been ordered directly from the pages of a catalog—a clean, white desk with only a computer monitor on it, a Swedish-inspired couch, and a plain white bookshelf. A piece of art on one wall, and an indoor plant in the corner. Despite the recently laid gray carpet and freshly painted walls, there was still a sense of history in the office, a sense that any argument between the lawyers had already happened a hundred times before.

"Mr. Joe Hennessy," Garrett indicated to the seat in front of his desk before he sat down on the other side. "The man that's lucky enough to have two big cases, despite just starting a law firm."

"I notice a tinge of jealousy in your tone." Hennessy placed his briefcase on the floor and sat down.

"Who wouldn't be jealous? Most lawyers work decades to get the cases you've gotten since you've come back."

"My hard work was done many years ago, probably before you were even born."

"And I guess we're about to find out if you still have the skills." Garrett reached across to the drawer of his desk and pulled out a notepad. "How's the murder case for Zoe Taylor coming along?"

"That's none of your business."

"I work for the Circuit Solicitor's office. We all talk in here. This is a small city. Everyone in the prosecution's office is talking about the pretty young girl that stabbed her ex-boyfriend, but none of us can understand why you haven't claimed it was self-defense." Garrett shook his head. "You landed two big cases, Joe. You're a very busy man, having to juggle those two large cases by yourself. So, how's it looking?"

"It's still none of your business."

"Come on, Joe. We're both lawyers. I just want to know where it's going," he said. "And you're lucky she's pretty, young, and white. The only one she's missing is 'rich.'"

"What are you saying?"

"Don't pretend that you think the system is perfect. Bias matters. Nobody is going to convict a young white girl of murder. All she has to say is that it was self-defense, that her black ex-boyfriend was beating her, and she walks away. I don't understand why you haven't convinced her to plead self-defense. Any good defense lawyer would've done that. Why haven't you pushed her to change her plea? She goes to court in a matter of weeks."

"It's still none of your business." Hennessy stared at him. "And I'm only here to talk about the ridiculous charges against Henry Cruise."

"Right, your big money case. The one that will make you rich. There'll be a lot more work from Cruise after this one."

"This is the only case I'm doing for him."

"Come on," Garrett exaggerated his surprise, throwing his hands up in the air. "I know you're not that stupid. Cruise has gotten weaker, and people are coming after him. If he wins this case, you know that there'll just be another one waiting around the corner. And the way I hear it, you could do with the money."

He waved his finger in the air. "I tasted one of Luca Vineyard's Merlots last year. A beautiful drop. Strong, but full of delicate overtones."

"You're a talker, aren't you, Aaron?"

"I do love a chat."

"Well, I'm not here to chat. I'm a busy man," Hennessy said. "I'm here to talk about new deals for Cruise's case."

"Alright, alright. There's a deal on the table." Garrett laced his fingers together, cracked his knuckles, and then produced a sheet of paper from another drawer. "There's a copy of the plea agreement in front of you. He pleads guilty to this charge: possession of stolen goods under Section 16-13-180, and gets ten years."

"Ten years? The maximum sentence for possession of stolen goods worth more than $10,000 is ten years. That's not a deal, that's just pleading guilty."

"Ten years for each offense."

"You're not pulling that one over on me, young man," Hennessy said. "I know the law. Section 16-13-180 D, states that the receipt of multiple items in a single transaction constitutes a single offense."

"You do know the law," Garrett expressed his surprise. "They warned me you were good, but I didn't expect you to be that good. But hey, you can't blame a guy for trying." He reached back into the drawer and pulled out another piece of paper. He placed it on the table and took the other sheet of paper away. "This one might interest you more—five years in prison for an early guilty plea."

"Five months, not years, in prison for an early plea," Hennessy retorted. "That's the starting point of negotiations."

"No way. This is a solid case against him. He has no chance of winning this with a jury," Garrett leaned back and smiled smugly, sure that he had the upper hand. "So I advise that you look it over more thoroughly."

"My client won't take it. It's clear that Cruise was set up during the raid. We all know that."

"There isn't enough evidence that it was a setup. If you take this to court and he loses, he's looking at ten years. He'll die behind bars. I suggest you get it to him quickly, this deal is only good for the next week. After that, it's off the table." Garrett sighed, shook his head, and leaned forward. "Come on, you know as well as I do that Cruise is a guilty man. He's run a money-laundering racket through Charleston for years."

"That may be, but he's not guilty of this."

"Man, oh, man," Garrett leaned back again. He laced his hands together behind his head. "It's unfortunate that Jason Norris went missing…" He eyed Hennessy, waiting for a hint of knowledge to be detected on his face. "Norris was the final clinch point. He was going to be the star witness. He witnessed Cruise buying stolen paintings in the past."

"Your missing witnesses aren't my problem."

"Anything you want to tell me about that?"

"We have no idea where Norris is."

"Or was. We don't even know if he's alive anymore. Nobody has seen him in five weeks." Garrett sighed. "Do you have any idea what kind of monster you're going into business with? But I suppose it doesn't matter to you, as long as you get more clients added to your roster. You're just here in

Charleston to make money."

"You said in your email that you had an updated witness list for me," Hennessy was blunt, ignoring the jab. "That's what I came to see."

"This is the updated witness list," Garrett reached back into the drawer and removed a manilla folder. He placed it on the table and pushed it across to Hennessy. "I'm sure it'll make good reading for you."

Hennessy squinted as he read the first page, and then flicked over to the second page. "The names are redacted?"

"Suppressed."

"Why?"

"On advice from the Charleston Police Department. Testifying against Henry Cruise invites a lot of danger, and we don't want these witnesses to go missing. The witness statements are attached for you to review; however, any identifying information has been withdrawn. We've made the decision, based on the safety of the witnesses, to suppress their names until the trial."

"I'll file a motion to have them made available."

"I excepted nothing less," Garrett said. "But we're going to protect these witnesses. That's our job. After what happened to Jason Norris, we're not giving Cruise the opportunity to do it again."

Hennessy ran his eyes over the first witness statement, with numerous lines blacked out. "This person is associated with Richard Longhouse."

"I can't tell you that."

"They mention working with a senator here in Charleston, off King St." Hennessy raised his gaze to stare at Garrett. "That's Longhouse's office."

"Or a senator from another area that's visited

here."

"You don't need to tell me any more than that," Hennessy smiled and stood. "I have enough information already."

CHAPTER 14

HENNESSY STOPPED a block down from Longhouse's office, taking the first available space he saw. Parking was hard in tourist season. He stepped out of his truck, took off his jacket, and loosened his tie. The sun was blaring down on the streets, pushing past ninety-five again, and well on its way to a hundred. Summer had just about arrived.

As he approached Longhouse's office, he saw local news crews had gathered on the sidewalk outside the building. Longhouse was up on a make-shift podium, front and center, speaking into an oversized mic, while behind him, a large banner displayed his last name along with blue and red stripes.

"…by the end of October, we will deliver fifty new beds for homeless people in South Carolina with this new initiative." As soon as Longhouse spotted Hennessy in the small crowd, he froze. Longhouse stopped talking, and all color drained from his face within seconds. "I'm afraid I'm going to have to wrap it up, folks. Thank you for coming out today and supporting us."

There were still more questions from the crowd, and one local journalist with a large, outdated camera stood in front of Longhouse, almost taking his head off with a large boom mic. Longhouse pushed past, disgruntled, and Hennessy marveled at how quickly the mask fell once the cameras stopped rolling.

"We need to talk," Hennessy called out once he was in earshot.

"No, we don't." Longhouse turned to face him, his expression devoid of all niceties. "I don't want to hear anything you have to say."

"I've just seen an updated witness testimony in Cruise's case," Hennessy's voice was loud enough for the reporters to hear. "And it appears that you're connected to it."

Longhouse stopped at the door to the Meeting St. building. He paused for a moment, and then turned around. The reporters were all staring, waiting for his next move. Longhouse glanced at the crowd, then offered Hennessy a fake smile, before opening the door for him. "Why don't we go inside and talk? It's a little more private."

Hennessy stepped inside the foyer. The foyer was large with tall ceilings, with a small breakaway area at the side of the room—three brown couches sat next to the far wall, and next to them, two tall indoor plants.

"I shouldn't be seen in public with you," Longhouse grunted once the door closed behind them. He glanced around, stress bursting from his face, and indicated to the couches. He sat down and waited for Hennessy to do the same before he began talking. "I hope you're not here about Cruise's case. You should be focused on trying to find out who really killed Andre Powers."

Hennessy tilted his head, surprised that the conversation started with Zoe Taylor's murder case. "What do you know about that case?"

"I know that Zoe Taylor didn't kill Andre Powers." He lowered his voice. "I don't know who killed him, but I know she's innocent."

"What's your connection?"

"Andre had worked for me here and there. He was a good kid, willing to work hard to make some money. I know he got caught up in something, and then someone covered their tracks to make it look like Zoe killed him. But I met her once—there was no way she was a killer."

"You're not telling me everything." Hennessy stared at his former colleague. "You know something else."

"That's all I know." He looked over his shoulder to make sure there were no prying ears nearby. "And just to be clear—I'm not going on the record to say that."

Hennessy kept his glare on Longhouse, trying to work out the connection.

"Alright, Hennessy. It's clear you're here for something else," Longhouse kept his voice low. "What have you seen on Cruise's case?"

"I've seen a redacted witness statement that mentions a meeting with a Senator on Meeting St. that has to be you." Hennessy leaned forward, resting his elbows on his knees. "Who is testifying against Cruise?"

"You don't know yet?" Longhouse smiled. "Well, that's unfortunate."

"It'll be unfortunate if I expose your criminal connections before you run for Governor."

Longhouse's smile disappeared, and he leaned forward again, pointing his index finger at Hennessy. "I'm not your puppet. Anytime you want information, you can't just threaten me with that."

"Then tell me who is testifying against Cruise."

"I can't." He shook his head and looked away. "I'm not allowed to talk about it."

Hennessy's eyes focused on Longhouse as a realization sunk in. "Is it you?"

"Me? As if I would do that," Longhouse brushed the tip of his nose and turned away from Hennessy's glare. "Cruise is a dead man walking. There are a lot of people trying to sink his ship. I suggest you jump off while you still can."

"I don't know why everyone keeps making that excuse. You don't get to play with the law. If you're involved in setting him up, I'll make sure that's exposed before the court." Hennessy shook his head. "That's how the justice system operates, and no amount of connections or money will stop it."

"Joe Hennessy, the great moral compass," Longhouse scoffed. "Everything was black and white to you. This is good, or this is bad. Sorry to be the one to break it to you, Joe, but the world doesn't work like that. Business, politics, relationships—they all exist in the gray. They exist in a world where good isn't always respected, and bad isn't always frowned upon. Our lives, the lives of the rich, exist in that area where you always refused to go."

"Corruption."

"No," Longhouse scrunched his face up and waved him away. "I exist in a world of freedom. True freedom. You don't get to where I am without doing a few deals. That's freedom. The ability to do what you want, when you want to do it."

"The law exists so that freedom can thrive. Freedom occurs within the bounds of moral capacity, not the bounds of corrupt dealings."

"Always so simple," Longhouse shook his head.

"Cruise has had a good life. It's time for him to pay for his sins."

"You know something," Hennessy pressed. "What do you know?"

"I'm not talking," Longhouse looked away again. He stood and ran his hands over his hair. "But I will tell you something—I heard a rumor that Jason Norris is still alive, and he's still going to testify in Cruise's trial."

Hennessy raised his eyebrows.

"I thought that might surprise you," Longhouse laughed. "So stop worrying about me because you're going to have to deal with that before Cruise's trial starts next week."

CHAPTER 15

OUTSIDE THE confines of Charleston, Jason Norris felt like he could breathe for the first time in years. A breeze brushed over the lake and settled on his hardened face. There was a storm on the horizon, building above the mountains and threatening the lands below. His own storm, the storm of recovery, the one that he'd avoided for so long, was now so close that he could smell its heavy and humid stench. There was no use running from it. If he wanted to come out the other side, if he wanted to redeem himself, he had to accept what was coming.

He felt like jumping in the lake and forgetting everything. Lake Marion did that to him. It was familiar, like a long-lost family member, like an old dream, like a fantasy that didn't seem quite real anymore. Full of so many childhood memories. Full of so many smiles. Full of so many yesterdays.

His Aunt Sally had snapped the property up for a steal back in the 70s, only a few thousand dollars. Despite the rising real estate prices around her, Aunt Sally had no intention of selling, no matter how many estate agents knocked on her door, with offers that most would find too tempting to pass on.

He wished his mother was alive to see his redemption. He smiled when he remembered her. It'd been years since he smiled, or maybe it was closer to decades. Really smiled, that is.

He heard the door to the home shut behind him, further up the grassy hill. It was his brother. There was a twinge of nervousness in the way his brother was walking towards him, wearing a shirt buttoned up all the way to the collar, holding two freshly squeezed lemonades, one in each hand. He walked barefoot through the grassed yard, watching for any small stones.

"Sammy." Norris nodded to his brother, feeling like a kid again.

"You haven't called me that in years." Samuel looked down into his lemonade. The large square ice cubes clattered together. "No one has called me that in a long time."

Norris handed one glass to his brother, and they clinked them together.

Jason breathed in, filling his lungs with the fresh air. His heart was not empty. He still knew there was love in the world, no matter how many decades he'd tried to hide from it. There was more than enough here to fill him. There would always be more than enough here.

"Y'all good?" Samuel asked.

"I'm as happy as a pig in mud," Norris replied, and turned to his brother. "But you look worried."

"Not worried," Samuel shrugged. "I just got news that someone vandalized the building behind the church. Completely tore the place up trying to get inside."

"Don't they lock that place up after hours?"

"Sure," Samuel nodded. "But teenagers can be pretty ingenious."

"You sure it was teenagers?"

Samuel took a sip and stared at his brother. "Who

else would it have been?"

"No one. Is your house okay?"

"I—I have no idea. Do I need to check if it's okay?"

Jason opened his mouth to speak, then shut it again and shook his head. "Nah, of course not. I'm just being overly cautious. I'm sure it was just teenagers."

Lake Marion seemed like the safest place to hide. People would be looking for him, and they'd be watching his place in North Charleston, and anyone associated with him, including Samuel.

"Are you going to tell me why you are really here? I think you owe that to Aunt Sally, at least." Samuel asked. "We haven't asked you because maybe you just needed to work something out. But it's been five weeks now."

"You invited me, remember?"

"I invited you to the Sunday BBQ. You arrived one Friday night, without so much as a bag packed. And with a torn jacket sleeve."

"Aunt Sally tell you all that?"

"She told me because she's worried."

"She ain't in any danger. I swear. I wouldn't do that to her."

Samuel took a moment to consider it, and then nodded. "She's not worried about herself, Jason. She's worried for you."

"I can take care of myself."

"Is it money that you need? Are some people chasing you because of a debt? I have some money saved up, and I could help you."

Jason scoffed quietly to himself and bit his tongue, hard. If only money could solve his problems. That would be an easy fix.

"I'm not here to take Aunt Sal's house off her, if that's what you're implying. I just wanted to pay a long-overdue visit."

"And the bruises you arrived with?"

Jason turned his face away so that the scar wasn't so visible. He reached his hand up and felt his cheekbone, and the memories came screaming back.

The two men.

Nowhere to run.

For the first couple of seconds, he thought he was done, but self-preservation had set in. One right fist to a left cheek, a knee to the ribs. Jason was not as quick as he'd been as a young man, but he still remembered how to throw a punch. One of the thugs had made the mistake of wearing a chain around his neck. Jason had pulled back on it just long enough for the guy to fall to his knees, gasping for air. He then ran to the end of the street like a man three decades younger. He fled Charleston, taking three buses and one taxi to arrive at Lake Marion.

Aunt Sally had tears in her eyes when he knocked on her door.

"Redemption isn't a magic trick," Samuel said as they stared out into the depths of the lake. There was a rising, agitated tone in Samuel's voice. "You have to put the work in."

"You told me that I could be redeemed. Forgiven, even."

"And you do that by making things right, not by running away. You have to face your demons and your past."

"You think life is so simple and easy, don't you?" Jason shook his head. "That's because, for you, it always has been."

"A good life is earned, Jason." Samuel tightened his jaw. "I didn't take any shortcuts to get here."

Jason hung his head and stared at the lemonade his Aunt had squeezed by hand. He bent down and picked up a flat stone and skipped it across the water. He counted; one, two, three, four, five skips before it sunk.

Samuel scavenged around for the perfect stone on the ground, brotherly competition setting in. He slid it into the water and counted till he reached six, one better.

"Beaten by my kid brother," Jason shook his head. "I reckon God helped you on that last skip."

Samuel laughed and sat down on a large rock nearby.

"So, what do I do?" Jason leaned against a nearby tree. "I'm ready to face my past, but I just don't know what to do."

Samuel paused for a moment. "I find that thinking about others always helps. Gets you out of your own head. Minimizes your own struggles. Try volunteering your time someplace."

There was a twinge in Jason's guts. "That's good advice, little bro. Trouble is, other people are the very reason I'm in this predicament." He drank the rest of his lemonade. "If it was just me, well, then it wouldn't matter so much."

"Oh?"

"I've got my kids to think about."

"Your kids?"

"Yeah yeah, I know they want nothing to do with me…" Jason said, letting out a long sigh through his nostrils. "And that's my fault. I've hardly been a good dad to them, but I still have to protect them."

"You think that James and Jenny are in danger?" There was a squeak in Samuel's voice that he quickly tried to conceal with a cough.

"Let's just say that it's better if I am assumed dead."

"Dead?"

"I said 'assumed,'" Jason said. "If anyone knows that I'm alive, they won't just come after me. They will come after Jimmy and Jen as well."

"You told me that—"

"Boys!" a shrill voice called out. Aunt Sally still called them 'boys,' even though they were now firmly settled into their fifties.

Samuel cast a sharp glare in Jason's direction.

"I promise you. Aunt Sal is not in danger," Jason said. "Not here, anyway."

"And what about all of us back home? I've got kids as well, Jason."

"I'm going to take care of all that."

"I sure hope so. I hope you're going to do the right thing."

"But what's the right thing to do? I don't have many options."

"If you're serious about redeeming yourself, you've got to go back and tell the truth."

Samuel started to walk towards the home, but Jason hung back for a moment.

Going back, testifying against Henry Cruise based on the statement he provided to the police was tantamount to a suicide mission.

Unless, he thought to himself, he changed sides.

CHAPTER 16

THERE WAS always more than one case, always more than one file to focus on. Running his own law firm, Hennessy anticipated that juggling cases would be his hardest challenge. He needed to focus on one case in the morning and then switch to the second case in the afternoon. He'd called Barry Lockett that morning and asked him to track down Jason Norris, but once that phone call ended, he had to shift his focus back to Zoe Taylor's case.

Zoe Taylor stood on the sidewalk in front of the Charleston County Judicial Center, dressed in her best skirt and jacket combination, staring at the front doors. Tourists passed her in the street, happily going about their day and snapping pictures, unaware of the anguish occurring next to them.

"This is where it all happens?" Zoe said, looking up at the building. "This is where people will judge me?"

"That's right," Hennessy responded, standing next to her. He wiped his brow with the back of his hand. The heat was only getting worse.

"What are we doing today?" Frank asked, standing tall next to his daughter. He was dressed in his best suit, which was at least fifteen years old, and wearing too much Old Spice cologne. "Are you trying to get the case thrown out?"

"We're lodging an application to change venues in

an attempt to receive a fairer trial. But what we're really doing is sounding out the opposition and forcing them to stop making public comments about this case. We're also signaling our intention to fight this case on every front. If they think that we're going to fight it, and we have some grounds for an appeal, then they're more likely to present a better deal."

"I thought we told you that we weren't taking a deal?" Frank looked at Hennessy.

"My job is to get the best outcome for you. It's up to you whether or not you accept the deal, but we have to leave it open as an option."

Zoe nodded slowly, staring at the building. "Then let's do this."

They entered the courthouse. It was quiet and subdued inside, almost like a library. Nobody spoke a word out of turn. Nobody raised their voices. The conversations were hushed, and the tones were low. After the security checkpoint, Zoe and Frank proceeded to the side of the foyer, looking for a place to sit and have a cool soda before the case began in thirty minutes.

As Hennessy stepped through the metal detector, past the Deputy Sheriffs, he noticed a woman waiting for him. She was early thirties, with tanned skin and slicked back brown hair. She smelled pleasant—her soft perfume had vanilla, sandalwood, and citrus tones—and she'd dressed well, professionally in a black skirt with a white blouse. She stood with a confident posture, her back straight and head held high, but it was the look on her lips, a stealthy grin, which alerted Hennessy to trouble.

"Mr. Hennessy," she held out her hand as an introduction. "My name is Nadine Robinson. I've taken over as the Lead Solicitor for Zoe Taylor's case."

"Miss Robinson," Hennessy offered his hand to the prosecutor. "I hope you're ready to have this case thrown out. This is your first murder case, I hear."

"That's right," Robinson shook Hennessy's hand. "But no case is going to get thrown out today, and if you believe it is, then you're going to be sorely disappointed. It must be strange for you to be back here." She pointed down the hallway, directing him to the courtroom, and walked alongside Hennessy as they approached the edge of the foyer. "But by all reports, you've been in a lot of fights in these courtrooms. A great lawyer in your day, I hear, until the loss of your son."

Hennessy stopped, tilted his head, and squinted at Robinson.

"Don't worry, Mr. Hennessy. I research all my opponents to make sure I can expose every little crack in their armor." The niceties were already gone from Robinson's voice. "We're in courtroom five at the end of the hall. I look forward to our little debate and showing you how much has changed in the last twenty years."

Robinson stepped away from Hennessy, walking back towards the other side of the courthouse foyer, where Richard Longhouse waited next to the far wall. Longhouse didn't take his eyes off Hennessy once. Hennessy kept his stare on Longhouse for a few moments before he turned and walked into the courtroom.

Once inside the almost empty courtroom, Hennessy paused for a moment, drawing in a long breath. He scanned the room. The room felt dull, lifeless, and deliberately so. This was not a place to party, and it was barely a place to smile. Cream and brown were the dominant colors in the room. The walls were painted a light cream color, and the furniture was dark brown. They were a stark contrast, perhaps even a mismatch. There was a monitor on the wall to the left of the room and the jury box to the right. The judge's seat was raised, but not too much, and sat slightly to the left, in front of the Great Seal of the State of South Carolina. The American flag sat on one side of the seal, the flag of South Carolina on the other. The ceiling was high, and the room felt spacious.

Hennessy went through the gate to the defense table, where Jacinta was waiting for him in the first row of chairs. He greeted her, and she handed him a file.

He opened his briefcase and sat down on the dark brown leather chair. He reviewed his case notes for the next twenty-five minutes, reading over his application to move venues. At 1:55pm, Robinson entered the room with two female assistants. Zoe and Frank arrived next. A number of people filed in the doors after them. The clerk at the front of the room read the case number in a robotic fashion and then asked the room to rise for Judge Jane Whitworth.

Judge Whitworth walked into the courtroom, sat down, and then picked up the file in front of her. She smiled slightly. Her brown hair was thin and short, her skin tanned by the sun, and she wore bright red glasses. She'd spent four decades in the courtroom, dedicating her life to justice, once working alongside Hennessy in the Circuit Solicitor's office.

Zoe sat next to Hennessy at the defense table, her

leg bouncing up and down.

"Firstly, I must say welcome back to the courtroom, Mr. Hennessy. It's a pleasure to see you back here." Judge Whitworth was still reading the brief as she acknowledged the lawyers. "I see you've entered an application to change the venue."

"Thank you, Your Honor, and it's great to be back," Hennessy stood at the defense table. "We've lodged an application for a change of venue, pursuant to South Carolina Code of Laws, section 17-21-80, supported by an affidavit, because we believe the jury pool for this trial will be heavily prejudiced against the defendant. We wish to apply to have this trial moved to Richland County, to the 5th Judicial Circuit."

"Can you please explain why you believe the jury pool of the 9th Judicial Circuit would be tainted against your client?"

"A junior solicitor within this jurisdiction has taken it upon themselves to talk about this case in the media and has made the case an example of how a murdered black man can't receive a fair trial in the South. These comments have since been taken on by two politicians, who seem to be making these comments for political point-scoring. The extensive media coverage within the jurisdiction has reached a point where it's impossible for the defendant to receive a fair and impartial trial."

"Interesting argument," Judge Whitworth commented. "Do you have a response to that, Miss Robinson?"

"Yes, we do, Your Honor," Robinson stood and buttoned her black jacket. "The prosecution is strongly opposed to moving the venue on the basis that the death occurred within this jurisdiction and both the defendant and the deceased were residents of the jurisdiction. We still have to go through voir dire, and during that selection process, the defense will have the opportunity to question the jurors and any perceived prejudices at that time. If a potential juror proves to be influenced by the comments made in the media, he or she is dismissed from serving on the jury during voir dire."

"Your Honor," Hennessy argued. "This would severely weaken the capacity for a fair trial, and the defense would be at a major disadvantage if the case was to remain in this county. The South Carolina Code of Laws provides the judge the discretion to approve this application if there's a substantial risk to the fairness of this trial."

"I'm aware of the ruling," Judge Whitworth responded. "However, I agree with the argument that the jury selection process should eliminate any such problems. The application is denied."

"Your Honor," Hennessy picked up two pieces of paper from the table. "The defense would also like to make an application under Section 17-21-85, supported by an affidavit, for an order for jury selection in the criminal case to be conducted in another county. Under this Section of the South Carolina Code of Laws, a circuit judge may order that jury selection go forward in another county and the jury, when selected, be transported to the county in which the indictment was returned for the duration of the trial." Hennessy handed the pieces of paper to the bailiff, who passed the first copy to the judge and then the second copy to the prosecutor. "The potential jury pool within this county has seen five headline reports about this trial, including how this case is solely about the death of a black man, alleged at the hands of a white woman. These are turbulent times for race relations within our country, and any reference to such bias places undue pressure on the jury, creating an unfair trial for the defendant."

Judge Whitworth read the application, scanning her eyes over it and nodding.

"Again, Your Honor," Robinson argued, still standing. "This is why we have jury selection. We have processes within the judicial system to deal with any undue bias the jurors may have."

Judge Whitworth nodded and drew a long breath. "I understand your trepidation, Mr. Hennessy. I have also seen these media reports mentioning race relations, however, I will agree with the prosecution that the reason we have the jury selection process is to eliminate any potential bias." Judge Whitworth paused for a long moment before she continued. "This application is denied, pursuant to the powers under the South Carolina Code of Law Section 17-21-85, however I will warn the prosecution that public comment from their office is not to be made in reference to race relations. Mr. Hennessy has made a valid point on the media reports, and I will state that there may be grounds for a reversible decision if comments continue to be publicly made by representatives of the Circuit Solicitor's Office, and it's shown that the jury was unduly influenced by those comments. Agreed?"

"Yes, Your Honor," Robinson stated. "Your decision is noted."

"Thank you, Your Honor," Hennessy replied and looked across to the prosecutor's desk.

Robinson was packing up her laptop, nervous like

a student told off by the Principal. After Judge Whitworth dismissed the hearing and left the room, Robinson glared at Hennessy. Her cutting stare told him one thing—this case was going to be a fight to the end.

CHAPTER 17

JOE HENNESSY stepped inside his office's conference room.

Damien Bates was standing by the window, staring out at the people passing by on the street below. Bates smelled like cheap whiskey, perhaps with the scent of vodka mixed in. His jeans were dirty, his boots were scuffed, and his once white t-shirt had been stained to a light yellow color.

"How'd it go in court?" Bates turned to Hennessy and sat down on one of the office chairs. "Have you got that pretty little girl free yet? I bet the ladies in prison are going to love her. She's fresh, innocent, young, and so pretty. It'd be really hard for her behind bars. Almost makes you want to be there to watch what happens to her."

Hennessy stared at him for a long moment, resisting the urge to shove him into the wall.

"We're trying to make sure that she doesn't go to prison," Hennessy said as he sat down at the other end of the long table. "The prosecution seems determined to take this all the way. The media attention is heating up, and it's turning out to be a bigger factor than I expected."

"Why don't you just say she stabbed him in self-defense?" Bates lounged on the chair like it was his living room. He tucked one hand inside the top of his trousers. "That's what everyone is saying happened. If she gets up in court and says that, then she walks away. That's what you should encourage her to do. In my twenty-five years as a private investigator, I've seen many women lie to get what they want. It shouldn't be a problem for her."

"We're not going to lie in court. There were no physical marks on Zoe. The prosecution has indicated that if we go down that path, they'll still go for manslaughter. That's still a minimum sentence of two years. Right now, our best chance is to fight the murder conviction and raise reasonable doubt about her guilt. She's decided to plead not guilty, and that's what we're proceeding with. So what have you got for me, Bates?"

"I've got something good." Bates rolled his tongue around his mouth. He leaned forward with a shifty look in his eyes. "I got the name of a lead."

"And who is it?"

"It'll cost ya."

"Cost me?" Hennessy said. "This is the job I'm already paying you for. I'm not paying you extra for the information I've already paid you for. You need to tell me what you know, and you need to tell me now."

"Alright. Alright. Settle down, big guy," Bates threw his hands up. "I just thought I'd ask."

Hennessy stared down at the short investigator. He had no doubt that Bates would do anything to make a quick dollar, and he'd have no problem with betraying anyone or everyone.

"The lead is in Atlanta," Bates said. "Her name is Nicole Clifton. Drug user. She lived next door to Andre and knew him well. She moved the day after the murder happened. Seems like she's on the run to me."

"What makes you think that?"

"I spoke to her friend in the same building. She said Nicole was a lifelong South Carolina girl, and she left suddenly the day after Andre was murdered. Packed all her stuff in the car and just drove away. She's worth talking to."

"Phone call?"

"I tried that, but I've had a run-in with Nicole in the past. You'll need to go there and talk to her." Bates pulled a stained piece of paper from the back pocket of his jeans and slid it across the table. "You'll find her here."

"Isn't that what I'm paying you for? To investigate and talk to these witnesses?"

"Like I said, she won't talk to me. She'll shut up the second I step near her. It's best if you go."

Hennessy picked up the piece of paper and looked at the address. "I feel like you're sending me on a wild goose chase."

"No wild goose chase. Just a lead."

"This had better be a good lead." Hennessy leaned forward. "Because you are, without a doubt, the worst investigator I've ever worked with. You've given me nothing during the entire preparation of this case, and now you tell me there's a possible lead in another state, but you can't talk to her. It's like you want Zoe to be convicted."

"But I'm cheap," Bates shrugged like it wasn't the first time he'd heard that evaluation. "Just talk to this girl, Nicole Clifton."

Hennessy stared at Bates. Bates shifted uneasily under his glare.

"You could've sent an email with this

information," Hennessy sighed. "You didn't have to come to the office."

"I know." Bates looked around the room and then to the door. He stood and moved a seat closer to Hennessy, leaning forward and lowering his tone. "I came here because I wanted to sound you out about something."

"What's that?" Hennessy leaned back, distancing himself from Bates' bad breath.

"I wanted to talk about Henry Cruise," Bates whispered. "I can help you with him."

Hennessy squinted. "What do you know about Henry Cruise?"

"Everyone in my business knows Cruise. He's the man that people talk about. Sure, he's older now, but he still has money, and money talks. I've worked with Cruise before, pulled some jobs for him in the past. And I know that you're defending him as his lawyer."

Hennessy nodded, wary of giving too much away. He didn't expect Bates to be talking about the Cruise case.

"Well, I thought I could help you. You see," he looked over his shoulder again and lowered his voice to a whisper. "There's a rumor floating around that someone is willing to pay top-dollar to throw Cruise under the bus." Bates rubbed his fingers together. "And I'm talking big money."

"You're saying you'll cross Cruise for the right price?"

"I'm saying that I'll do anything for the right price. I could hook you up with the right people, and you could make a lot of money from it. All you'd have to do is ensure that Cruise goes to prison. And by the sounds of it, he's going there anyway. You see, you'd just be making money off a bad situation," Bates leaned even closer. "You and me, Joey-boy. We could strike it rich with this one."

"No thanks. That's not what I do as a lawyer," Hennessy stood and walked to the door of the conference room. "It's time for you to go."

Bates shrugged slightly and then stood up and walked out the door. "If you change your mind, you know how to find me."

Bates winked at Hennessy and then made a step towards Jacinta's desk. Jacinta leaned back, trying to create distance between her and the investigator. Hennessy called out before his investigator could begin to spread his sleaze all over Jacinta. "Goodbye, Damien."

Bates paused before he turned around and raised his hands in surrender again. He walked out of the office without saying another word.

"Thanks," Jacinta said once the door had closed behind Bates. "I hate spending any time around that creep. He stinks, and the way he licks his lips while looking at me is disgusting."

"If he gives you any trouble, let me know," Hennessy said. "I'd happily put my fist through his nose."

Hennessy turned back into the conference room. He sat back down at the table and wrote a name in the middle of a blank piece of paper. He stared at the name before putting a large circle around it.

Henry Cruise seemed to be at the center of everything.

CHAPTER 18

HENNESSY TOOK a flight west.

While he read Zoe Taylor's case files on the plane, his thoughts kept drifting back to Henry Cruise, the stolen artworks, and his other cases. Over the past month, Hennessy had beaten a DUI charge for another client, and another man walked through the door earlier that week with a request for a defense on a fraud charge. His reputation as a lawyer was growing in Charleston. Hennessy liked being busy, he liked the idea that the money kept rolling in, but he was almost at his limit.

Despite his workload, he needed to talk to Nicole Clifton face to face. With media attention on Zoe's case continuing to build, he needed a breakthrough, one big enough to smash open the case, and he couldn't trust Bates to deliver it.

He'd been to Georgia many times in his life, but had mostly remained on the tourist trail. He remembered a family holiday when he was young—visiting the Atlanta Zoo and seeing the lions, tigers, and bears, strolling around the headquarters of Coca-Cola, and sweltering in the summer heat. He remembered the style of the people on the streets, the swagger of confidence that people had, and overhearing the street language that seemed a world away from his schooling. But most of all, he remembered the food. The ice-pops in the middle of a summer's day. The barbequed burgers after a long day of activities. And the fried chicken. Oh, the fried chicken. His mouth salivated at the thought.

But there'd be no food tour on this visit. He would venture as far from the tourist scene as possible, visiting the darker side of the state. Once he landed, he hired the cheapest rental car, knowing that a nice car wouldn't last long in the places he was going.

Nicole Clifton was staying with her brother in Washington Park, a neighborhood just outside Downtown Atlanta. It was an area well-known for gang issues. According to the news, shootings were rampant, drugs were in abundance, and trouble was on every street corner. As Hennessy drove through the neighborhood, he passed home after home that looked cared for, some with fresh coats of paint, and didn't see any trouble. But as he turned down the street for Nicole Clifton's address, that view changed. The sidewalks were cracking, the street was littered with potholes, and trash filled most people's yards.

Hennessy stopped outside the address Bates had provided. The single-story home was run-down, beaten down by weather, time, and neglect. The front window of the home was boarded up. A section of the roof had blown off. There was no front fence. Hennessy parked the rental car near the entrance, locked it, and walked up the weed-infested path to the front door.

A short black man in his forties opened the door before Hennessy could knock, staring up in surprise at Hennessy's towering figure.

"Hello," Hennessy was cordial. "I'd like to talk with Miss Nicole Clifton."

"That depends on who's asking," the man was

weary of Hennessy's presence. "You're dressed like a cop. You a detective?"

"I'm not."

"A government worker?"

"No."

"Child safety?" the man raised his eyebrows. "Cause my kids have grown now. I've nothing to say to you guys anymore."

"I'm not from child safety," Hennessy said. "My name is Joe Hennessy. I'm a lawyer in Charleston. Miss Clifton might be able to help me."

"You've wasted your time coming out here." The man looked Hennessy up and down again, and then scoffed. "She won't talk to you."

Hennessy saw a figure appear over the man's shoulder inside the house. She was dressed in a dark purple dressing gown, and her black hair was a mess. It looked like she'd only just rolled out of bed, despite the sun passing its highest point of the day.

"Nicole Clifton," Hennessy called out. "I'd like to talk to you about why you left Charleston."

She was hesitant, but she approached the door. Her arms were folded across her chest, and she was wary of his tall presence.

"You're not in trouble, Miss Clifton, and it won't take long."

She came to the door and nodded to the other man. She had the dry skin of a drug user. She scratched constantly. And her eyes couldn't focus on anything for more than a few seconds.

"You want to know about that night with Andre, don't you?" Her voice croaked.

"Anything you can tell me could be helpful," Hennessy confirmed. "I understand you lived next door to him, and I understand you were friends. I'd just like to ask you a few questions about why you left Charleston the day after his death."

"I don't know if I should talk to you." She rubbed her arms and stepped out onto the porch. "Or if I should talk to anyone about Andre."

"Why not? Who are you afraid of?"

She looked out at the yard in front of her, leaning on the railing. "You got a smoke?"

Hennessy shook his head.

"I could do with a smoke." She bit her lip. "I lived next door to Andre for a year. He was a good guy, but like a lot of guys around there, he struggled to find work, so it led him to work for some bad people. It was the only work he could find around those parts."

"Was he working for a man named Henry Cruise?"

"Andre never told me who he worked for, but I know it was dangerous. I'd sometimes see him with bruises on his face or cuts on his arms. He was always carrying, just in case, you know? He told me once that he was involved in setting some people up. He said something about working for rich old men fighting each other, but that's all I know."

"Then why did you leave the night after Andre's death?"

"Are you kidding? I knew Andre was working for some powerful people, and when someone like that dies, you don't stick around to find out who did it."

"Are you saying his girlfriend didn't kill him?"

"Zoe?" She scoffed. "No chance. Zoe's little weak arms could barely pick up a knife, and she sure couldn't stab someone like Andre multiple times. Andre was so much bigger than her."

"Any ideas who it could've been?"

"No, but I know the day after the stabbing, a guy named Damien Bates was lurking around the building asking questions of all sorts of people. That's when I knew I had to get out of there. I didn't want to be messed up in it all."

"How do you know Damien Bates?"

"He's sold me a hit in the past."

"Of drugs?"

She nodded. Hennessy groaned. He'd been played by his investigator, and he didn't like it one bit.

"Do you know him?" Nicole looked up at Hennessy.

"He sent me here."

Nicole's face went white. She turned and reached just inside the door, grabbing a pack of cigarettes. Fishing a smoke from the pack, she held it to her mouth, and then lit it with a lighter. She took a long drag of the cigarette, and then blew a large puff of smoke.

"Bates is the worst. He'll do anything to make a dollar, and I mean anything. He'd pimp out his own grandmother for a dollar." She puffed hard on her cigarette. "And if there's something that needs to be taken care of, people send in Bates."

"What are you saying?"

"I'm saying he'll sell anything to the highest bidder."

Hennessy's fist clenched, and he leaned it against the porch railing, punching it lightly.

"So you're defending Zoe?" Nicole asked. "In court?"

Hennessy nodded. She puffed on her cigarette again.

"I liked Zoe. I only met her once or twice, but she

was nice." She paused while the thoughts went through her head. "I don't want to get involved, but you might want to talk to Dwayne Fox. He lived on the same floor as me. He was the one who told me he was moving out of the building, and I should do the same. Dwayne moved around a lot more than I ever have. He came from Florida and was only in the building for five months before he got out of there. He was the one that told me Andre was dead."

"And where is Dwayne Fox now?"

She looked up at Hennessy, and then slowly looked away. "He works over in Grove Park, not far from here. He's working at a store owned by his brother. We drove out here from Charleston together. We talked about who could've killed Andre, but we both knew that we didn't want to be in the apartment building when the cops came asking questions."

"Have you got an address?"

She reached inside and grabbed a small notepad. She scribbled the address of the store, tore off the piece of paper, and held it out for Hennessy to take.

"Look, Mister, none of this information came from me. And if you try to make me testify about anything, I'll deny it all," she said. Hennessy reached for the piece of paper, but she held onto it for a long moment. "All I know is that if Bates is involved, then there'll be trouble following close behind."

CHAPTER 19

HENNESSY CALLED Jacinta, and she worked her magic on the internet. Within minutes, she had Dwayne Fox's address, work history, social media profiles, family contacts, and past criminal convictions. After fifteen minutes of traffic in the rental car, Hennessy pulled into an outdoor lot and parked closest to the street. Two of the cars in the lot looked abandoned. Another looked like it was lived in. He doubled-checked his car was locked and then made his way inside. The top-half of the door to the drugstore was boarded-up, and electrical tape ran across a large crack in the main window. After walking through half the store, Hennessy found his intended target stocking shelves.

"Dwayne Fox?"

The man turned in surprise.

"Yes?"

"My name is Joe Hennessy. I'm a lawyer in Charleston." Hennessy looked around. "Is there somewhere we can talk in private?"

"What's it about?" Dwayne took a step back. "Am I in trouble?"

"No trouble," Hennessy said. "It's about Andre Powers."

A look of shock flooded over his face. "Mister, I don't know anything about that."

"I've just spoken to Nicole Clifton, and she

suggested otherwise."

He stepped back further. "Ok, ok." He tried to calm himself down. He looked at Hennessy's tall figure again, and then towards the end of the aisle. He was scanning for an escape route. His breathing shortened. "Did you say you were a cop?"

"No, I'm a lawyer. You're not in trouble." Hennessy slowed his speech pattern in an attempt to calm Dwayne down. "I'm representing Zoe Taylor, the girl accused of murdering Andre Powers."

"Ok, ok." Dwayne hushed him. "Just keep your voice down. I can't get into any trouble around here." He walked to the end of the aisle and called out to another worker stocking the shelves. "Anthony, I'm going to take my afternoon break now."

Dwayne waved for Hennessy to follow him through the back of the store. They walked through the storeroom, and Dwayne opened the roller-door used for deliveries and continued outside. He closed the roller-door behind Hennessy, and walked a few more feet before he stopped next to a dumpster and a large pile of discarded cigarettes. Dwayne pulled a cigarette from his pocket and lit it. He offered Hennessy one, but he declined.

"Do you know what happened to Andre Powers?" Hennessy began.

"No." His answer was reluctant. "I didn't see him get stabbed."

"But you were around there that night?"

He nodded, and sucked in more of the smoke, avoiding eye contact.

"What did you see?" Hennessy pressed. "Is there anything you can tell me?"

"I can tell you there was trouble."

"What sort of trouble?"

"There was a heavy walking around the building that night."

"A heavy?"

"Yeah. A heavy—that's someone that's employed to do the heavy work. Heavy lifting, you know?"

"Had you seen him before?"

"Yeah. I'd met him before. His name was Jason Norris."

Hennessy raised his eyebrows.

"Norris came knocking on my door and said he was looking for Andre Powers. I knew right then and there that it was trouble, and I wanted no part of it. When a heavy like Jason Norris knocks on your door, you get out of there."

"What did you tell Jason Norris?"

"Nothing, but that wasn't enough for him. He tried to force his way into my apartment, but one of the guys hanging out in my place was carrying. He showed Norris his piece, and Norris changed his mind about coming in."

"What happened next?"

"Nothing. We just went about our night like usual."

"But you left the next day?"

"That's right." Dwayne sucked back hard on the cigarette. He looked over his shoulder to make sure nobody was listening. "The next morning, the cops are crawling all over the street saying that they're going to charge someone with Andre's murder. I knew it was time for me to get out of there. I wanted to get out of there for a while, but that was the clincher."

"Then why take Nicole?"

"She was… we were good friends, sometimes we were more than that, you know what I'm saying? She came to my apartment the next morning and said she saw someone near the cars that night. I told her not to say a word, and she said that she'd already told her neighbor that she saw something. That's when I told her we had to go."

"If you had nothing to do with it, then why run?"

"Are you serious, man?" Dwayne scoffed. "That's what Jason Norris does. He sets people up. That's what he's known for. And if he was sniffing around my place, then I was a target. Nicole said the same thing. Jason Norris was sniffing around her place the night before. That means we were targets to be set up for Andre's murder."

"Are you saying Norris was the person who set up Zoe?"

"I'm saying that's a possibility."

"But once Zoe was charged, why didn't you return to Charleston?"

"Because Zoe is a pretty white girl. No jury is going to convict her of stabbing a poor black guy. And that means someone else would be charged, and I didn't want that to be Nicole or me. We have to stay out of Charleston until this blows over."

"Is there anything else you can tell me?"

Dwayne paused, shifting uncomfortably from one foot to the other.

"Dwayne," Hennessy said. "You know something. What is it?"

"I saw a guy named Damien Bates there that night." He looked around to make sure nobody was listening. "And I saw him the day before talking to Andre at his apartment."

Hennessy clenched his fist. "Thank you, Dwayne."

His trip to Atlanta had been helpful, but now he had more questions than answers.

But there was one thing that had become abundantly clear—Damien Bates wasn't telling the whole truth.

CHAPTER 20

DAMIEN BATES' office was located in a half-empty strip mall in North Charleston, next to a small shop on one side, and an empty laundromat on the other. Hennessy wasted no time in finding Bates, driving straight from the Charleston International Airport. Hennessy stepped out of the car and scrunched his nose. The parking lot was littered with trash, and it smelled like there was a broken sewer pipe nearby. The sign above the door said, "Private Investigator. Cheap." Hennessy banged hard on the closed wooden door, and it barely stayed on its hinges.

"Alright, alright," Bates shouted from behind the closed door. "I'm coming. Don't break it down."

Bates opened the door to be confronted by the towering figure of Hennessy standing over him. It only took a moment for Hennessy to grab Bates by the collar and push him back into the office.

Hennessy's right hand gripped Bates' collar. Within a split second, Bates found himself squashed against the wall inside his office, a hand gripped around his collar, unable to call for help. Hennessy pressed his knuckles into Bates' throat. "You lied to me."

Bates tried to struggle, tried to get free, but Hennessy was too big, too strong, and too determined, to allow Bates even the slightest of movements.

Bates tried to take a large breath, but gagged as Hennessy's hand pushed deeper. His eyes became wide as he tried to fight back. Bates lunged his knee towards Hennessy, hitting his thigh, but Hennessy didn't flinch. Rage had engulfed him.

"I need the truth."

Bates moved his eyes towards the table. Hennessy released some of the pressure from Bates' throat, allowing him to draw a breath. Hennessy held the investigator against the wall, waiting for him to continue.

"I can't talk while you're assaulting me," Bates swallowed hard. "Let me sit down."

Bates avoided eye contact as Hennessy held his stare on him for a long moment. When he was satisfied that Bates felt threatened, Hennessy released his grasp from Bates' throat.

Desperate to draw breath, Bates put his hands on his knees, sucking in deep gulps while struggling not to gag. When he finally regained his composure, Bates stepped away from Hennessy, back towards his office table, and most likely towards a gun. Hennessy stepped in his path and indicated that Bates should sit on the chair next to the door.

"Alright, alright," Bates was breathless, but held his hands up in the air. "Settle down, big guy."

Hennessy shoved him into the chair. "Talk."

"Alright, alright," Bates' voice rose to a higher pitch. He brushed his hand over the tip of his nose and sniffed. "What do you want to know?"

"You were outside Andre Powers' apartment the day before he was murdered."

"Did Nicole Clifton tell you that?" he asked. "I

know that she's lying because she wasn't there that day."

"It wasn't Nicole that told me."

"Who then?" Bates squinted.

"It doesn't matter who told me. What matters is why you were there."

Hennessy stood over the seated Bates. Bates looked around the office—he was too far from the weapon that he kept handy in the top drawer of his desk.

"I'm not going to ask you again, Bates. You need to start talking."

Hennessy understood that men like Bates lied as much, and as often, as they could, until they were unsure of the truth themselves.

"It was a coincidence," Bates pulled on his earlobe. "I was just looking around America St., and then there I was, at the corner of Harris and America."

"You lying prick," Hennessy brought his face to Bates' again. "You wouldn't know the truth if it slapped you in the face. You've been giving me false information this whole time. You were there. You know something and you're not telling me."

"There's nothing I can tell you," Bates looked away.

"You're off this case," Hennessy made a movement towards the door. Bates wasn't going to talk. "I never want to talk to you again, you dirty lying dog, and I'll make sure that whatever you're involved in is exposed in court. If you witnessed something, then I'm going to expose that to everyone."

"Be careful with the threats you make." Bates' tone changed as he sat in the chair. "I know something that may just hurt you."

Hennessy rested his hand on the door and paused for a moment. He opened the door, not wishing to engage Bates any further, but Bates continued anyway.

"Roger East," Bates called out as Hennessy stepped out the door.

Hennessy stopped and turned back to Bates, staring at him.

"I thought that might get your attention," Bates smiled. "You don't think I know about that? I know about everything that happens around here. And it'd be really unfortunate if Henry Cruise found out about your meeting with Roger East."

Hennessy stared at the dirty investigator.

"If you employ me again, and say, double my wages, I can forget all about it. I never heard a thing," Bates grinned. "But if you walk out that door and cut me loose, I'll be on the phone straight to Cruise, and you're going to have a lot of explaining to do."

"I won't be blackmailed," Hennessy said. "Not by you, and not by Roger East."

Hennessy walked into the parking lot, back towards his car.

"Good luck explaining that to Cruise," Bates laughed as he jumped to his feet and stood in the doorway. "Henry Cruise is not a very generous man when it comes to mistakes."

CHAPTER 21

THE CALL came later that afternoon.

Cruise wanted to meet, although he wouldn't say what it was about over the phone. From his tone, Hennessy could tell right away. Bates had made good on his promise to call Cruise. There was no use hiding the fact, and there was no use running from it. Hennessy had no choice but to meet with Cruise and explain the truth.

The Medici Ristorante in Hampton Park, north of Downtown Charleston, was not a tourist destination. They didn't welcome people they didn't know. The tables were small, the lighting was low, and the smell was musty. There was a bar at the front of the room and fifteen small round tables towards the back. The pictures on the wall were mostly of the Italian countryside, with the occasional picture of a family.

Henry Cruise sat in his empty restaurant, puffing on a cigar. The cigar smoke trailed up like tendrils, beckoning Hennessy towards the tired-looking mobster, a half-empty plate of pasta in front of him. There were two other men in the restaurant—the bartender, and a man stationed by the door, ensuring that no customers mistakenly wandered in off the street.

Cruise paused for a moment as Hennessy sat down. "I like you, Joe. There's something about you that makes you likable, and I don't like many people."

Cruise tapped the cigar on a small plate, avoiding eye contact. "But you're also a defense lawyer. Most defense lawyers I've met have been as dirty and corrupt as me."

Hennessy waited for Cruise to direct the conversation to his call from Bates.

"Order a whiskey, Joe. It's on the house."

Hennessy nodded and turned towards the bar. "A Talisker."

"Ah," Cruise said. "A good Scottish drop. Smoky. Peaty. And just enough punch to burn your throat. Good choice."

Cruise held up two fingers to the bartender, who poured the drinks and took them across to the table. He placed the drinks on the table and left.

Cruise smelled the whiskey and then took a sip. Hennessy did the same.

"I wanted to talk to you about the trial that starts next week," Cruise kept his eyes on the whiskey. "You going to get me off this thing, aren't you?"

"That's the plan," Hennessy replied. "We've got a strong case, although the prosecution has indicated that another witness has come forward."

"Another new witness," Cruise scoffed. "They just keep bringing witnesses forward. We're a week out from the trial, and they just keep adding to the case."

Cruise brought the cigar to his mouth and took a long puff before he blew the smoke back into the air.

"Listen, Joe. I'm sure you knew my reputation before you took the job. I like intimidation, and I like revenge. Those two things make me a very happy man, and in my old age, I enjoy them even more. Those two things have kept me in business for decades. Intimidation and revenge. They make me happier than a pig in mud." Cruise turned his glare to Hennessy, staring at him with the intensity of a threatened lion. "My question is—are you a trustworthy man, Joe?"

Hennessy nodded his response, not breaking eye contact.

"You aren't going to throw this trial on me, are you?"

"I'm not."

"Word on the street is that you've been approached with certain offers from certain people. People who want to see me go down. Lots of money has been talked about."

"Someone offered me a large sum of cash to throw the case, but I didn't take it."

"Who?"

"Roger East."

Cruise nodded slowly and puffed on his cigar again. He looked at the end as he continued talking. "Think how it looks to me. You come back to Charleston because you need money to save your vineyard, and someone offers you a lot of it to throw this case. Probably even enough to save the vineyard you love so much. So you take my money, then take their money, lose the case, and walk away from Charleston forever. That sounds like a sweet deal to me, almost a chance too good to pass up."

"That's not what I'm going to do."

"Good." Cruise leaned forward and made eye contact. "Because if you lose this case, then that's what it looks like to me. And people who cross me don't live for very long. Win the case, or I'll think you double-crossed me. And if you double-crossed me, I'll give you a chance to meet your dead son."

CHAPTER 22

AFTER ANOTHER day in the office working on case files, Hennessy walked home through the streets. It was hot again. The heat was baking the sidewalk, burning heat rising off the pavement. Joe took off his tie, undid the top two buttons, and rolled up his sleeves.

He received a call from Wendy. She said she would be down for the weekend. He told her it was a long drive to make just for the weekend, and she should stay at the vineyard, but she wouldn't listen. She knew he was going to need support before the trial started the following week. On Friday morning, he'd already planned his night ahead—lose himself in the haze of a bottle of Mr. Johnnie Walker and dig a huge hole of despair. Perhaps it was Wendy's sixth sense that made her drive down, or perhaps it was a coincidence, but he was glad she was coming to stop him.

As he walked through the Friday evening crowds, the previous week's events were still running through his head. He never should've accepted Cruise's money. That was becoming clearer now.

He arrived at his apartment a little after 7pm, and walked in to find Wendy in the kitchen. She was wearing a floral apron, her hair pulled into a tight bun on top of her head and a touch of pasta sauce on her shoulder. She was cooking, sipping on a glass of red wine, and stirring the pot. It might've looked normal, average, but to Joe, it was so much more than that. At that moment, she was the only thing holding his universe together.

Hennessy's rental was a small, no-frills, two-bedroom apartment on a quiet tree-lined street, two blocks from the action of Wentworth St. While it only had a small kitchen and living area, it also had a lovely view of the nearby park from the front porch.

"Looks like you're cooking up a storm," he kissed her on the cheek as she stirred the pot. "And thank you for coming down."

"I knew you would need it," she responded. "It's seafood fettuccine, along with a bottle of our Merlot from two years ago."

"Oh, nice choice," Hennessy smiled. "Out of all the seasons we had for the Merlots, that was my favorite. I was going to have a Caesar salad tonight, but this smells so much better."

"What do you call a rooster looking at a pile of lettuce?" Wendy smiled. "A chicken-sees-a-salad."

He laughed as he grabbed another wine glass from the cupboard.

Wendy finished cooking, Joe fixed the plates, and they ate at the eat-in kitchen countertop while sitting on tall stools. They told each other stories of their week, laughing as they went. Joe complimented Wendy's cooking, saying it was the best pasta he'd had in years. Over the meal, they talked about the heat, the news, and the local gossip. They chatted about the vineyard, and how the season was looking amazing. It was the best meal Joe had had in months, but it wasn't just the food. He missed his wife. Even after decades of marriage, he still missed her. He missed her laugh, her smile, and her stories.

After they placed the dishes into the dishwasher, Joe led Wendy out onto the front porch. There was a small two-seater couch on the raised porch, and they sat, sipping wine in the cool night air. They looked over the quiet street, enjoying a moment of calm in the city. They sat in silence for a few moments before Wendy asked the question that she'd been thinking about all evening.

"Have you been to the bridge?"

Joe didn't respond, staring out at the moon.

"Joe?"

He drew a long, deep breath before he replied. "No. I can't. I can't even go near it. If I have to travel that way, then I'll drive the long way. I just... there are too many bad memories there."

Wendy nodded and then looked into her glass. "I'm going to go there tomorrow and say a prayer. Do you want to come with me?"

"I'm sorry," Joe shook his head. "I can't. Not yet."

Wendy understood. The grief of losing their son had been repressed for so long, but being back in Charleston, the pain felt so fresh again.

"I still miss him." Joe struggled, one tear escaping his grip. The tear rolled down his cheek. He didn't wipe it away. "I miss the man he would've become, and I miss the times that we could've had together. All that was stolen from us."

"I would've liked to have seen his wedding," Wendy smiled, tears of her own sliding down her cheeks. "Can you imagine that? Little Luca waiting for a woman at the end of the aisle. She would've been amazing, I bet."

"The best," Joe whispered.

He rested his head on Wendy's shoulder, and they didn't say another word until the moon had passed behind a large cloud.

CHAPTER 23

AFTER SPENDING much of the weekend with his wife, Joe Hennessy's desk was elbow high with folders and papers. He had gone back into the office at 2pm on Sunday after he waved Wendy off, and then worked till 2am, before he arrived back at his desk at 9am the next morning. He'd managed five hours of sleep, not that it was a problem.

When life was pushing so hard, with no margin for error and no chance to make a mistake, Hennessy's focus increased. He was working so frantically that adrenaline was his driver, singing through his body, tingling his senses, forcing him to push past his limits. It was in the adrenalized excitement of a trial that he found himself, unable to sleep but not needing to. He needed to work, he needed to challenge the justice system, and he needed to push himself past the edge.

Anything to avoid the feelings of grief that bubbled under the surface.

"Aaron Garrett is here to see you." The intercom in his office buzzed. It was Jacinta. "He says he has new discovery material to present to you."

Not what he wanted to hear as he prepared for the case, but not unexpected. "Let him in."

Garrett entered the office with a swagger, a spring in his step, dressed in a well-fitted suit. His tie was bright red, and he was wearing an extra shot of cologne, a heavy punch of woody aroma.

"Looks like you've been nice and busy, Joe." Garrett nodded towards the mountains of paperwork on the desk. "I hear that you've got more work than you can handle?"

"I'm a busy man, Aaron, so what have you got for me?"

"No time to be nice? Most lawyers around here like to have a bit of a chat first," Garrett smirked as he sat down in front of Hennessy's desk. "You and I could be friends, Joe. We could work together, putting away all the criminals in Charleston. I present you a deal, and you convince your clients to take them. That's the way justice should work. We work as a team. Do you know what 'team' stands for? Together Everyone Achieves More. That could be you and me, working together to clean the streets. We could be like a superhero duo. Maybe even get a statue made in our honor one day, right in town, so that people can talk about the great partnership of two successful lawyers. They could put us next to the bust of Gedney M. Howe, in front of the Judicial Center. Imagine that? People would talk about us for generations. Maybe they'd even study our cases at college."

"What have you got, Aaron?"

"Still no time to chat?" Garrett smiled and crossed one leg over the other. He waited a moment for Hennessy to respond, and when he didn't, he continued. "That's fine. I won't take it personally. The non-redacted witness statements are now available. And a new witness has come forward."

"What a surprise," Hennessy leaned back in his chair. "Here we are, five days before Cruise's trial begins and a new witness has come forward. What a coincidence."

"I don't know what you're implying, Joe, but there's nothing untoward here. If you think there is, I'd like to see you prove it."

"I bet you've covered your tracks well."

"Indeed. We have a witness who will testify that they saw Henry Cruise dealing with stolen artworks." Aaron laced his hands together and rested them in his lap. "Five days is enough time to conduct a deposition with this new witness and prepare for the statement at trial. My assistant will send through the electronic copy, but I wanted to drop this off myself." Garrett reached forward, opened his briefcase, and removed a manilla folder. He placed it on the table and tapped his hand on top of it. "But you can't touch this witness."

"You must know that I'll object to this new witness. We haven't had the chance to depose him, nor check their background."

Garrett shrugged. "Then I'll guess we'll have to see what the judge has to say about that."

Hennessy stared at the prosecutor, considering if he was giving too much away.

"Is Jason Norris still going to testify?" Hennessy questioned. Lockett had no luck finding out if Norris was still alive. There was no trace of him.

"We don't know where he is. We haven't talked to him in weeks. In fact, we have assumed he's dead. But that doesn't matter. We still have enough evidence to prove that Henry Cruise arranged for the theft of those stolen artworks and was in possession of them when he was arrested."

Hennessy leaned forward. "You know as well as I do that Henry Cruise was set up. Someone took an opportunity to plant the stolen paintings at the Five Corners before the PD performed the so-called 'raid.' This whole case stinks of corruption."

"A life like the one that Henry Cruise has lived has a way of catching up with a man. Eventually, you have to pay the piper. A lifetime of crime gets paid one way or another."

"Not for this."

"Sure, the world's perfect. We only catch criminals in the act," Garrett scoffed. "The world is a lot more complicated than that. Do you think the general public cares what a criminal is put away for? No. They don't care. They just want their streets safer. And that's my job—to make the streets of Charleston safer."

"If you wanted to make the streets safe, you should've become a traffic warden."

"Nice advice, but I don't think I'll take it up. And I guess that's like the old saying—if you want to make crime pay, become a defense lawyer." Garrett smiled. "I have to say, Joe, you look a lot older than the last time I saw you. There's a lot more gray in your hair. Is the stress of being a lawyer starting to get to you?"

Hennessy ignored his comment. He reached across the table and picked up the manilla folder. "I trust this statement isn't redacted?"

"No, all the unredacted statements are available now," Garrett stood to leave. "Henry Cruise has made a lot of enemies in his lifetime. There are a lot of people that'll be happy to see him rot in prison. The threats that Cruise makes mean nothing to these people. They've already lost too much at his hands—business, money, sons, daughters. They're not scared anymore. Not of Cruise, not of you, and not of the courts. They want justice." Garrett's words sunk to the floor. "See you in court next week, Joe. I'm looking forward to it."

Garrett walked out of the room, and Hennessy waited a moment.

He opened the paper file, scanning his eyes over the unredacted statements. There were no surprises on the first few pages, but page five made his mouth drop. It was the new witness, the new testimony of someone who had stepped forward to testify against Henry Cruise.

"Of course," Hennessy's fist clenched as he said the name aloud. "Richard Longhouse."

CHAPTER 24

INDICTMENT

STATE OF SOUTH CAROLINA
COUNTY OF CHARLESTON
IN THE COURT OF GENERAL SESSIONS
NINTH JUDICIAL CIRCUIT
INDICTMENT NO.: 2022-AB-02-155

STATE OF SOUTH CAROLINA, V. HENRY DAVID CRUISE, DEFENDANT.

At a Court of General Sessions, convened on 10th of March, the Grand Jurors of Charleston County present upon their oath: Receiving stolen goods, chattels, or other property; receiving or possessing property represented by law enforcement as stolen.

COUNT ONE
S.C CODE SECTION 16-13-180.
RECEIVING STOLEN GOODS, CHATTELS, OR OTHER PROPERTY; RECEIVING OR POSSESSING PROPERTY REPRESENTED BY LAW ENFORCEMENT AS STOLEN.

That in Charleston County on or about 10th of March, the defendant, HENRY DAVID CRUISE, did possess property represented by law enforcement as stolen, in violation of Section 16-13-180 South Carolina Code of Laws (1976) as amended. To wit: HENRY DAVID CRUISE did take possession of stolen artworks which he knew, or should have known, were stolen and the said artworks had an estimated value greater than ten thousand dollars per Section 16-13-180 (C) (3).

FINDINGS

We, the Grand Jury, find that HENRY DAVID CRUISE is to be indicted under Section 16-13-180 South Carolina Code of Laws (1976) as amended.

*****

THE CHARLESTON County Judicial Center sat behind the Four Points of the Law, a historic intersection and tourist destination in Downtown Charleston. The Four Points had a notable building on each corner, representing God's law, city law, state law, and federal law, where a person could get hitched, ditched, taxed, and imprisoned all in one intersection.

On the southeast corner of the Four Points sat St. Michael's Episcopal Church, representing God's law. Constructed in 1751, the church had a well-photographed 180-foot-tall white steeple, which had become representative of the city of Charleston. Joe Hennessy paused in front of the church as he passed, looking up to the famous white steeple, feeling a sense of history, standing in front of the same church where George Washington and Robert E. Lee once attended. There were tourists around, snapping photo after photo, not looking where they were going, unaware that just behind the intersection, the modern story of crime and justice was unfolding.

After months of bluster, after months of pretense, Henry Cruise was to have his day in court. The prosecution had offered several deals to avoid the trial, all including prison time of five years plus. Cruise refused each deal, stating that he wasn't going to prison for something he didn't do.

Hennessy walked into the Charleston County Judicial Center and into courtroom number five. Cruise, dressed respectfully in a fitted suit, waited at the defense table to discover his fate. His arrogance was still there—he still presented himself as the most powerful man in the room—but the cracks were beginning to show in his armor. Hennessy noticed a moment of nervousness, a moment of vulnerability, as Cruise waited for the jury selection process to begin.

During a deposition two days earlier, Richard Longhouse had given nothing away. He barely said a word that wasn't already listed on the witness statement. Yes, he saw Cruise deal with stolen paintings. Yes, he was sure they were stolen. Yes, he was telling the truth. No, he didn't buy any himself. No, he wasn't trying to frame Cruise. Very factual, very lackluster, and nothing of substance.

The prosecution team walked into the courtroom, their conversations jovial. Their confidence was clear, and they weren't threatened by the case, the evidence, or Cruise. They were already marking it down as an easy win.

"Five minutes," the bailiff called out, alerting everyone that Judge Curtis Blow would soon enter the courtroom, and the trial was about to begin.

The courtroom filled behind them. Media, onlookers, and law students filled the gallery. There wasn't an empty seat. There was a buzz in the crowd, a frantic murmur of anticipation for the trial. Cruise had five people there for support, but none of them were family. He told Hennessy that he had children and grandchildren, but Hennessy had never seen a photo of them, nor had he ever heard them mentioned by name.

"All rise. The court is now in session, the Honorable Judge Curtis Blow presiding."

Judge Blow walked into the courtroom, head down, and focused on his desk. He stood behind his chair for a moment, looked over the courtroom, and then sat down. He moved the files in front of him, stared at Henry Cruise for a long moment, then took off his glasses and wiped them with a cloth. Once he placed his glasses back on, he moved the microphone closer, and welcomed the parties to the court. He let the lawyers introduce themselves, asked Cruise if he understood the charges against him, and once satisfied, he called for jury selection to begin.

The morning was spent in voir dire, the jury selection process. While Hennessy was concerned with jury bias in Zoe Taylor's murder trial, he was happy to fill Cruise's jury box with local Charleston residents. Henry Cruise, despite his criminal faults, was a Charleston man through and through. Locally born and raised on the Peninsula, he'd never lived anywhere else. He talked like a Charleston local, dressed like a Charleston local, and went to church every Sunday, just like a Charleston local. While some members of the jury pool were excluded for various reasons, including knowing Cruise personally or a poor understanding of legal terms, the remaining twelve jurors were selected without much hassle.

Ten jurors were middle-aged, two were older. Some of them were single, some had families, one was divorced and childless. There was a manager of a souvenir shop. A hairdresser with six children. A taxi driver, a retiree, and a stay-at-home mother. A Black banker, a Cuban cleaner, and a former Las Vegas Casino owner who moved to Charleston to live a slower pace of life. Five women, seven men. Alternatives were also selected—they were the people who would listen to the evidence but take no part in the deliberations, unless required by the court.

After jury selection, the court took a brief recess.

Fifteen minutes later, the crowd was settled, as were the lawyers. Cruise leaned back in his seat, nodding to himself, running his hands up and down his suspenders. The seats in the courtroom were almost full, the spectators whispering to each other in hushed tones.

When Judge Blow returned, the crowd hushed.

When instructed, the bailiff walked to the door in the front corner of the room, guiding the members of the jury to their seats. Some appeared nervous, some appeared confident, but all appeared ready.

They took their oath, under instruction from Judge Blow, "Madam Foreman, Ladies and Gentlemen of the Jury. Please stand and raise your right hand to be sworn: You shall well and truly try, and true deliverance make, between the State of South Carolina, and the defendant at bar, whom you shall have in charge, and a true verdict give, according to the law and evidence. So help you God."

After they confirmed their oaths, Judge Blow continued, "Under the constitution and laws of South Carolina, you are the finders of the facts in this case. I do not have the right to pass upon the facts or to even express any opinion that I might have as to them because this is a matter solely for you, the jury, to determine. As jurors, then, it is your duty to determine the effect, the value, the weight, and the truth of the evidence presented during this trial."

The jurors confirmed their understanding, and Judge Blow invited prosecutor Aaron Garrett to begin his argument.

*****

"Your Honor, ladies and gentlemen of the jury. My name is Aaron Garrett, and these are my colleagues, Michelle Saltmarsh and Maxwell Smith. We're here to present the charges against the defendant, Mr. Henry Cruise. As Judge Blow has explained to you, Mr. Cruise is charged with possessing property represented by law enforcement as stolen as defined by the State of South Carolina Code of Laws. I'm standing before you to make an opening statement, and this statement will provide an overview of the trial, as nothing I say now is considered evidence.

I represent the Circuit Solicitor of the Ninth Judicial District in the State of South Carolina. As their representative, I work to enforce the law as it is written, ensuring that those who break the law are convicted, regardless of race, gender, or wealth.

Now, Mr. Henry Cruise is indeed wealthy. He has amassed a large property portfolio, including his home in Downtown Charleston, a vacation home in Florida, a rental home, a restaurant, and most importantly in this case, his property portfolio also includes the Five Corners Art Gallery.

It was in this art gallery, the art gallery owned by Mr. Cruise, that police found five stolen Stephen Scully paintings. Mr. Scully was a world-renowned artist in the 1940s and 1950s, who was respected for pushing boundaries and paving the way for a lot of modern art that we see today. These paintings, especially as a set of five, were highly sought after by art collectors and had an individual value of an estimated one million dollars each. In total, the paintings were worth more than an estimated five million dollars.

Three of these paintings were stolen in the 1980s from an art gallery in Florida, and had never been located since, and two of the paintings were stolen on the 1st of March from an apartment in Manhattan, New York. This was the first time they'd been together for almost forty years.

These paintings were found in the storeroom of Mr. Cruise's art gallery, wrapped in brown paper, perhaps in an attempt to hide them. Due to a tip-off to the police, a raid was actioned on the property on Broad St., in Charleston, led by Detective David Duncan of the Charleston Police Department. During this trial, you will hear from Detective Duncan, and he will explain to you the process of the raid. You will also hear from other police officers who were there on the day of the raid, and they will tell you what they saw in the art gallery.

The stolen paintings were in the storeroom of the Five Corners Art Gallery. That is a fact, and that is not up for dispute. We have body-camera footage from the officers who conducted the raid at the gallery, and we will show that to you during the trial. It will show, clearly, where the paintings were found.

Mr. Cruise was the only person in the art gallery at the time of the raid. He is the sole owner of the art gallery, and he was in control of those artworks.

Now, at this point, it's important to make a clear distinction of law for you. You will hear the term 'possession' a lot during this trial, and when you hear it, I want you to remember that this is a legal reference to the term. In law, here in this court, constructive possession means that the defendant had dominion and control or the right to exercise dominion and control over the stolen item. I will repeat that so it's clear for you—constructive possession is the ability and intent to exercise dominion and control over the item or the premises on which the item was found while knowing the items were there.

That's an important distinction to make—say, the police did not need to catch Mr. Cruise with his hand on the item to prove he was in possession of it, rather, they only have to ensure that it's proven that the stolen items were under his knowledge along with dominion and control.

As such, you will hear from witnesses who will state that Mr. Cruise discussed the stolen items. You will hear from witnesses who will state that Mr. Cruise offered to sell them the items and that he knew they were stolen. And you will hear from witnesses who will state that Mr. Cruise had every intention of selling the stolen items.

These charges require reasonable control of the items in question, and Mr. Cruise clearly had that.

Possession of stolen property is not a victimless crime.

It affects each and every one of us. The trickle-down effect of behavior like this encourages more crime on our streets. There are insurance amounts to pay out from the people the artwork was stolen from, which in turn, affects how much we all pay for insurance. There are black market activities that are related to dealing with stolen goods. We don't want these activities on the Peninsula. We don't want them in Charleston County. And we don't want them in the great state of South Carolina.

It's my job to ensure this behavior doesn't continue, and it's your job to listen to the facts, understand the case, and ensure that Mr. Henry Cruise is convicted of this crime.

Over the coming days, we will present witnesses to you, and they will provide the evidence in this case. As I mentioned, you will hear from the police officers that conducted this raid. You will see footage from their body cameras, and footage from other officers' body cameras during the raid. You will see, with your own eyes, the moment the stolen artworks were discovered. You will hear from undercover police officers who will testify that they heard Mr. Cruise discussing his possession of the stolen paintings. You will also hear from associates of Mr. Cruise, and they will testify that Mr. Cruise discussed selling the stolen paintings with them.

You will hear from Mr. Cruise's ex-wife, Ms. Hamilton, who was the former manager of the Five Corners Art Gallery. She will explain that Mr. Cruise advised her that he wanted to purchase stolen items. You will hear from Mr. Adriano Castellano, a former politician, who will explain that Mr. Cruise offered him the option to buy the artworks. You will hear from expert witnesses who will explain the worth of these paintings.

This was an unjustifiable crime, and Mr. Cruise deserves to be punished by the law.

At the end of this case, I will address you again and ask you to consider all the evidence we have presented and to conclude beyond a reasonable doubt that Mr. Henry Cruise is guilty.

Thank you for your time."

*****

During the jury selection process, Hennessy had identified two strong leaders. The first, juror number five, was likely to side with the prosecution, and the second, juror number ten, was likely to side with the defense. Number five was a straight-laced retiree—tall, fit, and strong—who'd spent his entire life working for various government agencies and had never even so much as had a parking ticket. He was likely to believe anything that came out of Garrett's mouth. Juror number ten appeared equally as strong in character—he'd spent his twenties in the Air Force, but after that, he spent years fighting for every dollar, fighting to survive, balancing on the line of the law.

Leaders were important in the jury room, as the jurors weren't just twelve individuals submitting twelve different votes. If that were the case, a jury would be split up, kept in different rooms, and left to vote without a discussion. Rather, a jury was a panel of people who worked towards a general consensus. A juror with a strong character could lead some people to change their minds, swaying other opinions with their passion and delivery, rather than factual evidence.

As soon as Garrett finished his opening statement, Hennessy stood and walked to the lectern near the jury box, ready to deliver his opening.

When invited by Judge Blow to begin, Hennessy looked to the jury, nodded, and then began.

*****

"Ladies and gentlemen of the jury, Your Honor, my name is Mr. Joe Hennessy. I'm a criminal defense attorney, and I'm here to represent the defendant, Mr. Henry Cruise.

I want you all to remember something very important as we progress through this case—this is a court of law. As such, we are here to judge the law. We're not here to talk about feelings, or intuition, or our thoughts. We're not here to use our 'gut.' We're not here to guess.

We're here, in this court, to judge a man based on the evidence that is available against the laws that are applicable. Regardless of where the stolen items were found, it is the law to judge a man based only on the available evidence.

Evidence is defined as the body of facts that indicate whether a belief is true or valid. That's evidence. An assumption is defined as a thing that is believed without proof. Without proof. In this court of law, you cannot convict a man based on assumptions. You must only use evidence to make your determination.

You cannot use the defendant's looks, his family situation, his business interests, or your gut feeling to form a decision. You cannot use assumptions. You cannot guess. You must only use the evidence presented in this court. And in making your decision, you must be unprejudiced. You must be fair. And above all else, you must be just.

In the State of South Carolina, it's only a crime to knowingly possess a stolen item. A person cannot be convicted if they were not aware of the stolen item being present on their person or within their control. The prosecution must prove, beyond a reasonable doubt, that Mr. Cruise knew the paintings were in his art gallery.

They won't be able to, of course, because he didn't know that they were there.

What the prosecution has failed to highlight in their 'roadmap' is the fact that Mr. Cruise only managed the art gallery for five days. You will hear from witnesses who will state that Mr. Cruise had very little involvement in the art gallery until five days before the police raid. These witnesses will tell you that before the 5th of March, the manager of the art gallery was Mr. Cruise's ex-wife, Ms. Hamilton. At the time, they were going through a messy divorce, and Mr. Cruise retained the art gallery as part of the settlement.

You will hear from witnesses who worked at the Five Corners Art Gallery, and they will testify that the paintings weren't there the day before the police raid.

You will hear from witnesses who will testify about their doubts on the authenticity of the paintings. Mr. Ivan Allen will explain that the paintings have all the characteristics of a series of fakes. If you have reasonable doubt about the validity of the paintings, then you cannot convict Mr. Cruise on a charge of possession of stolen goods. If the paintings are proven to be fakes, which the witnesses will tell you they are, then they're not the paintings stolen from the location in New York. Rather, they are replicas of those paintings.

You will hear from witnesses who will tell you the Stephen Scully paintings were about to become worthless, due to allegations of child sexual assault against the artist. These allegations were to be published in a book next year by five of the people he abused.

Throughout the testimonies, you must remember this is a court of law. This is not a court of guesses. If there are gaps in the prosecution's case, then you must find Mr. Cruise not guilty. If there are gaps in the evidence, then you must find Mr. Cruise not guilty. If there are gaps in the evidence given in the testimonies, then you must find Mr. Cruise not guilty. This is a court of law, where we listen to the evidence, and only the evidence. This isn't where you decide an outcome based on assumptions.

You require sufficient evidence to make a decision. You will not have enough evidence to make a decision in this case. At the end of this trial, your only choice will be to find Mr. Cruise not guilty.

Thank you for your service to this court."

CHAPTER 25

DETECTIVE DAVID Duncan was a broad-shouldered man in his late thirties, with a jaw slightly too large for his face and eyes that were slightly too close together. There was something lifeless about his eyes—he had a cold, distant stare—but years of police work could do that to a man. He walked to the witness stand with confidence, swore his oath loudly and proudly, and when he sat in the witness box, he provided a nod to the jury.

"Thank you for talking with us today, Detective Duncan. Can you please begin by telling the court your profession?"

"My name is David Duncan, and I've been a detective in the Charleston Police Department for more than ten years. It's been my honor to serve the people of this city, and I'm proud to do my service to the people of this beautiful state. I'm a patriot, and I love my country."

"Thank you, Detective Duncan. In your many years of experience as a detective, have you ever led a raid on a property?"

"Many times. I couldn't tell you how many exactly, but it would be more than twenty raids. Usually, it's drug raids, but I've performed around five raids on properties searching for stolen goods. Those stolen goods have been things from cars, to tools, to household items."

"And on the 10th of March, did you lead a raid on the Five Corners Art Gallery?"

"That's correct. I led a team of ten officers during that raid." His chest puffed out as he spoke with pride about his job. "We'd received a tip-off that there were stolen artworks in the Five Corners Art Gallery, and after conducting preliminary investigations into the gallery's dealings, we were satisfied with the high likelihood that the items were located in the storeroom of the gallery. We had to move quickly because we were told that the artworks were worth a million dollars each, and we didn't want the gallery owner to sell the artworks before we had a chance to intercept them. "

"And where did this tip-off come from?"

"An anonymous source in New York via a phone call to my desk at the office."

"Thank you, Detective," Garrett said. "Can you please describe what happened on the 10th of March?"

"The actual raid preparation started three days before when we stationed two plain-clothed officers outside the address to monitor who was coming and going from the gallery. We had an undercover officer go into the gallery the day before the raid, and when the gallery attendant was distracted, the undercover officer walked into the storeroom. It was at this point that they identified five paintings wrapped in brown paper, like the tip-off had described. Based on the information that we had, we determined that these must be the stolen Stephen Scully paintings."

"Why not just go into the gallery at that time to seize the stolen goods?"

"Because we needed information that the paintings

were going to be sold."

"And did you get that information?"

"We bugged the phones in the gallery, but we found no information about a sale. However, at the same time, we were also monitoring the owner and the staff of the Five Corners Art Gallery. One of our undercover officers heard Mr. Cruise, the gallery's owner, say that he was going to sell five paintings for five million dollars within the next day."

"And did this transaction take place?"

"No," Duncan sat up straight. "We intercepted the paintings before the transaction could take place."

"Detective Duncan," Garrett stood and walked to the area in front of the jury. "For the benefit of the jury, can you please explain why you didn't wait until the transaction had taken place on the day of the raid before you went into the property?"

"We had a gap in our monitoring due to a technical mishap," Detective Duncan looked to the jury. "It happens. We don't have the big city police budgets of New York or Los Angeles, and this means that some of our equipment is outdated. And that's ok. We work with what we've got. And we still get results. We weren't able to monitor the premises as we would've liked, so we were left with a choice—should we wait and risk losing the paintings, or raid the premises before we were ready? We chose not to wait."

"Can you please describe what happened on the morning of the raid?"

"After we realized that our electronic monitoring system had failed, we scrambled to get it back up and running. It was only once we got the system functioning again that we saw that Mr. Cruise had entered the Five Corners. Unfortunately, we'd been distracted by the issues with the monitoring system, and we were unsure if the buyer was also inside the premises."

"Detective Duncan, constructive possession means that the defendant had dominion and control or the right to exercise dominion and control over either the drugs itself or the property upon which the drugs were found—"

"Objection!" Hennessy leaped to his feet. "Misleading and prejudicial! Your Honor, that instruction from the prosecutor is not correct. The indication that constructive possession means control over the property where the stolen goods were found is simply false."

"Sustained," Judge Blow stated. "Mr. Garrett, you need to be very careful with your phrasing of the law." Judge Blow turned to look at the jurors. "Members of the jury, I wish to make it very clear that constructive possession does not, I repeat, does not, mean control over the property where the goods were found. Rather, it means control of the stolen items. The onus is on the prosecution to prove the control over the stolen items, not the building in which they were found. Raise your hand if this definition is unclear?" Judge Blow waited but no juror raised their hand. "You may continue your questioning, Mr. Garrett, but step carefully."

"Apologizes, Your Honor," Garrett drew a long breath. "Detective Duncan, can you please explain what happened next in the raid?"

"That's when we made the decision to raid the premises. We couldn't risk losing the paintings when they were so close, and we couldn't risk letting Mr.

Cruise escape." Duncan cleared his throat. "On the basis of the information available to us, we made the decision to raid the property at 10:05am."

"Thank you, Detective," Garrett moved back to his desk. He typed a number of commands on the laptop, and a series of pictures were displayed on the monitor at the side of the room. "Detective Duncan, are these the photos that a member of your team took during, and after, the raid?"

"That's correct."

"Can you please describe the pictures as we move through them?"

"Of course." Detective Duncan removed a glasses case from his suit pocket and put on a pair of thin-rimmed glasses. He studied the first picture of the storeroom and then began his description.

For the next two hours and five minutes, Detective Duncan took the jury through photo after photo, describing each picture in detail. He described where the paintings were found, how Mr. Cruise was the only person in the art gallery at the time, and how Cruise reacted after he was arrested.

After the testimony, which had started to bore the previously bright-eyed jury, Judge Blow invited Hennessy to cross-examine the witness. Hennessy stood and moved to the lectern. He took his time, ensuring the jury had their eyes focused on him before he began.

"Detective Duncan, can you please tell the court if you have evidence that Mr. Cruise purchased the paintings?"

"They were in his possession."

"Were they?" Hennessy exaggerated his surprise. "And on the previous day when your undercover officer entered the premises, was Mr. Cruise on the property?"

"No."

"So when you first identified that the stolen paintings were at the Five Corners Art Gallery, they were not in the possession of Mr. Cruise?"

"They were in his constructive possession, which is the ability and intent to exercise control over the item or the premises on which the item was found with the knowledge the items were there." Detective Duncan sat up a little straighter. "He was the owner of the art gallery. It's his responsibility to determine what comes and goes from there."

"But you have no evidence that he acquired the paintings?"

"He was in possession of them."

"You didn't answer my question, Detective Duncan." Hennessy looked at the jury. "I asked whether you have evidence that Mr. Cruise acquired the paintings?"

Detective Duncan shook his head.

"Please answer the question verbally, Detective Duncan."

"No."

"No? Despite conducting surveillance on the premises for two days prior, you have no evidence of Mr. Cruise acquiring the paintings?"

"The tip-off said that Mr. Cruise had taken possession of the items five days before the raid."

"The anonymous tip-off?"

"That's correct."

"Do you have any evidence that this was correct?"

"No," Detective Duncan shook his head. "We don't."

Hennessy squinted. "So you have no evidence that Mr. Cruise acquired the paintings?"

"That's correct."

"Detective Duncan, I understand you were wearing a body camera during the raid. Can you please tell the court what Mr. Cruise said when you showed him the Stephen Scully paintings?"

"He said that they weren't his."

"He said that as his first reaction?" Hennessy moved back to the defense table and removed a piece of paper from the table. "In fact, he said, 'I have never seen those paintings before. They're not mine.' Is that correct?"

"Something like that."

"Yes or no, Detective Duncan. Is that what Mr. Cruise said to you?"

"Yes," Detective Duncan lowered his voice. "That's what he said."

"And when you entered the gallery, where was Mr. Cruise?"

"In his office."

"And the paintings were in the storeroom?"

"That's correct."

Hennessy paused. Silence was an important weapon in the courtroom. Silence calls attention to a moment, and focuses the attention of the crowd, allowing the information to seep in. Hennessy moved back to the lectern before he continued.

"Detective Duncan, how did you establish that Mr. Cruise had planned to sell the paintings?"

"One of our undercover officers overheard this conversation."

"Was there a recording of this?"

"Unfortunately not."

"And where did this conversation take place?"

"In the Civic Lantern bar in Charleston at around 5pm."

"That's interesting," Hennessy said. He moved to his table and typed a number of commands into his laptop. A video of the inside of the bar was displayed on the monitor. "This is the surveillance footage from inside the Civic Lantern bar at 5pm that evening. It looks quite busy, wouldn't you agree?"

"I would."

"Can you please identify where your undercover officer was seated at this time?"

Detective Duncan hesitated.

"Detective Duncan?"

"He's there," Detective Duncan groaned and pointed to the screen. "Seated by the bar."

"Seated by the bar?" Hennessy questioned. "He's at least fifteen feet away from Mr. Cruise at this time. Are you suggesting that your officer overheard a conversation fifteen feet away in a busy bar?"

"He must've gotten closer."

"Really?" Hennessy let the footage from the bar play out. It was on double-speed. He let it play out until Cruise had left the bar. "As you can see, Detective Duncan, your officer didn't come within fifteen feet of Mr. Cruise at any time during his time in the bar. Are you saying that your officer heard Mr. Cruise across a busy bar?"

"I don't know." Detective Duncan shrugged. "If you need any further clarification, you'd have to ask him."

"And we will, Detective Duncan," Hennessy said. "No further questions."

CHAPTER 26

ON THE morning of the second day of the trial, the courtroom smelled sterile, almost like a hospital, like the cleaning staff had drenched the room in disinfectant the night before. The air conditioning was working overtime, with the temperature already at 85 degrees by 9am, and the room was filling up with onlookers.

With the case building, Aaron Garrett stood to call his second witness, crime scene expert Dr. Daniel Hayes. Daniel Hayes was early forties, black hair balding halfway to the back of his head, with long sideburns clinging onto the side of his face. He'd worn a white button-up, barely ironed, underneath a brown leather jacket that he probably thought looked 'nice.'

Aaron Garrett stood with his body half turned to the jury, half towards Daniel Hayes.

"Thank you for taking the time out of your busy schedule to talk with us today, Dr. Hayes," Garrett began. "Can you please tell the court about your professional background?"

"My name is Dr. Daniel Hayes, and I have a PhD in Forensic Science from West Virginia University. I've been employed by the Charleston Police Department for the past fifteen years in the Forensic Services Division, and I've lectured regularly at the University of South Carolina, which I'm very proud to do. I love inspiring the next generation of crime scene analysts. It's a very interesting field—everything is always changing, and the key is to stay one step ahead of the criminals."

"Thank you, Dr. Hayes," Garrett typed into his laptop, remaining seated behind his desk. "Were you present during the raid on the Five Corners Art Gallery on the 10th of March?"

"I was." Dr. Hayes straightened his tie. "While the initial raid took place, I stayed in a police sedan, and once the site was secured, I entered the premises and began to conduct initial investigations. I took samples of DNA, dusted for fingerprints, and took photos of the scene."

"And are these the photos that you took?" Garrett indicated towards the monitor again. A series of photos scrolled through on the screen.

"That's correct."

"And is this the report that you built for the crime scene analysis?" Garrett held a piece of paper in the air. He handed a copy to the witness and introduced it as evidence.

"Yes, it is."

"Can you please tell the court what you included in this report?"

"Certainly." Dr. Hayes moved to become more comfortable in his chair and began to explain the report in detail.

Over the next thirty-five minutes, Dr. Hayes explained how Cruise's DNA was found in the storeroom, how his fingerprints were found on the wall next to the paintings, and how long he assumed the paintings had been stored in the room. Due to their location at the front of the stack and the lack of dust on the brown paper that was wrapped around the outside of each painting, he estimated that the paintings had been stored in that position for less than a week.

Garrett closed the testimony without fanfare or any big statements, but the testimony was convincing to the jury. He was a solid witness. A doctor. An expert with years of experience. And his testimony was an important piece of the puzzle, a piece of evidence to add to the growing pile.

Hennessy stood and moved to the lectern, taking his time before asking his opening question. Dr. Hayes waited patiently before he eventually raised his eyebrows to the judge, indicating to Hennessy that he was taking much too long.

Hennessy waited a moment longer and then began.

"Dr. Hayes, in your extensive review of the crime scene and the stolen paintings, did you find Mr. Cruise's fingerprints on the paper that was wrapped around the paintings?"

"We found his fingerprints around the area where the paintings were stored, yes."

"Dr. Hayes, I didn't ask whether you found fingerprints around the area. I asked whether, in your extensive analysis, you found Mr. Cruise's fingerprints on the paper that was wrapped around the paintings?"

"No," he shook his head. "However, it must be noted that we didn't find any fingerprints on the paper."

"And in your extensive analysis, did you find Mr. Cruise's fingerprints on the frames that held the paintings?"

"We didn't find any fingerprints on the frames, but that was expected. We theorized that the people who handled these paintings would wear gloves. These paintings are worth around five million in total, after all."

"No fingerprints. Interesting," Hennessy noted. "In your extensive review of the crime scene and the stolen paintings, did you find Mr. Cruise's DNA on the paper that was wrapped around the paintings?"

"Objection," Garrett called out. "Asked and answered."

"I argue that it wasn't, Your Honor. The prosecution has presented an expert witness to talk about their subject of expertise, and the defense would like to confirm whether their analysis concluded that Mr. Cruise's DNA was found on the items."

"I'm inclined to agree with the defense," Judge Blow stated. "The objection is overruled. You may answer the question, Dr. Hayes."

"No," Hayes shook his head. "However, again, it must be noted that we didn't find any DNA at all on the paper."

"And in your extensive analysis, did you find Mr. Cruise's DNA on the frames that held the paintings?"

Garrett groaned audibly in the background.

"Again," Hayes shifted in his seat. "We expected that whoever handled the paintings would wear gloves."

"You seem to be avoiding my question, Dr. Hayes," Hennessy looked to the jury. "So I'll ask it again—did you find Mr. Cruise's DNA on the frames around the paintings?"

"No," Dr. Hayes conceded. "But like I said, we would expect anyone to be wearing gloves when they handled the paintings. We found his fingerprints in the area around where the paintings were stored."

"In the gallery storeroom?"

"That's correct."

"Were you at all surprised that you found Mr. Cruise's fingerprints or DNA in the storeroom of the gallery he'd been the owner of for the last five years? Did that, in any way, surprise you?"

"Of course not." Dr. Hayes shook his head.

"And does the presence of his fingerprints or DNA in the storeroom of the gallery that he owned indicate that he was guilty of this crime?"

"They were around the paintings."

"But not on them?"

Dr. Hayes drew a breath and conceded. "That's correct."

Hennessy nodded slowly for the benefit of the jury. "Dr. Hayes, in your extensive analysis of the crime scene, did you find anything that directly pointed to who stole the paintings?"

"I'm sorry, I don't quite understand the question."

"Let me be clear then—did any of the evidence that you found, anything in this extensive five-page report, anything in the fifty-five photos that you took, indicate that Mr. Cruise stole or handled the paintings at any time?"

Dr. Hayes sat back a little and looked at the prosecutor's table. Garrett avoided eye contact.

"No," he conceded.

"Thank you, Dr. Hayes," Hennessy said. "No further questions."

CHAPTER 27

MAIRE HAMILTON was a problem.

Hennessy was able to identify that from the start. Maire Hamilton was Henry Cruise's fourth ex-wife, and there was a saying about hell hath no fury. Hennessy had found it never held truer than when a court and a judge were involved. She was a wildcard, but not only in her hatred, but also in her previous employment as the former manager of the Five Corners Art Gallery.

When called, Maire Hamilton entered the courtroom and looked to the jury. She offered them a large smile before being sworn in. She had been a swimsuit model in her twenties, and as she entered her mid-forties, she was desperately clinging onto the ideals of youth—her lips were pumped full of collagen, her brow barely moved when she raised her eyebrows, and her breasts were clearly paid for. Her blonde hair was straight, and she wore a fitted black suit, with a floral-scented perfume following her.

"Thank you for coming here today, Ms. Hamilton," Garrett began. "Can you please describe your relationship with the defendant, Mr. Cruise?"

"I was married to Mr. Cruise for five years before we separated and then finally divorced."

"Have you agreed to waive your spousal privileges under South Carolina Code of Laws, Section 19-11-30, Competency of husband or wife of party as witness?"

"That's correct," she responded.

"Were you employed in the Five Corners Art Gallery?"

"I was the manager of the gallery for the entire five years I was married to Mr. Cruise," her face barely moved as she talked. "He bought the gallery as a wedding present for me. I'd always wanted to own a gallery, and I managed the gallery for five years, although it remained under his name in terms of ownership."

"And did you take ownership of the gallery after your divorce?"

"No. Mr. Cruise," she said his name with cold disdain. "Wanted to keep the gallery as part of the divorce settlement."

"Was that an issue of contention during the divorce proceedings?"

"The biggest. It was the one issue we couldn't agree upon. Eventually, I had to give up trying to settle on it. Upon advice from my divorce lawyer, I agreed that Mr. Cruise could keep the gallery, despite all the hard work I'd put into it." Her jaw clenched. "I guess he wanted to keep it so he could continue running his criminal activities and buying stolen paintings."

"Objection," Hennessy stood. "Assumes facts not in evidence."

"Sustained," Judge Blow stated. He turned to face the witness. "Please only describe the facts as you know them, Ms. Hamilton, and try not to make any accusations in court."

Maire nodded, and Garrett moved on quickly. "Ms. Hamilton, during the time that you managed the gallery, did you ever hear about your former husband using the business to break the law?"

"Objection. Leading the witness and hearsay," Hennessy called out. "There's no evidence of this, and the witness cannot testify to something that doesn't exist."

"Sustained." Judge Blow grunted. "Mr. Garrett, you know better than to ask a leading question like that."

"Yes, Your Honor," Garrett nodded and turned back to the witness. "Did Mr. Cruise ever directly discuss buying stolen paintings with you?"

She stared at her ex-husband, the hatred for him clear. "Yes."

Cruise's jaw clenched, and his fists tightened into balls. "Liar," he whispered.

"And when Mr. Cruise discussed buying stolen paintings with you, what was your response during those discussions?"

"Objection. Hearsay," Hennessy said. "The witness is being asked to talk about something they haven't witnessed."

"Your Honor," Garrett said. "The witness is allowed to talk about what she told the owner of the art gallery."

"Overruled. I'll allow the questioning to continue for the moment, however, Ms. Hamilton can only comment on what she said."

Maire nodded. "I told him I wanted nothing to do with it, and I wanted nothing to do with any criminal activity. I told him that if he wanted to sell stolen paintings to make money, then he couldn't do it through my gallery."

"And what was his response to that?"

"He said that if I ever left the gallery, he would start selling stolen artworks from the storeroom."

Garrett raised his eyebrows and nodded. He was putting on the display for the benefit of the jury. "Did it surprise you that only five days after you signed the divorce papers, giving Mr. Cruise full control of the gallery, stolen artworks were found in his possession?"

"Objection," Hennessy said. "Leading the witness, hearsay, and not to mention that this question assumes facts not in evidence. There has been no established fact that the artworks were in Mr. Cruise's possession."

"Sustained," Judge Blow said. "Mr. Garrett, don't make me warn you again about those types of questions."

"Withdrawn," Garrett said. "No further questions."

Hennessy reviewed his notes for a moment, looked to his client, and then moved to the lectern near the jurors. He looked at them, nodded, and then turned to the witness.

"Ms. Hamilton, before the divorce was finalized, how long were you and Mr. Cruise separated?"

"Around a year."

"And during that time, how would you describe your relationship?"

She took a moment, and then drew a long breath. "Strained."

"Strained?" Hennessy questioned. "Did you say that you wanted him out of your life forever?"

"Nothing like that, but we didn't get along."

"Nothing like that?" Hennessy made a surprised face to the jury members. "Ms. Hamilton, I should remind you that everything that is written online has the ability to be stored, retrieved, and re-read at a later date, even if you have deleted it before the trial began. So, I'll ask you again, did you make the following statement, and I quote, 'I want that piece of trash out of my life forever. I'm going to put him behind bars?'"

"I could've said that." She looked away from the jury and shifted uncomfortably in her seat. "There are a lot of emotions that come out during a divorce, and sometimes you say things you don't mean."

"And sometimes, you say things that you do mean," Hennessy responded. "On the 5th of October last year, did you also write on a Facebook post that you, 'want your ex-husband locked up for life,' and, 'that would take care of all your worries?'"

Maire looked at the prosecution table. They hadn't prepared her for that line of questioning, and she sat in the stand, alone and afraid, with the eyes of everyone in the courtroom burning into her. "I don't know. I could've said that."

"I have the copies of the statements here." Hennessy walked back to his desk and held up a piece of paper. "Shall we continue with what else you wrote about Mr. Cruise?"

"No," Maire stopped him from going on. "Ok. I said it. I said that I wanted him behind bars, and that I wanted him out of my life forever."

Hennessy nodded. "While your divorce was being finalized, did you still manage the gallery?"

"That's correct."

"And when was your last day in the gallery?"

"The 5th of March."

"Only five days before the raid?"

177

"That's correct."

"Ms. Hamilton. When you were the manager of the Five Corners Art Gallery, how many hours a week did you work?"

She shifted uncomfortably, then shrugged. "About 15 to 25 hours a week."

"So not full-time then?"

She shook her head. "No. Not full-time."

"And were you the only manager?"

"Well, I was the senior manager—"

"But you were only there 15 to 25 hours a week. So there must have been managers when you weren't around."

"There were a number of other staff, yes," she said. "I wasn't there all the time to monitor the gallery."

Hennessy drew a long breath and looked at the jury. He then nodded, indicating that he was coming in with a heavy left hook.

"Ms. Hamilton, do you still know the codes to the gallery?"

"I don't know the answer to that question. Henry could've changed the codes in the time before the raid."

"At the time of the police raid, the code for the alarm, which has since been changed, was '1555.' According to the data files, this code was set two years ago. Was this the code you set?"

"Ah," she looked down at her hands. "Yes."

"And the code for the back entrance at the time of the raid was '2555.' And again, according to the data files, this code was set two years ago. Was this the code you set?"

"Yes."

"So you had access to the gallery even after the divorce was finalized up until the raid."

"I can't confirm that. I—"

"That wasn't a question, Ms. Hamilton," Hennessy interrupted. "But this is—did you tell anyone the codes after you were no longer the manager of the gallery?"

"Not after."

"Before?"

"Maybe," she whispered.

"Maybe? Ms. Hamilton, you've sworn to tell the truth, the whole truth, and nothing but the truth. Did you give the codes to anyone before your divorce was finalized?"

"Yes," she conceded. "But I don't remember who I gave it to. I just wrote the codes on a piece of paper, and then someone gave me fifteen thousand dollars in cash."

"I'm sorry?" Hennessy's mouth hung open for a moment. "Are you saying that someone paid you for the codes?"

"Yes."

"Who?"

"Like I said, I don't know. I just got a message on my phone that asked me to sell the codes. I went to the location the person asked, which was in Brittlebank Park, next to the water. It was night, and this guy with sunglasses was waiting there with two thick envelopes. I gave him the codes, and he gave me the money. That was all there was to it."

Hennessy turned to look at the prosecutor. Garrett shook his head, indicating he had no idea about the codes. "And what date was this?"

"The 4th of March."

"And you just gave this person the codes?"

"Yeah, I thought if I don't manage it anymore, I don't care what happens to the gallery. I did nothing wrong. I didn't break in there, and I didn't do anything with the paintings. I'm in the clear."

"You have done something wrong, Ms. Hamilton, and the police will need to talk to you after this," Hennessy said, shaking his head. "No further questions."

"Redirect, Counselor?" Judge Blow was quick to ask.

"Just one question," Garrett stood. "Ms. Hamilton, did you access the gallery after the 5th of March, the date of your finalized divorce?"

"No."

"Thank you, Ms. Hamilton." Garrett looked at the judge. "Nothing further."

CHAPTER 28

THE NEXT days of the trial were full of activity. Expert crime scene analysts talked the talk, members of the Charleston PD testified about the intensity of the raid, and art professors discussed their knowledge of the Stephen Scully paintings. The art experts declared the paintings as legitimate, despite their flaws, and the jury appeared convinced.

By the morning of the fifth day of the trial, the prosecution's case was becoming a masterpiece of its own—the specialized experts and trusted authoritative figures were painting a clear picture of the events on the 10th of March. Hennessy objected where he could, breaking Garrett's rhythm at every chance, but there was little he could do about the increasing weight of the evidence.

It was 8:05am on Friday when Hennessy arrived at the courthouse. He was about to take a sip of his strong coffee when he spotted Jacinta—early as well—striding towards him with an apple in her left hand.

She passed him the apple. "I read once that eating an apple first thing in the morning does a 200% better job of waking you up than a cup of coffee." She took the coffee out of his hands, threw it in the trash, and then nodded down towards the apple in her open hand. She had a broad smile stretched across her face.

"You threw my coffee in the trash?"

"The apple is better. Trust me. It's good for your health. It doesn't have any caffeine, and it's fat-free."

"Cigarettes are fat-free, and cigars have no sugar, but that doesn't mean they're good for you." He took a bite of the apple. It was golden and red, slightly out of season, just a little too tangy. As he chewed it, he skeptically pondered her claim that it was better than caffeine. Objection, he thought, speculation. "I'm going to need another coffee."

"You'll be running on adrenaline today," Jacinta smiled. "Because I have something for you. I found it online last night."

"What is it?"

Jacinta led her boss into the courthouse foyer and then into the empty conference room nearest to the first hallway. Once inside, she shut the door and opened her laptop. She clicked open a picture. "I spent around five hours last night going through old photos of Richard Longhouse. Friends, family, associates, that sort of thing. I was just looking for anything that may help us today, and well, I think I found it."

She turned the laptop towards Hennessy.

Hennessy's mouth hung open before a smile spread over his face. "Jacinta, you're a star."

For the next hour, Hennessy and Jacinta prepared for Richard Longhouse's testimony, who was likely to be called as the last witness of the week. When the time ticked past 9:35am, they left the conference room and walked into the courtroom.

Hennessy didn't make eye contact with Henry Cruise as he arrived. He nodded vaguely in his direction, only acknowledging him as much as he had to. Hennessy would do his job. He would do it professionally. But he would do no more, as far as Henry Cruise was concerned.

The crowd had gathered behind them. The media were closest to the door, notepads ready, paying attention to everyone that walked in or out of the doors. Judge Blow arrived, and the bailiff guided the jury to their seats. Aaron Garrett was smiling as he called his first witness of the day. Hennessy sat up straight and tried not to think too far ahead.

"The prosecution calls Adriano Castellano."

Garrett had planned his week perfectly. A former politician and media personality, well-liked by everyone, Adriano Castellano was a trusting face to end the week. He oozed Southern charm. He was polite, well-mannered, friendly, and respected by everyone.

However, there were also rumors of corruption decades long.

He built his wealth in property development, building estates on parcels of empty land, encouraging councils to change their zoning laws, no doubt with large envelopes of cash swapping hands behind closed doors. The public turned a blind eye to those rumors, seduced by his almost stereotypical presentation of a good Southern gentleman.

Castellano had fallen out with Cruise a number of years before, like most of the rich and powerful over the past decade, and was happy to sink his boots into a man who had been a thorn in his side for a long time.

"Mr. Castellano, thank you for coming into court today. I understand that you're a very busy man," Garrett began. "Can you please tell the court how you know Mr. Cruise?"

"Henry was a former business associate, and someone that I've known for many years, perhaps even decades. My, how time flies," he looked at the jury and smiled. They offered polite smiles in return. "Where do all the years go?"

"And when was the last time you interacted with Mr. Cruise?"

"It was the 9th of March, the day before the police raid. I was walking on King Street to go to lunch, and I saw Mr. Cruise on the street. He had just exited his car, and we saw each other. He greeted me, and we chatted for a few moments. He asked if I was still wealthy."

"And what was your response?"

"Well, a true gentleman never talks about money," Castellano smiled. "But I told him I was doing well."

"What did Mr. Cruise ask you next?"

"He grabbed my elbow and took me to the edge of the sidewalk, away from everyone else. He leaned in and asked if I was interested in buying five Stephen Scully paintings."

"That lying prick," Cruise mumbled under his breath. "He'd say anything to take me down."

Hennessy wrote the word 'calm' on his notepad and placed it in front of Cruise. They couldn't afford an outburst. The jury wouldn't respond well to a surge of emotion from the defendant.

"And what did you say when he offered that to you?"

"I was shocked, but I thought he must've come into the paintings legitimately."

"And did you offer to buy them?"

"No. To be honest, I didn't trust Cruise. I

assumed the paintings were probably fakes."

"And were you convinced that he was in possession of the paintings?"

"Objection," Hennessy called out. "Hearsay."

"Withdrawn," Garrett was quick to reply. "Let me rephrase that. Did Mr. Cruise tell you he was in possession of the paintings?"

"Yes. He said that he had the paintings waiting for me."

"Those were his exact words?"

"Yes."

"Thank you, Mr. Castellano. No further questions."

Hennessy began once invited by Judge Blow. He knew it wouldn't take much to tear the testimony apart. Castellano had come to kick Cruise when he was down, nothing more.

"Firstly, Mr. Castellano, did you see Mr. Cruise handled the paintings?" Hennessy asked, seated behind his desk.

"No, but he told me about it."

"You didn't see it?"

"That's correct."

Hennessy nodded slowly. "Mr. Castellano, would you call Mr. Cruise a calculated man?"

"I suppose."

"Would you call him a careful man?"

"I guess so," he shrugged. "We've known each other for years, so I guess I could say that."

"You mentioned that you've known Mr. Cruise for many years. Can you please tell the courts how many arguments you've had with Mr. Cruise over that time?"

"I couldn't tell you." He shook his head. "That's

not something I keep track of."

"Is that because the number of arguments you've had is, in fact, quite a lot? Enough to even classify your relationship as enemies?"

"I wouldn't say enemies, but yes, it's true that Mr. Cruise and I haven't seen eye-to-eye on occasion."

"And why is that?"

"We... have competing business interests."

"Mr. Castellano, you claimed to have spoken to Mr. Cruise on the day before the raid. Were you aware that the paintings were stolen?"

"At that point in time, no."

"Can you please tell the court the exact moment that this interaction took place?"

"Just before lunch, on the lower end of King St."

"Are you saying that Mr. Cruise, who you claim is a careful and calculated man, made you an offer to buy stolen artworks worth five million dollars on the street, where the conversation could be overheard by many people?"

"Yes." Castellano rubbed his collar and then cleared his throat. "That's what I'm saying."

"How long did you talk to him for?"

"A few minutes."

"Only a few minutes? And you expect this court to believe that a man you haven't seen for years, a man you've had many disagreements with, just offered you these million-dollar paintings on the street?"

"Yes." He shrugged. "That's what I said."

"And can you please tell the court how that interaction started?"

"Um," Castellano had started to sweat on his brow. "He just said he was looking to off-load some artwork."

"Really? He just came out and said that to you after the two of you had no contact for a number of years?"

"That's right." Castellano removed a handkerchief from his jacket pocket and wiped his brow. "He asked if I was still wealthy, then offered to sell me the Stephen Scully paintings. That's what really happened."

"Do you have any evidence that this interaction took place?"

"No."

Hennessy groaned and looked at the jury. "Mr. Castellano, you took an oath to tell the truth on this stand. Can you please tell the court how long this interaction lasted?"

"Only a few minutes or so."

Hennessy shook his head. Castellano sat on the witness stand, his face red and looking like it was about to explode.

"No further questions, Your Honor."

CHAPTER 29

RICHARD LONGHOUSE. Hennessy had thought long and hard about how to question him on the stand, and all the possible tactics were coming down to one option—keep pushing his buttons until he snapped. Longhouse had a history of exploding when challenged, he had a history of vicious outbursts, and Hennessy needed to break the man who seemed to be at the center of everything.

Garrett had planned his week well. He intended to finish with two strong personalities, two good South Carolina men, who could talk the talk and convince the jury of anything.

Richard Longhouse walked to the stand with his shoulders back and his head held high. There was an expression of confidence on his face. He was there to sink his former associate, he was there to lie through his teeth, and he was going to enjoy it as well. Longhouse swore his oath and then sat on the stand. He was dressed in a well-fitted suit, complete with a skinny tie that hung straight down the middle of his white shirt.

"Mr. Longhouse, thank you for making an appearance in the court today," Garrett walked to the lectern. "Can you please provide a brief introduction about yourself?"

"My name is Richard Longhouse, and I'm a Senator for South Carolina. I'm a patriot, I love my country, and I'll do anything for the people of this county, this state, and this great country."

"And can you please explain how you know Mr. Cruise?"

Richard Longhouse hesitated for a moment and shot a look in the direction of the defense table. "Mr. Cruise is a former associate of mine."

"Associated in what way?"

"He donated to some of my campaigns, early on in my career. Well, via his business."

"Which business was that?"

"His restaurant, The Medici Ristorante."

"And would you say that you were friends with the defendant?"

After considering the question for a moment, he nodded. "Yes."

"Are you still friends with Mr. Cruise?"

The jurors had given the witness their full attention. Several blinked and sat up straighter. The question had caught Hennessy's attention as well. For one, he wondered why the prosecution would want to establish this.

"Until the start of this trial, I would have said we were friends, yes." He shrugged a little.

Hennessy glanced at Cruise. He was so red in the face that it looked as though his blood pressure was about to erupt.

"What was the nature of the friendship?"

"I would often frequent his restaurant. I was a patron in return for his support." He cast a look towards Cruise. "He helped me out, and I helped him out."

"In what way did you help him out?"

"I would support his business interests." If

Longhouse had started shaky, he was now hitting his stride. Now he was ready for the killer blow. "And then one day, he asked for my financial support. I asked what it was about, and he asked if I wanted to buy the Stephen Scully paintings. He knew I was an art collector, and he offered them to me."

"Did Mr. Cruise reveal why he was selling these artworks?"

"He said there was a lot of money in it."

"And when did this interaction take place?"

"On the Wednesday before the raid. I went to his restaurant and dined with him over lunch. We discussed numerous things, including what he wanted to do with the art gallery now that he was managing it. He said..." Longhouse sat up straighter. "He said that he was going to sell stolen artworks out of it. There was big money in stolen artworks, he told me. I asked him how he would get his hands on the artwork, and he said that he already had his hands on the five stolen Stephen Scully paintings. That was a surprise to me because I knew that three of the Stephen Scully paintings were stolen in the 80s. The sale of the complete set of the five paintings would've been invaluable, a truly rare event in modern art."

"Did you say you were interested in buying the paintings?"

"I told Mr. Cruise that I loved the Stephen Scully series, but I had no interest in dealing with stolen artworks."

"Thank you for your honesty, Mr. Longhouse," Garrett said. "The prosecution has nothing further."

Garrett ended his questioning and returned to the prosecution table.

Hennessy could feel Cruise was about to stand up

and shout something out. He was muttering under his breath, cursing and spluttering. "Who does this jerk think that he…" Hennessy reached out and gripped Cruise's arm. When Hennessy felt Cruise calm down, he began his questioning.

"Mr. Longhouse," Hennessy asked, remaining seated. "Do you currently own any other Stephen Scully paintings?"

"I own two older paintings by Stephen Scully," Longhouse said. "The two Stephen Scully paintings that I own are not worth a lot of money, maybe fifteen thousand a painting. The stolen series of paintings, along with another series that is on display at The Met in New York City, were his signature series."

"Is it fair to say that you're a fan of Stephen Scully's artwork?"

"Absolutely. I love his artwork."

"Do you have a private gallery in your home, Mr. Longhouse?"

He drew a breath. "I do."

"And do you know the contents of that gallery?"

Longhouse stared at Hennessy for a long moment, trying to figure out where he was going with the testimony. "I know most of the contents, but probably not all the paintings in storage."

"So it's fair to say that art is a passion of yours?"

"That's correct."

"And how many paintings do you own?"

He shrugged. "Maybe two hundred and fifty paintings. Thirty-five are on display in my private gallery, while the others remain in storage. I also loan some of my private collection out to various galleries for display."

"And the ones not on display, where are they stored?"

"In a specialized facility in Atlanta. When I wish to change the paintings in my gallery, they take them down and exchange them for other ones. The paintings are changed every five months or so."

Hennessy paused, letting the testimony sink into the minds of the jurors. "Mr. Longhouse, you stated that you're friends with the defendant, correct?"

"That's right."

"And you are also friends with the defendant's ex-wife, is that correct?"

Longhouse's eyes narrowed, but he nodded and leaned in closer towards the mic. "Yes. Ms. Hamilton and I have several mutual friends."

"And Detective Duncan. Do you know him?"

Longhouse blinked a few times before answering. "Yes. He's a friend of my son."

"And Mr. Hanson, the former manager of the Five Corners Art Gallery, do you know him?"

"I know a lot of people."

"Please answer my question."

"Yes." Longhouse nodded.

"And Mr. Castellano?"

"I know him."

"Did you have lunch with Mr. Castellano five days before the raid occurred, on the 5th of March?"

Longhouse squinted. "I'm not sure what you're implying."

"Mr. Longhouse, please answer the question."

"Perhaps I had lunch with him. I'd have to check my calendar."

"I have a copy of your calendar here, Mr. Longhouse." Hennessy stood and raised a piece of paper in the air. He moved across the floor towards the jury. "It's listed here that you had lunch with Mr. Castellano five times in the three weeks before the raid."

"And why is that a problem?"

"Mr. Longhouse, do you know Mr. Mailings, the owner of the two Stephen Scully paintings that were stolen from Manhattan on the 5th of March?"

Longhouse nodded.

"Please answer verbally for the court."

"I do."

"And what is your association with Mr. Mailings?"

Longhouse shrugged. "We're friends."

"Did you have lunch with Mr. Mailings in the three weeks before the raid?"

He nodded again. "Maybe."

"And you said that you've never seen any of these paintings before?"

"That's correct."

"Do you know former Senator Mr. Gerald Smith?"

"We're good friends. I've had dealings with him in the past."

"And is this a photo of you and Mr. Smith in your home?" Hennessy walked back to his desk, typed a number of commands into his laptop, and displayed a picture on the monitor at the side of the room.

"It's an old picture, but yes, that's us in my gallery. From the looks of that picture, it was from a time when I used to host an annual charity event in my home."

"The picture was taken in 1995 and uploaded to Mr. Smith's social media profile in 2015 as part of a 'Throwback Thursday' movement," Hennessy zoomed in on the picture. "Can you please tell the court if you recognize that picture in the background?"

Longhouse squinted. He paused for a moment and then sat back. He rolled his tongue around his mouth and then looked at Garrett.

"Mr. Longhouse?" Hennessy pressed. "Can you please tell the court if you recognize that picture in the background?"

"I do."

"And can you please tell the court what that picture is?"

"I guess that looks like No. 5 of the stolen Stephen Scully series."

"You guess?"

"I can't be certain."

"In your home?"

"Well, hang on now. That was a public charity function, and I had no dealings with what came and went from that charity auction. That event was to raise funds for our local church. I wasn't aware that there was a stolen painting in the room."

"Really?" Hennessy tilted his head to the side. "And did all the money raised from that event go to the church?"

Longhouse paused. Hennessy knew where the funds for his political campaigns came from. It was one of Hennessy's long-held secrets.

"I—"

"Before you answer that question, Mr. Longhouse, I will remind you that you're under oath." Hennessy reached down into his briefcase next to him and removed a folder that looked like it was at least twenty years old. "And I will also remind you that the truth has a way of finding its way out."

Longhouse moved uncomfortably in his seat. His mouth was hanging open, and he was working through the options in his head. "Your Honor," Longhouse looked up at the judge. "May I please request a recess?"

"A recess?" Judge Blow looked confused. "What on earth for?"

"I need to use the bathroom," Longhouse fished for an excuse.

"No," Judge Blow shook his head. "You can answer the questions of the defense attorney, and then, we can consider a recess."

Hennessy held up the folder. "Mr. Longhouse, did all the money raised from the charity event that included No. 5 of the stolen Stephen Scully series go to the church?"

"Objection," Garrett stood, trying to save his witness. "Relevance."

"Your Honor," Hennessy argued. "The witness claimed to have never seen the painting that was involved in an auction at his house, and we're trying to establish where the money from that auction, which clearly included the stolen painting, went."

"Overruled," Judge Blow turned to Longhouse. "You may answer the question."

He shook his head. "I don't recall."

"Mr. Longhouse, are you aware of what happened to that stolen painting after the auction?"

Again, he shook his head. "No. How could I? That's more than twenty-five years ago. I have no idea who bought that painting in the auction."

"Did you buy the painting at the auction?"

"No, of course not," he scoffed.

"No further questions, Your Honor." Hennessy drew a long breath. "However, we reserve the right to call the witness as a defense witness."

"Noted," Judge Blow said. "Redirect, Mr. Garrett?"

"Yes, Your Honor. Just a few questions," Garrett took a moment, circled something on his notepad, and then asked the questions still seated behind his desk. "Mr. Longhouse, do you recall ever having seen that painting before?"

"No."

"Do you recall ever having possession of that painting?"

"No."

"Did you realize that painting had been in your home, even though it was more than twenty-five years ago?"

"No."

Garrett turned back to the judge. "No further questions."

Judge Blow called a close to the day's proceedings, marking the end of a long week in court.

Hennessy didn't spend long in the courtroom after the day finished. He talked to Cruise briefly, assuring him that the case was on track, and then chatted to Jacinta before he headed outside.

There was a welcome fresh breeze as he stepped outside at 5:05pm. Hennessy took a moment to feel the cool air and took a deep breath, letting the stress of the week wash away.

He felt his phone vibrate in his pocket and fished it out.

"I've got good news for you, Joe." It was Barry Lockett. "I've just got word to confirm that Jason Norris is still alive."

CHAPTER 30

AFTER A delicious Frogmore stew at the Bowen's Island restaurant, Hennessy thought about turning in for the night, but when his mind started to wander back to thoughts of his son, he turned back to the office instead. It was either there or the closest bar, and he figured the office was the healthier option.

The weather had cooled. The soft breeze brought the smell of the ocean through the streets of Charleston, filling the air with the fresh, sultry fragrance of a late spring night. He parked on the street and walked into the foyer of his office building, turning off the alarm system so that he could step inside without sirens going off. He caught it just in time.

After walking up the stairs, he switched on the AC before he made his way to his desk and looked over the trial notes. Wendy had warned him to lay off the caffeine, especially at night, but he turned the coffee pot on out of habit. He missed her. She had stayed at the vineyard for the past few weekends, opting not to take the drive down to Charleston. They talked on the phone daily, but he still missed her caring touch.

Hennessy turned over a file on his desk, trying to focus back on Henry Cruise's case. He read through the file Barry Lockett had given him on Jason Norris. Joe shook his head and sighed a little.

Jason Norris had long been ingrained in Henry

Cruise's circles—the two of them had met when Jason Norris had first come to Charleston, when he was a young man of just fifteen. From what Lockett had pieced together, right from the start, Norris had been indebted to Cruise to the tune of 5 grand. A good chunk of change for a young man to pay back in the late 80s. Cruise had cashed in on the debt by getting Norris to perform jobs for him. Of course, each job had only gotten him in deeper. There were rumors of extortion, loan sharking, and drug deals that Norris had been involved in.

Of course, this was all 'alleged.' On Cruise's part, anyway. Norris had done five years in one stint, a year in another, and had been before a judge five times in total. Always the fall guy, Hennessy thought to himself.

He went to the small kitchenette at the back of the office, reaching for the coffee pot, but he heard a noise down in the streets below.

Distracted by the noise—it sounded like there was something banging against the outside door to his office building—he walked over to the window, hands casually in his pockets, rolling his shoulders back to stretch them out.

He glanced out the window to the small parking lot at the back of the building, with room for five cars parked against the fence. A light rain was falling. There was one small sensor light next to the back door of his office building, and it illuminated a man standing at the door. The man was wearing a hoodie, his face obscured, and he had his hands dug deep inside his pockets that were baggy enough to hide a gun. Baggy enough to conceal a weapon.

Hennessy froze.

He hadn't bothered to lock the front door behind him after he'd entered.

He could call the police—but at this time of night, getting the cops to show up in a timely manner was asking for the impossible. Maybe the man got the address wrong. Maybe he was just waiting for a friend. The man stepped forward again, trying to open the door.

No.

Hennessey watched as the man tried to open the back door. It was locked. He returned to his desk—he had a Glock 19 in his bottom drawer. Hennessy pulled the gun out of the drawer, checked that it was loaded, and placed the gun in his belt. He went back to the window. The man was circling around to the front of the building. The front door was unlocked.

Hennessy headed down the stairs. As he reached the ground floor, he ducked down, wishing he'd never turned the lights on. A passing truck stopped with loud brakes, and the light of the truck illuminated the front of the building.

Through the window next to the front door, Hennessy caught a glimpse of the man's face, and a faint flutter of recognition ran through his mind. The hoodie was still up, but it had slipped a little. Hennessy noticed the hesitancy in the man as he approached the front door. The man didn't try it. He turned to leave.

Hennessy moved on instinct. He opened the door.

"Hey," Hennessy called out as he stepped onto the sidewalk. The man was twenty feet away. "Hey!"

The man spun around, cringing a little as he reached down towards his knee. The movement had aggravated an injury. He limped a few steps, catching himself before he fell over.

Hennessy noticed a car across the street, parked in a no-parking zone with the lights on, and one window rolled down. His heart pounded. Something wasn't right.

The truck pulled away.

Hennessy looked back at the sedan. He spotted the barrel of a rifle sticking out of the car window.

A shot rang out.

Another followed.

Hennessy dove back into the building as a third shot rang out.

Tires screeched, and the sedan roared down the street.

He waited a few seconds, even after hearing the car speed away, before he resurfaced. He took in a few shallow breaths and edged his face around to check that it was all clear. He blinked a few times, looking for the man in the hoodie.

Hennessy crouched down and moved towards the edge of his building, checking for any sign of blood.

"Hello?" he called out, searching around.

But the man—whoever he was—had gone.

CHAPTER 31

THE METAL of the dumpster was cool against Jason Norris' sweat-soaked back. After taking in a few breaths so jagged that his lungs felt like they were ripping to shreds, he did a body check, running his hands along his arms, shoulders, and torso, still not quite believing that the bullets had missed him.

He checked his hands for blood. They were clean.

He leaned his head back, clanging it against the metal, thinking about how he'd managed to claw his way to safety. He was a block away from the lawyer's office now. A block away from the place he had so foolishly turned up at looking for help. He shook his head and laughed at his naivety. How could he have been so stupid? There was no one who could help him. No one was coming to save him. This was his fate.

He caught his breath and closed his eyes. His past was flashing through his head. He tried to get the images to stop, tried to calm it down, but they continued, surging through his brain like a kaleidoscope. His time in prison. The murders on his hands. The church that he prayed at as a kid. The fights with his mother.

If only he'd never left school and come to Charleston when he was fifteen. Just a boy who thought he could be a man. He should've never taken out a loan from Henry Cruise to buy a car. If he could go back in time to any moment, if he could change anything about his past, it would be that one decision. He would've found another way. Gone to a bank. Gone to a used car dealer.

Gone home to his mother.

Anything would've been better than taking money from Henry Cruise.

He wondered how much longer he could live like this. Always looking over his shoulder. Jumping at ghosts. How many more attempts on his life would it take? Maybe it was just time to give up. Let one of these guys take him out once and for all. Let the inevitable happen. Let fate take him.

But another set of images flashed before his eyes. A baby girl born thirty years earlier, kicking her chubby legs out. The little toddler girl laughing and trying to pick up her younger brother to soothe him. His kids. James and Jenny. They didn't deserve the hell he put them through. He had to make it up to them.

Or at least die trying.

He moved to stand up when a dark car slowed down at the end of the alleyway. He held his breath. The car paused briefly before it kept moving. Probably just someone trying to score a late-night drug deal, he reasoned.

Norris dusted himself off, blinking to adjust to the dim alleyway.

He hit a pole when he was running from the bullets, and his jaw ached. He reached up and rubbed it, grimacing at the sharp pain. For a second, he actually laughed to himself, wondering what a sight he would make now if he looked in the mirror—one side of his face bruised, the other swollen and cracked.

He wondered what the jury would make of a man who looked like him.

But he had made a choice. He wanted to return to his faith. He wanted to mend the wounds of his past.

It was time to tell the truth, and time to listen to his mother's words—no matter the cost.

CHAPTER 32

"YOU LOOK like you need sleep, Joe, more than you need a bourbon."

"Sleeping is for after the trial," Hennessy replied to Barry Lockett. "Right now, bourbon is the best answer."

Hennessy flagged down the bartender, who poured him another shot of bourbon. Lockett ordered a Westbrook IPA. They sat at the bar in the Blind Tiger after 11pm, only a block away from the office. It was a charming alehouse dating back to 1803, featuring a brick-walled courtyard at the rear and dark décor inside. The sort of place a man could get lost in—exactly what Hennessy needed.

"I was shot at tonight." He threw back the shot of bourbon and waved to the bartender, and pointed to the IPA tap. "I didn't think that's how my Friday night was going to go down."

Lockett sat back a little. "Who shot at you?"

"I don't know." Hennessy thanked the bartender for the beer and then took a sip. "But I wasn't the main target. At about 9pm, there was someone trying to get into my office to talk to me, and I went down to see them. As soon as I opened the door, someone in a black sedan started shooting at the other person."

"Did the other person get away?"

"I think so. The police responded quickly to the gunshots, and we searched the local area. There were no bodies, and no sign of blood, so I assume the person got away."

"Must be your lucky week," Lockett whistled, and then took a sip of his beer. "It's a messy business that we find ourselves in sometimes, isn't it? I bet you didn't get this kind of excitement on the vineyard."

"Hey, you can get quite dirty in the mud," Hennessy joked, but then his mood turned somber. "Cruise is trouble. I knew that from the start."

"But you didn't expect this much trouble, did you?"

The bartender flashed the lights behind the bar, calling last drinks. Hennessy looked at his watch. 11:05pm. He shook his head.

"Cruise has been a nightmare from the start," Hennessy said, his fingers wrapped around the glass. "I'm the guy's lawyer and even I want to turn against him." He let out a light chuckle at the irony of it before taking a long sip of the pleasantly strong liquid. "I recognized the face of the man at my office door."

"And are you going to tell me, or are you going to keep me in suspense?"

"It was Jason Norris."

"Are you sure?" Lockett's face showed his surprise. "I've been looking for that guy and I've found nothing. He's been doing quite a good job of keeping a low profile."

"It was him." Hennessy took a long drink of the IPA, knocking back a quarter of it in one gulp. "The question is—what was he doing there? What did he want to talk to me about at 9pm on a Friday night?"

Lockett nodded. "You think he wants to turn against the prosecution?"

"I'm not sure, but I know we need to talk to him.

He's still on the prosecution's witness list, and if they know he's alive, then they're going to call him up to testify."

"I'm on it, boss," Lockett said. "If he's in Charleston, I'll find him."

CHAPTER 33

"HOW HAVEN'T they thrown the case out yet?" Cruise shook his head as he walked into the courtroom, speaking loudly enough for the prosecution team to hear. He sat down at the defense table, ready to start the second week of the trial. "How can they keep going after Longhouse's testimony?"

"They still think they've got a case. Even after they had the entire weekend to think about it, they still think they've got a case." Hennessy looked across to Garrett. "Apparently, they want to go down with the sinking ship."

Garrett did his best to ignore them. He was finalizing his preparation for the week ahead.

"But it's obvious that Longhouse has set this all up," Cruise shook his head. "How can't they see that?"

"They're taking the gamble through the court. They want to take it all the way to the jury," Hennessy said, still looking at Garrett. "And if they withdraw the case, then they're admitting that you were framed. That leaves a big question about who set you up—and there's not one prosecutor in South Carolina that's going to face that question. They won't have a job if they accuse Longhouse of fraud. No, even if it looks like they're going to lose, it's better for the prosecution to see this one through."

"We'll have to see about that," Garrett said, finally turning to Hennessy. "We still believe Mr. Cruise is guilty of dealing in stolen art. And we have one more witness to prove it."

Hennessy turned to Barry Lockett, sitting behind him. Lockett nodded.

Cruise looked across at them and then adjusted his jacket. Hennessy turned back to his laptop, preparing for the day ahead. Judge Blow walked back into the courtroom and welcomed the jury back after the weekend. Garrett stood up, still confident, and called the week's first witness.

"The prosecution calls Mr. Jason Norris."

The courtroom doors opened, and Jason Norris walked in. He was wearing black trousers and a white shirt, unbuttoned to the third button. While the clothes covered up most of his tattoos, the unbuttoned shirt revealed his new piece of jewelry—a necklace with a large cross.

"Mr. Norris," Garrett began. "Thank you for coming to court today. Can you please tell the court when you first met the defendant, Mr. Cruise?"

"I first met Henry Cruise when I was fifteen years old, and he was in his late twenties," Norris paused. "That's more than forty years ago."

"How would you describe your relationship with Mr. Cruise during those decades?"

Norris took a deep breath. "We were... Well, that's the thing. I was taken in at fifteen. Mr. Cruise gave me a loan, a handout. I didn't realize the strings that were attached, and if I did, I wouldn't have taken it. I was embarrassed to have been fooled, now when I look back at it all." Jason bit down on his lip. "But everyone has a degree in hindsight, right?"

When he looked back up, he saw familiar brown eyes at the back of the courtroom. Samuel was there, sitting in the back row. Samuel nodded to him in a sense that said, 'This is the right thing to do.'

Norris sat up a little straighter.

"During your time working for Mr. Cruise, what sort of things would he ask you to do?"

"At first, when I was just a kid, he got me to do all his dirty work. When a member of the organization fell out of line, then sometimes they needed to be reminded of who was the boss. So I would be the one to show them. If one of the young guys down the bottom of the food chain thought he was clever by taking off with something to sell on his own, then he would need to be made an example of. No one ever got away with crossing Mr. Cruise. As I progressed up the so-called ranks, I didn't get my hands so dirty, I suppose you could say."

"What did you do instead?"

Norris shrugged. "I became his right-hand man. Once I served my time, I was allowed a little more leeway. Shown a little more respect."

"And during this work, what were you asked to do, specifically?"

"When I was younger, I was mostly paid to beat up people, but as I got older, my skill set changed. I still enforced debts, but I could also set people up for crimes they didn't commit."

"Did Mr. Cruise give you the authority, the autonomy, to make your own decisions?"

Norris thought about this. "Well. Now that I think about it, no." He shook his head. "I was always one step behind. Always trying to pay back a debt where the interest just kept getting bigger and bigger. Until I was drowning. Until I couldn't breathe. He threatened to hurt my children if I didn't do what he asked. What kind of man does that?" Norris shook his head. "If I could go back in time, I would do everything differently."

But he couldn't. And it was all out there. All out in the open for his brother to hear. He couldn't bear to look up. But when he finally looked up, there wasn't judgment in Samuel's eyes—there was forgiveness.

"And when was the last time that you worked for Mr. Cruise?"

"The last job I did for him was on the 15th of March."

"That's five days after Mr. Cruise was arrested for possession of stolen artworks. Is that correct?"

"Yeah."

"And what job was that?"

"I set someone else up for a crime they didn't commit."

"Why did you do that?"

"Because Mr. Cruise paid me to do it."

"Do you know why Mr. Cruise wanted you to do that?"

"No," Norris shook his head. "I never knew, and I never asked. It was best not to ask questions when things like that happen."

"Did Mr. Cruise ever pay you to commit a crime?"

"Objection," Hennessy called out. "Leading the witness. Relevance. Prejudicial."

"Sustained," Judge Blow was quick to answer. "Mr. Garrett, this is your witness, and I'm sure I don't need to remind you of the rules of this court. You're not to lead the witness."

"Yes, Your Honor," Garrett paused, ready to land

the decisive blow. He turned a piece of paper over. "Mr. Norris, you stated that you were employed by Mr. Cruise, did Mr. Cruise ever ask you to steal or sell stolen artworks?"

"Objection," Hennessy called out again. "Leading the witness again."

"Sustained," Judge Blow stated. "Mr. Garrett, I don't expect that sort of behavior in this courtroom."

"Yes, Your Honor, I withdraw the question." He paused, trying to reframe the question. "Can you please explain to the court what sort of work Mr. Cruise asked you to do?"

Norris took a moment and stared at his brother. His brother nodded. It was time for the truth.

"He asked me to do many things, but he never asked me to sell stolen artwork. I've never seen him deal with stolen artwork, and I've never seen him handle stolen artwork. He's never talked about stolen artwork with me."

Garrett stood motionless for a moment. When the shock subsided, he squinted at Norris and then looked back at his notes.

"Mr. Norris, you have stated in this police statement that you saw Mr. Cruise purchase stolen artworks in the past, and that you saw, in person, that Mr. Cruise paid for two of the Stephen Scully paintings. Is that true?"

"That's not true. I was paid to say that, and I was paid to make that statement to the police."

"Pardon?" Garrett scoffed. His expression hung suspended for a moment. He looked at Hennessy, and then back to the judge. "Your Honor, may we request a recess?"

"Approach," Judge Blow waved the lawyers

forward. Both lawyers walked in front of the judge's chair. He turned off his microphone and talked in a low tone to the lawyers. "And what is the purpose of the request?"

"The witness has provided testimony to the police that he's now recanting, and he's saying the complete opposite of what he told us earlier. We're not prepared for the change in his testimony. Either he's perjuring himself now, or he did so earlier when he signed a witness statement."

"He's your witness, Mr. Garrett. Did you not prepare him for this testimony?"

"We did, Your Honor. We talked to him last week, however, this is still unexpected."

"We would prefer that the questioning continues, Your Honor," Hennessy said, a slight smile escaping. "It's in the best interest of the court for the truth to come out."

"You knew this was going to happen," Garrett stated. He pointed his finger at Hennessy. "You've played us. You knew he was going to change his testimony."

"I have no idea what your witnesses are going to say," Hennessy said. "And as the defense team, we are well within our rights to question your witnesses."

Judge Blow looked across to the witness and then back to Garrett. "I will grant you a fifteen-minute recess, and not a moment longer. You can discuss the testimony with the witness; however, you must be prepared for the fact that the defense will also have the opportunity to question the witness."

Garrett turned back to his desk, his movements sharp and fierce. Judge Blow announced the recess, and Norris stepped out of the witness box before being escorted out the doors of the courtroom by one of the Deputy Sheriffs, closely followed by Garrett.

"What happened?" Cruise asked after Norris had exited. "What was all that about?"

"Jason Norris has found his faith," Hennessy said, and turned around to nod to Lockett. "And he wants to tell the truth, no matter the cost."

For the next fifteen minutes, the courtroom was hushed, waiting for the return of the prosecution and the witness. When they returned, Garrett's face said it all—he couldn't sway Norris.

When asked by Judge Blow, Garrett stood and declined to continue questioning Norris. "We have no further questions for the witness, Your Honor."

Judge Blow drew a long breath and looked over to the defense. "Then I guess he's your witness, Mr. Hennessy."

Hennessy turned a page in front of him, wrote a few lines of notes, and then looked up at the man in the witness box. "Mr. Norris, you've changed your testimony from the original witness statement that you made to the police. Why is that?"

"Over the past five weeks, I've rediscovered God in my life. I've found my faith, and I know that I have to tell the truth. It's my path back to redemption. I've done a lot of bad things, but it's time to change. No more lies. No more crime. I'm going to tell the truth, no matter the cost."

Hennessy nodded. "For the benefit of the jury, have you ever seen Mr. Cruise purchase stolen art?"

"No."

"Have you ever seen Mr. Cruise sell stolen art?"

"No."

"Did you ever see Mr. Cruise handle the Stephen

Scully paintings?"

"No."

"And can you please explain to the court why you told the opposite story to the police?"

"Because I was paid to do it."

Hennessy drew a breath. He was going to test how far Norris was willing to go on his journey of redemption. "And who paid you to make that statement to the police?"

"A man named Roger East." Norris paused as a gasp came from the crowd. "He paid me five thousand dollars to lie."

"And did Mr. East tell you why he wanted you to lie to the police about what you saw?"

"Because they wanted Mr. Cruise to be locked up behind bars."

"And who are 'they'?"

"I wasn't told who it was, but I was given five thousand in cash to testify. I took it and made the statement to the police."

"And have you been given a deal to tell the truth here today?"

"No."

"And are you aware that it is likely you will be charged with perjury due to changing your statement to the police?"

"That has just been made clear to me by the prosecutor."

"However, even though you will be punished for perjury, you still wish to tell the truth?"

"That's correct."

"Thank you, Mr. Norris." Hennessy sat back down. "Good luck on your journey of faith, and thank you for being brave enough to tell the truth."

CHAPTER 34

"THE STATE rests, Your Honor."

Garrett stood at the prosecution table, shoulders slumped, embarrassed by his star witness. He had a strong case, one that was building towards a guilty verdict, but the testimonies of Richard Longhouse and Jason Norris had undone all the hard work.

Hennessy turned to the prosecutor and raised his eyebrows. Garrett refused to turn and make eye contact. He knew what was coming next.

Hennessy stood. "Your Honor, the defense wishes to file a motion under Rule 19, a Directed Verdict. We have adequate grounds for this motion, and we apply for the court to make a verdict in the defendant's favor, as there has been a complete failure of competent evidence tending to prove the charge in the indictment. The defense calls for the court to consider the non-existence of evidence that has shown Mr. Cruise had any knowledge that the artworks were in his possession."

"And have you prepared the motion?"

"We have the preliminary information for this motion." Hennessy remained standing. "However, we request a short recess to finalize the details."

"Considering the case the prosecution has put forward," Judge Blow nodded slowly and then looked at his watch. "And given the time, we shall recess for forty-five minutes for lunch to allow the defense adequate time to finalize this motion."

"Thank you, Your Honor."

Judge Blow stood and walked out of the room while a buzz of activity began at the prosecution's desk. They were desperate, scrambling to save their skin, trying to frame an argument against the motion.

Cruise leaned closer to Hennessy as the crowd behind them filed out through the courtroom doors. "What's happening? What's all this talk about a directed verdict?"

"After the State rests their case, the defense can ask the judge to make a decision on a matter of law," Hennessy looked across at Garrett and then back to Cruise. "In a directed verdict, the judge makes a decision on a lack of evidence to prove the matters of law. He'll only consider the existence, or in this case—the non-existence of evidence—and not the weight of the evidence."

"I don't know what that means," Cruise shook his head. "Give it to me in English."

"It means that we're applying to the judge to dismiss the case because the State didn't prove that you 'knowingly' had possession of the stolen goods. Just because they were on your premises is not enough. Because the State didn't catch you in the act of buying or selling the artwork, they have to prove you had dominion over the items as well. No witnesses have proven that." Hennessy paused and looked over his shoulder again. "Usually, the motion is dismissed without even so much as a second thought, but given the judge has allowed time to prepare the motion means that we have some legal grounds to stand on. They failed in an error of law. Judge Blow will consider this motion and may throw the case out before we've even had to stand up there and argue our side of the case."

Cruise scrunched his nose, nodded, and then sat back in his chair, resting his thumbs under his suspenders. "Good job."

Hennessy turned back to his laptop and continued typing, preparing a document for the judge to review. He turned to speak to Jacinta a number of times, gathering information and continuing to type. Twenty-five minutes later, the crowd began to return. By the time the bailiff called the court to attention, the seats in the courtroom were full.

Judge Curtis Blow returned to his seat, looking out at the crowd from over the top of his glasses. The jury box remained empty. He checked his notes, grunted, and then moved the microphone closer.

"Mr. Hennessy," Judge Blow leaned forward to rest on his elbows. "Have you prepared the motion?"

"We have, Your Honor." Hennessy stood and picked up two sets of paper. "The defense submits a motion for a directed verdict."

The bailiff took the documents and passed one copy to Judge Blow, and then handed the second copy to the prosecution table.

Judge Blow sighed as he read over the motion, taking his time to read over every page. After five minutes, he groaned and placed the piece of paper down.

"Mr. Garrett, do you have any arguments you wish to present against this motion?"

"Your Honor, the prosecution team believes that we have adequately shown that Mr. Cruise had dominion over the stolen items." Garrett's voice delivered the statement without emotion. "We request that the case continues, and the jury is given the opportunity to make a decision of guilt."

"Noted," Judge Blow cleared his throat. "Given the State's apparent failure to prove that Mr. Cruise knowingly, and that is the key term here—knowingly—had possession of the stolen items, I will consider this motion." He turned to the bailiff and nodded. "We will recess for two days while I review this motion, before I make a decision on a matter of law."

CHAPTER 35

"WELL, THAT certainly was a good way to make a start back in the law profession. What a trial," Jacinta flipped her hair over her shoulder and shot Hennessy her best confident smile. "Jason Norris was the best witness that we could have asked for."

"Better than we'd hoped," Hennessy smiled and handed a Starbucks coffee to his assistant. "A Venti Latte, two shots, with almond milk and one sugar, just like you wanted."

"Perfect. Thank you," she smiled. "So, what do you think the judge will say?"

"You never know with judges." Hennessy sat down at the chair in front of her reception desk. "They're ruled by the law, but they can be swayed with their heart instead of their head. Sometimes, you can predict what they're going to do, but here, I don't know. Judge Blow was hard to read," he sighed. "There haven't been any more calls, have there?"

"No more calls this afternoon," Jacinta smiled and shook her head. "And here's the good news—this first case is just about over."

Over. Hennessy leaned his head against the back of the chair, staring at the ceiling as he thought about that word. Over. It implied that they would never have to deal with the consequences of this case again. That there would be a firm line drawn when the verdict was delivered, and they walked out of the courtroom.

But this was far from over.

If they won, he'd be off the hook for a little while. At least, until the next time Henry Cruise stormed into his office, demanding that he represent him. If they lost, well, he didn't even want to think about the consequences.

"What do y'all feel is going to happen?" Jacinta asked. "What do you think is the right thing—guilty or not?"

"Right?" Hennessy smiled. "There's no right side as a defense lawyer—there's only the side of the client."

"Come on," she said. "Don't take the easy way out. What do you think is going to happen?"

"It's a tough question. Cruise is guilty of a lot of things, but is he guilty of this? I don't think he is," Hennessy shook his head. "And that means, by the letter of the law, that he shouldn't be found guilty."

"But what do you personally feel?"

"Feel?" Hennessy laughed. "You young'uns and your feelings."

"I'm not that young," Jacinta smiled. "So, are you going to answer my question, or are you going to keep avoiding it like an old man who can't express his emotions?"

"Ouch," Hennessy chuckled. "Ok—personally and professionally, I need him to get off, but emotionally?" Hennessy shrugged again. "He should be behind bars. That's where he belongs. He's caused a lot of pain to a lot of people, and there should be some repercussions for that."

The office phone rang. Jacinta looked over at Hennessy and then at the phone. Hennessy nodded.

Jacinta reached across and picked up the call. She spoke briefly with the person on the other line and then placed the receiver down. "That was the courthouse confirming that Judge Blow has made a decision on the motion and would like us all back in court at 11am."

Hennessy nodded but didn't smile.

Within an hour, Hennessy and Jacinta were back at the courthouse, loaded with caffeine.

As Hennessy walked into the courthouse foyer, Cruise was leaning against the far wall, waiting in his finest suit. Cruise still had arrogance, he still had confidence, but his head had slightly drooped.

"This is it, isn't it?" Cruise asked as Hennessy approached. "The moment where we find out if you sold me out or not."

"I've presented the best defense that you could hope for in your situation," Hennessy responded. "If the judge rejects the motion, then we can still present our case."

"We'll see," Cruise said, a hint of fear lacing his voice. "What do you think they're going to say?"

"I think you're a man that's spent many years terrorizing the people of Charleston," Hennessy stared at him. "And if the decision goes our way, then today is my last day with you. I'm done working with you."

"You're done when I say you're done," the menace returned to Cruise's tone. "Nobody walks away from me."

Hennessy glared at Cruise for a moment, and then led his client into courtroom number five. Hennessy greeted the prosecution team and then sat down. Cruise was slow to sit down next to him, taking his time.

Five minutes later, the crowd quietened as the door to Judge Blow's chambers opened, and the Deputy Sheriff assigned to the Security Services Unit stepped out.

Hennessy's heart pounded against the walls of his chest. He wasn't sure what he wanted the judge to say. If Cruise was found guilty, he'd do a long stretch behind bars. A minimum of five years in the slammer, perhaps even ten, as Judge Blow was known to be particularly harsh on sentencing. But Hennessy also knew Cruise was set up. There was something inside him that said sending him to prison wasn't right either. Judge Blow entered the courtroom, but he was in no hurry, ambling forward without a concern for time. Hennessy tried to slow his heart rate with breathing exercises, but it wasn't working.

Jason Norris would need to run out of town as quickly as possible. Whoever set up Cruise would not be happy with Norris' change of testimony, and he would need to spend a long time looking over his shoulder. Hennessy had tried to contact Norris again, but he was already on the run. Norris had gone underground once, and he'd need to do it again.

If Cruise's case was thrown out, there would be people who would need to step carefully, none more so than Richard Longhouse. Cruise was known for his vengeful streak, and he wouldn't rest until he'd inflicted pain on the people that put him through the trial.

After Judge Blow welcomed the court, the bailiff guided the jury in. They walked with an uncomfortable focus, averting eye contact with Cruise. The bailiff instructed the jury and the court.

Hennessy and Cruise stood.

Judge Blow turned to the jury. "Members of the jury, I've been asked to rule on a motion that questioned whether the State has failed in its obligation to show that Mr. Cruise knowingly had possession of the stolen goods." He turned back to the prosecution. "Not one credible witness claimed that they knew Mr. Cruise had knowledge of the whereabouts of the paintings. Not one credible witness claimed that they saw Mr. Cruise handling the stolen items, and not one credible witness claimed that they discussed with Mr. Cruise whether he had possession of the items. And the key term there is 'credible.' The law is clear—for a person to be charged under Section 16-13-180 South Carolina Code of Laws, the prosecution has to prove that they knowingly had possession of the item and that they were able to have dominion over the item. In the eyes of the law, having the items on your property is not enough to prove guilt."

Judge Blow paused and then shook his head.

Guilty or not, Hennessy needed to end his association with Cruise. There was money to gain from the association, more than enough to clear the vineyard's debt, but money wasn't everything. He'd rather scrap and scrape for every dollar than have to work with Cruise again.

"Given the failure of the prosecution to present any evidence that showed Mr. Cruise knowingly had possession of the items," Judge Blow continued. "I have no choice but to grant this motion. Under South Carolina Code of Laws Section 16-13-180, possessing property represented by law enforcement as stolen, the charges are dismissed. Mr. Cruise, you're free to go."

For Hennessy, it took a second or two for the judge's decision to sink in. He'd had bittersweet victories in the past, but none had been as acrid as this. The wide, gleaming shark's grin on Cruise's face was enough to make Hennessy want to spin around and ask the judge if he'd made the correct ruling, but the hard slap on his shoulder brought him back to reality.

"We won," Cruise said. "You did it. I knew I could count on you, Joe."

Henry Cruise reached out to shake Joe's hand.

Hennessy couldn't decline. He gritted his teeth and reached out a stiff arm to shake the hand of one of the dirtiest men he'd ever met.

CHAPTER 36

JOE HENNESSY parked his truck at the front of the Five Corners Art Gallery, took a deep breath, and exited his vehicle. It was time to end his association with the owner of the Five Corners, and time to leave the nightmare behind him. Cruise was set up, that was clear to everyone involved, but if the corruption racket wanted Cruise in prison, Hennessy reasoned, they would need to do it legitimately and within the bounds of the law. A paper sign hung on the front door of the Five Corners, announcing it was closed to celebrate a private event. This was no time to entertain customers, this was no time to worry about money, this was a time for Henry Cruise to celebrate his latest escape from the clutches of the law.

Hennessy looked at the entrance to the gallery, shook his head, and rang the bell at the side of the door. A young woman, barely clothed and most likely an exotic dancer, answered the door. She giggled and appeared excited, or at least a little drunk. Hennessy walked through the wide entrance, running his hand along the wall, and stepped into the main room. Half the artworks had been taken down, and a number of chairs had been brought into the room.

Henry Cruise popped a champagne bottle, the excess fizz spraying onto one of the girls. She squealed with delight. Apart from the dancing girls, there were ten more people in the room, hangers-on, people who wanted to celebrate with free alcohol. The music was loud, the atmosphere was full of celebration, and the drinks were flowing freely.

"Ah!" Cruise shouted. "My new favorite lawyer!"

Cruise brushed one of the girls off his arm and walked towards Hennessy. Cruise was unsteady on his feet. He'd been celebrating for hours already, and it showed, but he'd still be celebrating long into the night. There was nothing like the threat of prison to help a person realize how much they valued freedom. Cruise approached Hennessy and held out his arms like he wanted a hug. Hennessy shook his head.

"I'm your ex-lawyer."

"Ex-lawyer?" Cruise grinned. "Forget about all that and come and celebrate with us."

"I did the job for you," Hennessy said. "And now I've come to tell you that I'm not going to work for you again. We're done."

"Don't be like that." Cruise's smile couldn't be wiped off his face. "I know you're emotional, but we'll talk again."

"We won't."

Cruise paused, looked down at his glass, and nodded at one of the girls with a champagne bottle. He held the glass out, and the young girl filled it up, the bubbles quickly overflowing the glass. Cruise's eyes lingered on her half-naked body for a while.

"You did well with Norris. I don't know what you threatened him with, but it worked. That was beautiful. The prosecution put him up there on the stand and expected him to lie, but he exposed the truth. That was magic," Cruise laughed. "But Norris needs to be careful now. Whoever asked him to lie won't be happy with what he did up there on the stand. He'll need to check over his shoulder at every corner, screen every phone call, and watch every car following him."

"Roger East was involved in setting you up."

"I don't believe he's behind it. He's just a gun for hire. He'll do whatever the highest bidder is asking. Nothing personal." Cruise sipped his champagne. "Why don't you stay for a while? Have a drink. Let off some steam. You deserve it after the performance you gave."

Hennessy shook his head. "What are you going to do with Longhouse?"

"Nothing yet," Cruise laughed. "Because I'm a threat if he becomes Governor. I have some dirt on him, and he knows I'm going to use it the second he becomes Governor. That's why he wanted me gone. All I have to do is keep my head down until then. If he wins the vote, then snap," he clicked his fingers. "With him under my control, I become one of the most influential men in this State again."

"You're the dirtiest person I've ever met," Hennessy shook his head. "We're done."

Hennessy turned to leave. If there was one thing he knew, it was that he wanted no part of Cruise's future dramas. But as he took a step towards the door, Damien Bates stepped in.

Hennessy paused for a moment, studying Bates. He was dressed in a wrinkled brown suit, but he was clean-shaven.

"I hear there's a party around here." Bates' eyes drifted to one of the half-naked girls. "And it looks like I'm just in time for some fun."

"Get a drink for my investigator," Cruise called

out to one of the girls. "The man deserves a glass of champagne!"

"Your investigator?" Hennessy turned slowly back to Cruise. "Damien Bates works for you?"

"See, boss?" Bates laughed and slapped Cruise on the shoulder. "I told you he knew nothing about it. The poor guy didn't have a clue."

Hennessy stared at them, switching his focus between Cruise and Bates.

They both laughed at him and then turned back towards the other people in the gallery.

CHAPTER 37

THE MID-MORNING sun peeked through the thick clouds, the light reflecting off the tall buildings in Downtown Charleston, and a gentle rain fell onto the window of his office. Hennessy leaned against the window, watching the street below. He loved Charleston's architecture. People from all around the world traveled to the city to admire the buildings, their style and charm unmatched. An architectural museum without walls, Charleston was home to thousands of historic buildings designed in an array of period styles, from Colonial, Georgian, Regency, Federal, Greek Revival, and even Art Deco. Block after block of beautiful homes were housed on the Peninsula, complete with Haint Blue and Charleston Green colors.

The following weeks had passed in a blur. While preparing for Zoe Taylor's murder trial, Hennessy couldn't stop thinking about Cruise. Was he going down? Or would he smooth things over with Longhouse? What was his connection to Bates? The night he saw them together was still making his head spin. Bates had cut his prices to work for Hennessy, and it all started to make sense. Cruise wanted him there.

Cruise had paid Hennessy's full fee, as he said he would, and the money took the pressure off the vineyard's bills. Wendy and Casey were more comfortable, but there was still a debt to pay. Without another good crop of grapes, Hennessy was looking at five years working in Charleston to get the vineyard established again. He figured he could do that, but there would be no more crime bosses and no more dirty secrets.

With Zoe's case due to hit the courts within a week, nerves were building for both Hennessy and the Taylor family. Three months of hard work was coming to a close. He'd spent the time building information on the witnesses, breaking down the crime scene piece by piece, trying to find enough evidence to cast doubt on everyone who was involved in the arrest of Zoe Taylor.

The closer the day came, the more anxious Zoe Taylor appeared. She was tense and panicky, sometimes breaking down in wheezing fits, and her anxiety seemed to rise with every day. And she had every right to be nervous—the case against her was strong, and she was looking at losing the best years of her life to prison.

Hennessy sat at the desk in his office. He was expecting the prosecutor any second. Although he had some leads, the witnesses were causing the most difficulties in his preparation for Zoe Taylor's defense. There was a witness that placed her at the scene of the crime, a witness that saw them arguing, and a witness that saw her running from the scene. They gave him nothing in their depositions.

The prosecution had offered a better deal the week before. Hennessy was surprised at the offer of a year in prison for manslaughter. It was a very good deal, and Hennessy encouraged Zoe to think long and hard about it, but she rejected it without a second thought.

She was innocent, she argued, and she didn't want to spend any time in prison for something she didn't do.

Frank Taylor wasn't easy to deal with, but Hennessy never assumed he would be. Every conversation was laced with rising anger, every comment made with angst, and every action performed with aggression.

But despite the evidence, Hennessy wasn't convinced Zoe was guilty. He just couldn't see her stabbing her ex-boyfriend in a fit of rage.

Jacinta's knock on his office door caught him by surprise.

"Prosecutor Nadine Robinson is here to see you."

Hennessy thanked Jacinta and asked her to send her through. Robinson walked in with confidence, a hop in her step. She was well-dressed in a dark blue suit, with her hair pulled back tightly.

"Still basking in the glory of your last win, Joe?" Robinson smiled as she entered the room. "I hear it was quite the surprise to everyone in the court."

"It was a great win," Hennessy said. "Defending an innocent man against an over-zealous Circuit Solicitor's office is always satisfying."

"We're doing nothing of the sort. Maybe that's how you see it, but that's not how we see it. Remember, life's all about perspective, Joe," Robinson said. "I once knew a guy that had the time to exercise twice a day, had time to read two books a week, and had all his meals cooked for him, and yet, he still complained about how much he hated prison."

Hennessy laughed. "And how can I help you today? Have you come to tell me that the charges have been dropped against Zoe Taylor?"

"Not quite, but I thought I would personally drop this file off," Robinson stood behind the chair in front of his desk. "There's new discovery information for Zoe's case, and it's quite the development. And to start, I must say that I know how this looks, but I can assure you there was no game playing with this information. We only discovered it this week, and I must say, we had to work through what it meant. It was quite the shock to all of us."

Robinson sat down carefully, resting her briefcase on her lap. She opened it and removed a large manila folder, and then placed her briefcase on the floor. She tapped her fingers on the folder as she looked around the room before bringing her attention back to Hennessy.

"In this folder is the list of the new discovery information. I'll have my assistant send the electronic file this afternoon, but I wanted to personally deliver the paper copy first and assure you that it's legitimate." She leaned forward. "And I'm not going to lie, it does strengthen our case. But I remind you, that it's not our job to put people away, it's our job to find the truth. We've reviewed the information, and our department still feels, strongly, that Zoe Taylor is guilty of Andre Powers' murder."

"What is it?"

"Someone was found in possession of Andre Powers' missing wallet."

"Who?"

"Someone you know." She drew a long breath but kept her hand resting on top of the file. "His five-page statement about the arrest is in this folder. The man was picked up during a traffic stop, and was under suspicion of carrying drugs. The officers then exercised their rights to search his car. Andre Powers' wallet was found in the glove box, along with five other stolen wallets. We took the man in, and he was charged with drug-related crimes."

"Does the statement say how the man came into possession of the wallet?"

"He said that he was walking past the car and saw that a man was sleeping in his vehicle with the window open. He was opportunistic and reached in and grabbed the wallet. He says it was before Powers was stabbed." She drew a breath. "But after he took the wallet, he says that he saw Miss Taylor running away from the scene with a knife in her hand."

"And do you believe his story?"

"Yes." She shrugged. "The man signed a deal to testify in exchange for a suspended sentence for possessing the stolen wallets and his drug possession charges. It's the man's third conviction in the last few years, and any judge is likely to come down hard on him, so he jumped at the chance to sign the deal. He didn't want to go back to prison."

"A deal to testify?" Hennessy leaned back in his chair. "You knew about this last week, didn't you? That's why you offered the deal for manslaughter."

"This discovery information only became officially available yesterday. The person in question only signed the deal to testify in the last twenty-four hours."

"And when was the traffic stop?"

She hesitated before she conceded. "Last Friday."

"Of course. You've known for five days, but it's only just come into discovery." Hennessy reached across for the information. "What's the man's name?"

"Someone you know well." Robinson lifted her hand from the file. "The man found in possession of Andre Powers' wallet is Damien Bates."

CHAPTER 38

INDICTMENT

STATE OF SOUTH CAROLINA
COUNTY OF CHARLESTON
IN THE COURT OF GENERAL SESSIONS
NINTH JUDICIAL CIRCUIT
INDICTMENT NO.: 2022-AB-02-145

STATE OF SOUTH CAROLINA, V. ZOE SAMANTHA TAYLOR, DEFENDANT.

At a Court of General Sessions, convened on 25th of March, the Grand Jurors of Charleston County present upon their oath: Murder.
That in Charleston County on or about the 15th of March, the defendant, ZOE SAMANTHA TAYLOR, with malice aforethought, did kill and murder ANDRE POWERS by means of stabbing, and ANDRE POWERS died in Charleston County as a proximate result thereof on or about 15th of March, in violation of Section 16-3-10 South Carolina Code of Laws (1976) as amended.

COUNT ONE
S.C CODE SECTION 16-3-10. MURDER

That in Charleston County on or about 15th of March, the defendant, ZOE SAMANTHA TAYLOR, did murder with malice aforethought. To wit: ZOE SAMANTHA TAYLOR did murder ANDRE POWERS per violation of Section 16-13-10 South Carolina Code of Laws (1976) as amended.

FINDINGS

We, the Grand Jury, find that ZOE SAMANTHA TAYLOR is to be indicted under Section 16-13-10 South Carolina Code of Laws (1976) as amended.

*****

THERE WAS nothing like the first day of a murder trial. The frenzied nature of the halls, the hectic and feverish atmosphere of the court, the intense buzz of the onlookers. People were attracted to crime and justice, needing to know that their system, the system that held the country together, was working as it should. And there was no other crime that captured the public's attention quite like murder.

The media pack outside the courthouse was desperate for a new angle on the story. They'd come from all over the state, corresponding to the newsrooms in the big cities, and they all wanted to report the information first. They pressed Hennessy for information as he walked into the courthouse, Jacinta by his side, but he ignored the reporters, not even giving a moment of his time. He needed to focus. He needed to keep his strength for the court. He needed to win.

He had no doubt that Zoe Taylor was innocent. That weight, that undeniable heavy burden, was pushing him to breaking point. Zoe's future, the future of an innocent girl, rested in his hands. If he lost, he would take on the appeal for free, he told himself over and over, trying to calm his nerves.

The crowd inside the courtroom was nervous and tense. There was a buzz in the air, an electricity coursing through the room. Zoe Taylor was waiting by the defense table. It was clear she'd been crying. She was dressed in her best black skirt and jacket; her hair pulled back tightly. She presented herself well and didn't look at all like a killer.

Nadine Robinson and her team were busy organizing files at the prosecution's desk. She didn't greet Hennessy as he walked past, instead focusing on her opening statement, rehearsing the lines under her breath.

When the bailiff called the room to order, the crowd rose to their feet. The thick and heavy tension in the room was unmistakable. Judge Whitworth walked into the courtroom, in no rush to begin the trial, and once she sat down, she looked over her notes, fixed her hair, and welcomed the parties to the court.

They spent the morning in voir dire, the jury selection process. Fifty-five potential jurors filed into the courtroom. Judge Whitworth began questioning the jury before she dismissed a number of people early. Both Robinson and Hennessy called for Judge Whitworth to exclude potential jurors with 'for cause' challenges. Robinson used five peremptory challenges after the pool was selected, and Hennessy used ten. The selected twelve that survived the questions all denied they'd heard about the case, and all denied seeing it on the various media channels. They were a mix of ages, a mix of education levels, and a mix of social classes. An odd bunch, if ever there was one. Two twenty-five-year-olds, who Hennessey hoped would side with the young defendant, two people in their thirties, five in their forties and fifties, and three in their sixties. Five men, seven women.

Hennessy studied them carefully. He knew which ones to target with emotions, and which ones to target with perceived facts, but most people didn't listen to the truth, jurors included. They heard what they wanted to hear. They saw what they wanted to see. They searched out stories that proved what was already in their subconscious, fulfilling their subtle biases.

After the jury was selected, Hennessy filed another application to move venues based on the makeup of the jury pool, however, Judge Whitworth took little time in refusing it. Whitworth barely spent five minutes considering the motion. It was further grounds for appeal, but that didn't help Zoe Taylor now.

Before the opening statements, the court took a brief recess. Frank Taylor was nervous, wiping his brow constantly with a handkerchief. Zoe seemed the calmer of the two, but she still looked near her breaking point. Some of Zoe's friends had arrived at court. They wanted to support her, but they kept their distance. A number of reporters sat by the back of the courtroom, most of them with their tablets ready, and two Deputy Sheriffs stood by the doors. Jacinta sat behind Hennessy, Barry Lockett next to her.

After the brief recess, Judge Whitworth instructed the bailiff to bring the jury in. The bailiff walked to the door in the front left corner of the room, opened it, and directed the members of the jury to their seats. The twelve people who would decide Zoe's fate walked in.

Judge Whitworth spoke to the jury about their responsibilities, explaining the charges were lodged under Section 16-3-10 South Carolina Code of Laws, and what that meant, "As the trial judge, it's my responsibility to preside over the trial of this case and to rule upon the admissibility of the evidence offered during the trial. You're to consider only the testimony which has been presented from this witness stand together with any exhibits which have been made a part of the record. As the presiding judge, I am the sole judge of the law in this case. It's your duty as jurors to accept my decisions as correct and apply the law as I now state it to you. Finally, I charge you in this regard that you should not be concerned with what you think the law ought to be, but rather what I charge you that the law is. However, I do not have the right to express any opinion on the facts or evidence of this case, because this is a matter solely for you, the jury, to determine. While I will guide you on the definition of the law, as jurors, it's your duty to determine the effect, the value, the weight, and the truth of the evidence presented during this trial," Judge Whitworth paused to arrange the files in front of her, and then continued. "We will now begin with the opening statements. The opening statement is not an argument, nor is it a testimony of evidence. It's merely a roadmap for the case, and a forecast of what the lawyers will present. The lawyers are not here to put on a show. They are here to simply tell you what the actual evidence will be."

Once Judge Whitworth was satisfied the jurors understood her instructions, she invited prosecutor Nadine Robinson to begin her argument.

*****

"Your Honor, ladies and gentlemen of the jury. My name is Nadine Robinson, and these are my colleagues, Maxwell Smith and Tanya Connelly. We're here to present the charge of murder against the defendant, Miss Zoe Taylor. As mentioned by Judge Whitworth, in this opening statement, I'll provide a roadmap of what the evidence presented during this trial will show, as nothing I say to you now can be considered evidence.

We are here today, in this court, to deliver justice. As a definition, justice is the idea that people are treated impartially, fairly, and properly. They are treated reasonably by the law, and it sees that the accused receives a morally right consequence merited by their actions. A moral consequence. I need you to remember that as we go through this trial. That no matter the background of the defendant, and no matter the background of the victim, you must make a decision impartially and justly. You need to make a just and fair decision without regard for race, wealth, or bias.

As Circuit Solicitors, my team and I represent the State of South Carolina. We work in the Ninth Judicial Circuit, serving Charleston County. We are responsible for the prosecution of criminal cases throughout this county. Murders, and violent crime, rarely happen in the city of Charleston. I'm thankful for that. I'm thankful that we are safe in this city. And we must strive to keep it that way.

Your job here, in this court, is to decide whether there's enough evidence to convict Miss Taylor of murder beyond a reasonable doubt.

Mr. Powers was murdered as he sat in his vehicle on a Sunday morning, at around 7am. From his autopsy, we can determine that he was stabbed five times, including a fatal blow to the neck, which severed his carotid artery and caused him to bleed out. Mr. Powers was in his car, outside his apartment on the corner of Harris Street and America Street, in the North-Central residential area of Charleston.

Over the coming days, we'll present witnesses to

you, and they'll provide the evidence in this case. You'll hear from the people who found the body, the detectives that investigated the case, and the paramedics who arrived at the scene.

You'll hear from Detective Knox, the lead detective on this case. He'll explain what he found at the scene and why Miss Taylor was arrested. He'll also tell you what she said when she was taken into custody. You'll see the footage from Mr. Knox's body camera, and the footage from other officers' body cameras during the arrest. You'll see, with your own eyes, the moment Miss Taylor was arrested at her home. You will also see the blood on Miss Taylor's sweater as she was arrested.

You'll hear from experts in the field of crime and justice. You'll hear from the South Carolina County Deputy Coroner, who performed the autopsy, you'll hear from crime scene expert Dr. Hayes, and you'll hear from numerous blood splatter experts. You will also hear from Dr. Morrison, who will advise the court that the blood found on Miss Taylor's sweater was a match for Mr. Powers.

You'll hear from the 911 dispatch caller, and she'll describe the call she received from Miss Taylor on the morning of the 15th of March. You will hear the recording of this call.

You'll hear from Mr. Damien Bates, who was at the scene of the crime that morning. He will testify that he saw Miss Taylor fleeing the scene around the time of death. He will testify that he saw Mr. Powers in his vehicle before his death, and he will testify that he saw Miss Taylor running from the scene holding an object that looked like a knife.

You'll also hear from a witness who will state that

Miss Taylor and Mr. Powers were previously a couple, however, they had separated. This witness will state that on the day before the murder, Miss Taylor had a very vocal argument with Mr. Powers, where she threatened to stab him.

Once we arrive at the end of this case, I have no doubt that you will have enough evidence to convict Miss Taylor of murder. But to do that, to make that decision, you must first let go of your biases and prejudices.

This was an unforgivable crime, and it warrants a conviction.

At the end of this case, I'll address you again and ask you to consider all the evidence we have presented and to conclude beyond a reasonable doubt that Miss Zoe Taylor is guilty.

Thank you for your time."

*****

A trial is a story told through two narrators, the prosecution and the defense, each one spinning the tale, slicing and dicing the facts, until one story seems more believable than the other. Robert Frost once said that, 'A jury consists of twelve persons chosen to decide who has the better lawyer,' and Hennessy believed that. He understood that if a case made it to trial, then the balance of evidence was likely to be unstable, enough for the prosecution to take it to court, but not enough for the defense to think they could lose.

Most lawyers rarely saw the inside of a courtroom.

They filed paperwork, made phone calls, reviewed legal precedents, and conducted meeting after meeting after meeting. For a case to make it to trial, to actually make it inside the courtroom, one of two things had to happen—either the client was hopelessly stubborn in the face of the prosecution's evidence; or the client genuinely believed they had a chance to win the case; but even then, most lawyers encouraged the client to take the deal and not to face the uncertainty of the courtroom.

Hennessy had asked numerous times if Zoe had wanted to take a deal. She refused each time, claiming her innocence. He didn't push her to sign the deal. He didn't strongly encourage her. He thought they had a better story than the prosecution, and he believed the evidence wasn't enough to convict her.

It was a risk, one with dire consequences, but it was a risk that Zoe had chosen to take.

Hennessy stood, made eye contact with the jurors, and nodded. Two automatically returned the nod. Standing behind the podium, Hennessy began his opening statement.

*****

"May it please the court. Ladies and gentlemen of the jury, Your Honor, my name is Joe Hennessy. I'm a criminal defense attorney, and I'm here to represent the defendant, Miss Zoe Taylor.

There's something important to remember during this trial—you need evidence, not theories, to convict Miss Taylor. You need facts, not stories. You need proof, not ideas, to make a decision of guilty beyond a reasonable doubt.

I want you to remember that, because there's a lack of evidence in this trial. The prosecution has decided to bring this case before the courts even though they don't have many pieces of the puzzle. Mr. Powers was murdered. We know that. That is clear. But we do not know who murdered Mr. Powers. And we don't know this because there's not enough evidence.

There is no murder weapon, there is no witness to the event occurring, and there is no footage of this event. There is no evidence that shows who committed this crime, there is no evidence that shows who stabbed Mr. Powers, and there is no evidence that demonstrates who was involved in his murder.

The absence of evidence is not evidence of its absence.

I'll repeat that for you, so it is clear—the absence of evidence is not evidence of its absence.

The prosecution team has not found a murder weapon. They theorize that Mr. Powers was stabbed with a knife, but they don't know. They don't know because they don't have the evidence. The missing knife could've been a box cutter. It could've been a sword. It could've been a sharp razor. We don't have that evidence, and as such, we don't know what killed Mr. Powers.

Just because the prosecution does not have the knife, does not mean it exists. Just because the prosecution has no eyewitness to the event, does not mean it took place. Just because the prosecution has no evidence of the murder, does not mean that Zoe Taylor committed the act.

The absence of evidence is not evidence of its absence.

As the defense team, we will present experts who will confirm that there is no clear evidence that a knife was used. We will present blood splatter experts who will show you that if the prosecution's theory was even close to correct, then Miss Taylor would've been covered in blood, instead of a few spots on her sleeve.

We will present expert witnesses that will demonstrate that the prosecution's evidence is doubtful, at best. Other expert witnesses will tell you that there is no way that Miss Taylor had the strength to overcome the much stronger Mr. Powers.

You will hear from the gas station attendant who saw Miss Taylor buying gas at 7:10am that morning. You will hear from Penny Jones and Gemma Vince, friends of Miss Taylor, who will testify that they rushed to Miss Taylor's home to console her after they were notified of the event. They were with Miss Taylor between the time Miss Taylor made the 911 call, and when the police arrived. These witnesses will tell you that Miss Taylor was in a state of shock.

You will hear from Mrs. Jodie Beckett, a psychologist, who will state that people react to distressing situations differently. She will tell you that shock causes people to act in strange ways.

Miss Robinson asked you to be fair and unbiased in your judgment of the evidence. I ask the same. I want you to study the facts of this case. Not how you feel. Not what you think must've happened. But the facts. And when we arrive at the end of this case, the facts will be simple—there's not enough evidence to convict Miss Taylor beyond a reasonable doubt.

The onus of proof is on the prosecution. They must present evidence that proves Miss Taylor committed this act. They won't be able to, because that direct evidence simply does not exist.

Direct evidence supports the truth of an assertion through its presence. The prosecution does not have this. What the prosecution has is a circumstantial case. That means the evidence relies on an inference to connect it to a conclusion. They have no direct evidence, and yet, they still chose to bring this case to trial.

In making your decision at the end of this trial, the only evidence you can consider is the evidence presented here. You cannot use evidence that isn't presented in this courtroom.

You cannot use the information you saw on social media. You cannot use your friend's opinion. You must make your decision based solely on what is presented in this courtroom. In making your decision, you must be unbiased. You must be impartial. And above all else, you must be fair.

Miss Taylor did not murder Mr. Powers. There is no evidence that she did, and you cannot convict her for it.

There are holes in the prosecution's case, and when this case is drawing to a close, I will stand up here again, and point to all the holes in their story. You will then be asked to make a decision on this trial, and you can only conclude that Miss Taylor is not guilty.

Thank you for your service to our great justice system."

CHAPTER 39

AT FIVE minutes past two, with the opening statements concluded, Robinson was instructed by Judge Whitworth to call the first witness of the murder trial. The adrenalized anticipation of the opening statements had created a restlessness in the crowd, and nobody was moving. Even after a short recess, the seats in the courtroom remained full. Nobody wanted to give up their spot to watch the show of the year in the Charleston courts. Hennessy's win in Cruise's trial had created an expectation, an anticipation, that he could deliver the impossible.

Nadine Robinson wasted no time in calling her first witness. She stood and called Detective David Phillip Knox. Knox walked to the stand as a proud man—his solid chest was puffed out, his shoulders were pulled back, and his chin was held high. He wore a black suit with a thin tie, white shirt, and brown shoes. He smelled like Old Spice. He presented an image of importance and competence, and more importantly for the jurors, dressed in a suit, he presented as a trustworthy man. He'd walked to the stand many times over his past thirty-five years in the force. He knew the drill, and he knew what worked. Knox went through the gate to the witness stand and was sworn in as routine dictated.

Presenting a strong first witness was essential to any prosecution case, and Knox appeared as solid as they came. As Knox swore his oath, Robinson scanned her laptop, reading over the lines and lines of notes, and then moved to the lectern near the jury to begin. She took a pile of papers with her and arranged them perfectly before she looked up. She looked first to the jury, then to the judge, and then to the witness.

"Detective Knox, thank you for coming to the court today," Robinson began. "Can you please tell the court your profession, and your connection to this case?"

"My name is Mr. David Phillip Knox, and I've been proudly employed by the Charleston Police Department for the past twenty-five years. I started there as a twenty-five-year-old, and a few years have passed since then," He smiled and looked to the jury. They responded to him with polite smiles. "I was assigned the title of Detective fifteen years ago, and before that I was part of the Patrol Team. I work within the Homicide Investigations Unit, and I'm also a member of the Crisis Response Team. I love working for the beautiful city of Charleston, and I'm very proud to serve this city." Knox checked that his tie was down the middle of his shirt. "And I was the lead detective on the investigation into Mr. Andre Powers' murder, and the subsequent arrest of Miss Zoe Taylor."

"Detective Knox, have you previously been the lead investigator on murder cases?"

"I've led many murder investigations in my long career. Perhaps as many as forty or fifty over the years I've been a police officer. I don't like investigating murder cases, but it's part of the job."

"Were you the first person to find Mr. Powers' bloodied body at the scene of the crime?"

"No."

"Do you know who was?"

"That was a man named Cooper Singletary. He found Mr. Powers' body in the front seat of his car near the corner of Harris and America Streets. He saw the window was open and checked on the body. It was at this point that he reported seeing blood, and he called 911." Knox cleared his throat. "Two officers arrived fifteen minutes after that first call, and then I arrived five minutes after them."

"What time did you arrive?"

"I arrived at 7:45am."

"What did you find when you arrived at the scene?"

"We found Mr. Andre Powers in the driver's seat of his red Chevrolet Cavalier. The car was a 1995 model, and it'd certainly done some miles. There was no blood on the outside of the car, however, it was clear once we approached the car that Mr. Powers was deceased."

"Did you take photos of the scene?"

"Yes."

Robinson turned to her junior prosecutor, who began typing on his laptop. She then turned back to the jury. "What you are about to see may be upsetting, and it may be distressing, however, it is important that you look at these photos. We're about to view the photos of the crime scene as Detective Knox found it. I understand if you need to look away, however, I ask that you take some deep breaths, and try to study the photos in detail."

She turned back to her assistant, who then typed a number of commands. The pictures of the crime scene appeared on the monitor. First, it was the street.

Second, a photo of the Chevy sedan. Then, a photo of Andre Powers, limp, bloodied, and lifeless. Two jury members gasped, as did some members of the gallery. A number of the jurors recoiled in horror at seeing pictures of a dead body. For the uninitiated, the scene was disturbing. Zoe dropped her face into her hands, unable to look at the photos of the man she once loved.

Robinson only introduced five photos of the deceased, as showing any more photos to the jury could be regarded as prejudicial against the defendant. Even with the five bloodied photos of Powers lying in his car, head slumped to the side, Robinson was treading a fine line.

"Are these the photos you took?" Robinson continued scrolling through the photos until she reached a distant photo of the car, without the body visible. She stopped on that photo.

"That's correct."

"At this point, was Cooper Singletary a suspect?"

"Of course. Everyone was a suspect. This was clearly a murder case; I could tell that the second I walked up to the window of the car. I talked to Mr. Singletary but was able to rule him out quite quickly. He was looking after his mother the night before and had only left his apartment five minutes before he found the body. Later, we confirmed his story. He was just walking by and was unfortunately the first one to notice the dead body."

"Did anyone else arrive at the scene?"

"The paramedics and a number of other police staff arrived next. We secured the area, and I instructed the other officers to begin looking for clues. I advised another one of my officers to take

253

photos of the body, and after that, I advised the paramedics to cover the body with a cloth before anyone else saw the distressing scene."

"What did you do next?"

"With another officer, I began to canvas the local area, taking the statements of anyone that we thought could've heard, seen, or known something. Other officers began to comb the area looking for any clues."

"Did you find the murder weapon?"

"No."

"At what point did Miss Taylor become a suspect?"

"Right after we started talking to the nearby residents. They reported that they saw Mr. Powers and Miss Taylor arguing nearby the day before. We went to interview Miss Taylor and found that she still had some blood on her clothes. That blood was later shown to match Mr. Powers' blood sample."

"And when you first talked to Miss Taylor, was she aware that Mr. Powers was deceased?"

"Yes. Just after Mr. Singletary found the body, Miss Taylor claims she arrived at Mr. Powers' apartment building to apologize to him. She told us that she saw his car window open, and she approached it. It was then that she saw he was deceased. She stated that she then got in her car and drove back to her house, before she made a call to 911."

"What time did Mr. Singletary make the first 911 call?"

"7:35am."

"And what time was Miss Taylor's call?"

"7:45am."

"However, by this time, you were already at the scene?"

"That's correct."

Robinson paused and looked at the jury. When she saw a number of expressions of surprise in the jury box, she continued. "After you surveyed the scene, what was the next step in your police investigation?"

For the next three hours and twenty-five minutes, Knox detailed the crime scene and the steps of the investigation, from how he established Zoe Taylor as the main suspect, to how he arrested her. He took the court through the process, step by step, describing every small detail that he'd observed. He talked about the evidence the officers had found at the scene, he talked about the state of Andre Powers' body when it was found, and he talked about the witnesses. He talked about when he first interviewed Zoe Taylor, he talked about the bloodied shirt she was still wearing, and he talked about how she was evasive in answering his questions.

Throughout it all, Knox kept looking at the jury, smiling, winking, and building a rapport with them. The jury warmed to Knox, trusting every word he said, as if he was an authority on all that was good. After Robinson finished questioning her first witness, Judge Whitworth recessed for the day marking the end of the first day of the trial. Robinson had deliberately stretched the testimony past 5pm, leaving the judge no choice but to recess before Hennessy had a chance to cross-examine.

It was a clear tactic—on day one, the jury had only heard the voice of one witness, and they left the court convinced of Zoe Taylor's guilt.

Hennessy would have to work hard to change that.

CHAPTER 40

HENNESSY'S RENTED apartment in Charleston felt lonelier each night.

Summer had arrived, bringing with it hot, humid, and sweltering nights. The air-conditioner in his apartment wasn't enough to cool him down. He spent the night after Detective Knox's testimony tossing and turning, half-asleep and half-awake, his mind drifting through his past in Charleston—his school years, his marriage to Wendy, his work as a lawyer, until his train of thoughts stopped at the memories of his son. He was unable to stop the intrusive thoughts from creeping into his head, unable to stop himself falling into the rabbit hole of pain and anger that beckoned him. At one point, after he finally drifted off, he woke to the screams of his son, calling out for his father to save him. That pain was becoming unbearable.

He missed Wendy's calming presence, he missed seeing his daughter every day, and he missed the divine serenity of the vineyard. It was a world away from the horrors of crime, a world away from the courts, and he missed the calmness that working on the land gave him. Being in Charleston, back near so much pain, was threatening to break down the strong emotional walls that he'd spent so long reinforcing.

He started most days with two strong coffees, along with an apple, thanks to Jacinta's advice, but it was no longer enough. Ice baths, the grocery store owner told him after his first day in court for Zoe Taylor's case, were the best way to wake up. It's worth a thousand coffees, he said. Hennessy took the man's advice, buying two bags of ice after court and storing them in the freezer. After his morning coffee, Hennessy filled the tub with cold water and dropped the bags of ice into it. He lowered himself in, shocking his body. He lay in the tub for ten minutes, trying to fight off the cold, before stepping out. He dried himself off, and once his body warmed up again, he realized the store owner was right—despite his lack of sleep, he'd never felt more alive.

Hennessy arrived at the courthouse for day two with a clear mind and an enthused determination, ready to find the truth about what happened to Andre Powers.

When invited by Judge Whitworth, he stood at the defense table, Zoe next to him, and thanked the detective for returning. The jury was awake and alert, paying attention to Hennessy's first questions of the case.

"Detective Knox, when Miss Taylor made the call to 911, did she say what time she saw the body?"

"Yes. She said she saw the body fifteen minutes earlier, but fled the scene in a panic."

"And when you questioned her, did she say what she was doing before 7:30am?"

"She said she had come from her home."

"Directly from home?"

"No, she said she stopped to buy gas."

"And, being a good detective, did you verify she had in fact bought gas that morning?"

He moved in his seat. "Of course. We checked the

cameras at the gas station that she said she went to. We saw her complete the transaction at 7:10am."

"And where was this gas station located?"

"In Mount Pleasant."

"Which is how far from the scene?"

"Around fifteen minutes' drive."

"So the earliest Miss Taylor could've arrived at the scene was 7:25am?"

"That would be a correct estimate, yes."

"Thank you, Detective," Hennessy turned a piece of paper over. "Can you please tell the court if you found the murder weapon?"

"No, we didn't locate it, but that's not unusual in this type of case."

"Do you know where it could be?"

"It could be anywhere, but considering we weren't far from the river, we theorized that the murderer may have thrown the knife into the water. If that was the case, there wasn't much chance that we would find it, however, we did look through the pluff mud at low tide, and we sent in one of our police divers to comb the lake. They found nothing."

"Thank you, Detective Knox," Hennessy moved in front of the jury box. "And can you please tell the court where the blood was found on Zoe Taylor's clothing?"

"We found blood on the sleeve of her sweater."

"And did Miss Taylor provide an explanation for the blood splatter?"

"She said that when she found the body, she reached into the car to take his pulse."

"She said that she reached into the car to take the man's pulse," Hennessy repeated and exaggerated his nod for the benefit of the jurors. "No further questions."

As he turned to sit down, Hennessy saw a familiar face in the crowd—Henry Cruise. Hennessey froze for a moment, unsure why his former client had an interest in the case. Cruise was seated in the back row, tucked behind five rows of onlookers. Cruise smiled slightly, and then nodded to Hennessy.

Hennessy sat back at the defense table, tapping his finger on the edge of his laptop, the possibilities streaming through his head.

CHAPTER 41

WHEN ROBINSON called the second witness, crime scene expert Dr. Daniel Hayes, her trial tactic was becoming clear. She would call local experts, people the jury could trust, before she brought out her star eyewitnesses. It was Hayes' second time confronting Hennessy in as many months.

For fifty-five minutes, Dr. Hayes answered questions about his analysis of the crime scene. Dr. Hayes explained the blood splatters, the way the body was found, and the likelihood that the murderer was in the passenger seat next to Powers when they began stabbing him. During the testimony, Hennessy struggled to pay attention. He checked over his shoulder twice—Cruise hadn't moved. He was paying attention to every word of the case.

When Robinson finished, Judge Whitworth invited Hennessy to cross-examine the witness. Hennessy picked up a folder and moved to the lectern, sorting through his notes before he began.

"Dr. Hayes, you found Miss Taylor's fingerprints on the vehicle, is that correct?" Hennessy questioned.

"Yes. We found her fingerprints inside the car and on the passenger door."

"Would it be reasonable to find fingerprints of Mr. Powers' ex-girlfriend in his car?"

"I guess that would be reasonable."

"Would it be reasonable to find her fingerprints on

the door?"

"Yes, I guess so."

"Were the fingerprints found on the car bloodied?"

"No," he shook his head. "They weren't bloody fingerprints."

"And did the presence of these fingerprints indicate that Miss Taylor murdered Mr. Powers?"

"They indicated that she had been in the car at an earlier time."

"An earlier time," Hennessy repeated. "As an expert, can you please tell the court how long fingerprints can remain on an item?"

"Unfortunately, there's no scientific way to determine how long a fingerprint will last. Some fingerprints have been taken off untouched surfaces more than forty years later, and some cannot be developed, even though they were handled yesterday. There are so many factors involved in determining how long a fingerprint will last."

"Up to forty years later?" Hennessy replied. "So, the presence of Miss Taylor's fingerprints on the car indicated that she had been in the car sometime during the past forty years. Is that correct?"

"Yes, that would be a correct assumption."

"We're not here to make assumptions, Dr. Hayes," Hennessy said. "We're only here, in this court, to discuss the facts. Can you confirm, as a fact, that the presence of Miss Taylor's fingerprints on the car indicate that she was in the car at some point during her life, and does not indicate anything else?"

Dr. Hayes paused and then nodded. "That would be correct."

"Did you find any fingerprints on the murder

weapon?"

"No, because we have not located the murder weapon."

"Are you a blood splatter expert, Dr. Hayes?"

"I've studied blood splatters, yes."

"Have you studied them enough to call yourself an expert?"

"I believe so."

"Can you please tell the court, if a man is stabbed in the neck, if his carotid artery is severed, how far would you expect that blood to spray?"

"That depends on how deep the wound to their neck was."

"Based on the evidence presented, we know how deep Mr. Powers' stab wound to the neck was. We know it was deep enough to sever his carotid artery. Can you please tell the court how far that blood would splatter?"

"Up to five feet."

"Enough to cover the inside of the car?"

"That's correct."

"Was there a section of the car not covered in Mr. Powers' blood?"

"Yes. The area around the passenger seat."

"So it would be reasonable to expect that the murderer was in the passenger seat?"

"That would be reasonable."

"Would it also be reasonable to expect that the passenger would've been covered in blood, given the wounds to Mr. Powers?"

"That is very reasonable."

"However, Miss Taylor's sweater wasn't covered in blood, was it?"

"I believe she had some blood on her sleeve."

"Is that the amount that you would expect, given the amount of blood that Mr. Powers lost?"

"No. I would expect that sweater to be covered in blood."

"But it wasn't, was it?"

"That's correct."

"Interesting. Not enough blood on her sweater." Hennessy paused and looked to the jury. "No further questions."

CHAPTER 42

THE TESTIMONY of the witness who found the body, Mr. Cooper Singletary, went as expected. Yes, he found Mr. Powers in the car. No, he didn't see anyone else in the car. Yes, he was distraught by what he saw. All very factual, all very credible; however, none of the facts pointed the finger at Zoe Taylor.

The next witness, neighbor Mrs. Marcy Milton, was much the same. Yes, she heard Mr. Singletary's scream for assistance. No, she didn't see anyone running from the scene. Yes, she saw Mr. Powers' body in the car, his neck cut open.

Solid witnesses, but nothing game-changing. Nothing that could swing a jury.

When the fourth witness of the day, Deputy Coroner Dr. Garry Wilson, walked to the stand, the jury was starting to lose focus. Robinson kept the questioning factual and her voice monotone. She questioned the doctor, and Hennessy objected where he could. When Robinson finished her examination of the autopsy report, she turned the witness over to the defense.

"Dr. Wilson," Hennessy began, seated behind his desk, laptop open in front of him. "In your report, it's noted that the paramedics declared Mr. Powers deceased at 8am. On page five of your report, you approximate the actual time of death was between 5am and 8am. Miss Taylor made the report to the 911 operator at 7:45am. When speaking to the operator, she stated that she saw the body of the deceased at 7:30am. Is there a time before Miss Taylor saw the body that Mr. Powers' may have been stabbed?"

"A simple deduction would tell you that, yes."

"According to your report, the death may have occurred before Miss Taylor arrived. How long after Mr. Powers was stabbed do you believe he died?"

"Within a very short timeframe after his carotid artery was severed. If not five minutes, then ten minutes at the most. The cut across his neck severed the artery, and this caused a massive hemorrhage, and the blood loss was fatal."

"That means, according to your report, there's a two-hour window, under darkness between 5am and 7:30am, when Miss Taylor was not present at the scene, when the deceased could've died. Is this correct?"

"I'm in this court to testify on the autopsy report. I can't comment on the whereabouts of Miss Taylor that morning because I didn't investigate her whereabouts. What I can tell you is the death occurred approximately between 5am and 8am."

"Thank you, Dr. Wilson." Hennessy turned to a file on his desk, opened it, and removed a piece of paper. "Did you conduct a toxicology report on the deceased?"

"We requested one. The toxicology report was provided by the South Carolina State Law Enforcement Division Forensic Services Laboratory."

"And what was found in the toxicology report?"

"The deceased's blood alcohol reading was 0.05, which indicates that he still had alcohol in his system when he died. This indicates that he either drank a lot the night before, or he had been drinking just before he died. We also found the deceased had high levels of diazepam, which is more commonly sold as Valium."

"How does alcohol interact with diazepam?"

"Not well. The body processes alcohol and diazepam in similar ways, meaning the effect of alcohol may be increased. Common side effects of this interaction may be drowsiness and fatigue."

"And what are the significant signs of a diazepam overdose?"

"When a person consumes too much of the substance, the body may react with certain signs. Each person is different, but the signature indicators of a diazepam overdose include a deep sleep and slowed breathing rate. Other signs may include fatigue, confusion, lack of awareness, and uncoordinated movements. Mr. Powers may not have been responsive at all before his death."

"With the levels of drugs in his system, would he have been conscious?"

"Drugs affect everyone differently, but with the levels we found in his system at the time of death, I don't believe so, no."

"No further questions," Hennessy said, closing the folder on the table.

Before Dr. Wilson could be excused from the witness stand, a man from the back of the crowd rose to his feet and yelled, "Don't let her go free! A black man deserves justice in Charleston!"

"Be quiet!" Judge Whitworth roared. Her face was red. "There will not be any shouting in my courtroom! Bailiffs, remove that man!"

"She killed him," the man continued. "Don't let

her get away with it!"

As the bailiffs removed the man from the courtroom, holding onto his arms, he continued to yell. Judge Whitworth turned to the jury and instructed them to disregard the interruption from the man, before she asked Robinson if she wished to redirect Dr. Wilson, which she declined.

The tension in the courtroom was sizzling, and it wasn't finished yet.

CHAPTER 43

ROBINSON CALLED Miss Stacey Anderson.

Anderson walked to the stand with her head down. She wore jeans, a black sweater, and gold jewelry, but all her clothes were loose on her skinny frame. Of Jamaican descent, her black hair was tied back tightly into a ponytail, and her make-up was poorly done.

"Miss Anderson," Robinson began after the witness was sworn in. "Can you please tell the court if you knew Mr. Powers?"

"Two years ago, I moved into a house five doors down from Andre, and we'd been friends ever since. He was a good man. Someone a girl could rely on."

"Would you describe yourself as close to Mr. Powers?"

"Yes," she dabbed her eye with the back of her hand. "We used to be really close."

"And did you know Miss Taylor?"

"She was dating Andre for a while, but I never really talked to Zoe."

"And when was the last time you saw Mr. Powers and Miss Taylor together?"

"The day before she stabbed him."

"Objection," Hennessy called out. "The answer assumes facts not in evidence."

"Sustained," Judge Whitworth stated. She turned to look at the witness. "Miss Anderson, a witness' testimony is limited to their personal knowledge of events, and as you are not claiming you saw Mr. Powers on the day of his death, you cannot make a comment on it. Is that understood?"

"Yes, ma'am," Anderson ran her hand over her hair.

"When you last saw them together," Robinson continued. "How was their relationship?"

"Objection," Hennessy said. "The question calls for speculation."

"Sustained," Judge Whitworth replied.

"Let me rephrase," Robinson paused and gathered her thoughts. "Miss Robinson, on the last day that you saw them together, could you hear them interacting with each other?"

"Yeah, because they were being super loud. They were yelling at each other on the street right in front of my apartment. I could hear every word they were saying."

"Do you remember any of the words that you overheard?"

"Yeah. Zoe was real angry and was yelling. I looked out the kitchen window, and I could see them. Zoe came close to Andre, but he pushed her back. That's when she said that she was going to stab him for what he did."

"Do you remember her exact words?"

"Yeah. She came at him, and she was all like, 'I'm going to stab you for what you did.' And then he pushed her away, and she said, 'I'm going to kill you.'"

One jury member gasped and then covered her hand over her mouth. Once Robinson heard this, she nodded to the witness and then turned to Judge Whitworth. "No further questions."

Hennessy waited a few moments before he started. He glanced over his files and then stood, waiting next to the defense table as he began. "Miss Anderson, what time of day was this interaction between Mr. Powers and Miss Taylor?"

"It was around five in the afternoon."

"And were you drinking at this time?"

"Yeah."

"Had you been using drugs that day?"

She stared at Hennessy, her mouth firmly shut.

"Miss Anderson?" Hennessy pressed. "Were you using drugs that day?"

"Maybe," she whispered.

"And what drugs did you take that day?"

"I might have had some crack."

"Crack cocaine?"

"Maybe."

"Do you usually use crack cocaine at five o'clock in the afternoon?"

"Objection," Robinson said. "Relevance."

"Your Honor," Hennessy argued. "The witness is claiming to have seen and heard something on the day in question, and we are merely establishing her mental state on that day."

"Overruled," Judge Whitworth didn't take long to consider the objection. "You may answer the question, Miss Anderson."

"Uh," Anderson stumbled over her answer. "Some days."

"Do you have children, Miss Anderson?" Hennessy questioned.

"Yeah, I got a five-year-old and a two-year-old."

"And were they with you on that day?"

"Hey, listen," Anderson sat forward and pointed

her finger at Hennessy. "I'm not getting my kids taken off me, ya hear? If y'all think that you can take my kids away, you've got another thing coming."

"I'm not threatening to take your children away." Hennessy walked to the lectern and rested one hand on it. "Let me ask another question. How high on drugs and alcohol were you when you claim to have overheard the conversation?"

"I don't remember."

"You were so high that you don't remember," Hennessy looked to the jury. "But you claim to remember the words spoken by Miss Taylor?"

"Yeah. I remember what she said. She said she was going to stab him."

Hennessy sighed and shook his head. "Miss Anderson, you weren't being truthful about your relationship with Mr. Powers, were you?"

"We were friends," she sat back in her chair. "I said that."

"Did you ever have sexual relations with Mr. Powers?"

"I…" she shrugged her shoulders. "Yeah. We hooked up a few times."

"In fact, you 'hooked up' just before Mr. Powers began dating Miss Taylor. Is that correct?"

"That's about right."

"And you were jealous of Miss Taylor. So jealous, in fact, that you once threatened to punch Miss Taylor. Is that correct?"

Anderson looked at Zoe, and then nodded slightly. She was beginning to sweat. "Yeah, I might have said that."

"You didn't like Miss Taylor. She was the girl that stole your 'good man,'" Hennessy stated. "You were high on drugs and alcohol at five o'clock in the afternoon while looking after your young children, and you claim to have heard Miss Taylor and Mr. Powers arguing. How far away were they when they were arguing?"

"Maybe fifteen yards."

"Were you inside your home?"

"Yeah, I was in the kitchen, but the window was open, and they were on the street right outside the window." Anderson was becoming flustered. "But I didn't have the tv on. I could hear them say everything. I could."

"And through the window, while high on drugs and alcohol, while looking after your young children, what were Miss Taylor's exact words again?"

"She said…" Her breathing had shortened. She looked to the doors of the court. She wanted to run out of there. "She said… Listen, I don't remember her exact words. She said something like—"

"You don't remember her exact words? You told this court, only moments ago, that you knew her exact words. So, are you guessing now?"

"No," she scrunched her face. "But I remember that she said she was going to stab him. That's what she said."

Hennessy sighed loud enough for the jury to hear his disappointment. "Your Honor, we have no further questions for this witness."

CHAPTER 44

THE REST of the week in court was filled with expert witness after expert witness. It appeared that Robinson was trying to bore the jury into a guilty verdict. She called another medical examiner, another blood splatter expert, a DNA analyst, and a weapons expert. It ended the first week of the trial in a mountain of facts, a mountain of assumed truths. Their case was building, but nothing pointed to the out-and-out guilt of Zoe Taylor.

Robinson was careful with her questions, careful where she directed the testimonies, and careful about who she brought to the stand. She called a forensic analyst from the South Carolina State Law Enforcement Division Forensic Services Laboratory. They provided a report in fine enough detail to put an insomniac to sleep. It was confirmed that Powers died as a result of exsanguination, the loss of blood causing death, after having his carotid artery severed. The forensic analyst provided a sound scientific overview of his report, never straying once into opinion, and never once raising his voice above a mundane tone. Hennessy objected where he could, but there was little he could do to question the report.

Expert after expert followed, and Robinson played her strategy well—build a mountain of small facts delivered by trusted specialists, in an attempt to convince the jury they must convict Zoe, before

Damien Bates came to the stand to seal the deal.

Cruise was there each day, intently listening to the trial. Hennessy wanted to confront him, but Cruise managed to avoid the lawyer, slipping out the doors early every afternoon. Hennessy called Cruise's cell phone a number of times, leaving messages, but he didn't receive a response.

After Judge Whitworth called an end to the week on Thursday evening, Hennessy was exhausted. Judge Whitworth didn't continue trials on Fridays, allowing the prosecution and defense teams an opportunity to work on their case tactics. Hennessy slept well but was called by Lockett for an early meeting on Friday morning.

Hennessy walked along the pier at Folly Beach. He stopped and talked to a tourist, a New Yorker, who wanted to tell everyone how beautiful the beachfront was. Hennessy laughed with the man, patted him on the shoulder and wished him well, before he continued along the pier.

Barry Lockett was waiting near the end of the long wooden pier, licking an ice cream cone, watching as a heavy swell rolled in from the Atlantic Ocean.

"Good ice cream?" Hennessy asked as he approached his investigator.

"The best. Chocolate chip. I haven't had an ice cream in years, but when I walked past the stall, I couldn't resist," Lockett said. The ice cream looked tiny in his huge hands. "Want one?"

"I'll pass," Hennessy smiled. They started walking along the pier back towards the beach. "Why did you want to meet out here?"

"Mate, are you serious?" Lockett smiled and opened his arms wide to look at the view of the

Atlantic Ocean. "Look at that. That's so beautiful and only twenty-five minutes from the office. Why wouldn't you meet here? We could meet in the office and sit in the air-conditioning, but out here is magical. Yep, I'd much rather be standing out here. You only go around once in life, mate. You might as well have a good time doing it."

"That's a good philosophy. You've got to know what makes you happy."

"The outdoors makes me happy. Just put me by the beach, barefooted, and with a surfboard under my arm. There's no better way to live. The ocean can be so angry, and then calm, and then destructive, and then joyful. I love it."

"You sure love going outdoors, don't you?"

"Well, it's safer than going out-windows."

Hennessy laughed. "An outdoor joke, eh?"

"You know, these two kangaroos go into a bar. And the bartender leans on the counter, and turns to the kangaroos and says, 'What'll it be, mates?' The kangaroos then kick down everything in the bar, breaking all the glasses, as they're wild animals and belong outdoors where they can do wild animal things."

"That joke took a different turn," Hennessy laughed. "So, what have you got for me?"

"I'm now sure that Richard Longhouse was behind the setup of Henry Cruise," Lockett finished the last of his ice cream. "I talked to a contact, and he said that Longhouse is making a run for Governor next year and has been cleaning out all the old dead wood. One of his old contacts was recently charged with fraud and is now in prison, one has moved to Canada, and another has fled to the Bahamas. He's cleaning house before he makes a run for the top job."

"And Cruise was the most dangerous."

"If anyone has secrets about Longhouse, he wants them gone."

Hennessy sighed. "I know some secrets about Longhouse from when we used to work together."

"Think he'll come after you?"

Hennessy shrugged. He stopped and leaned against the pier, the fresh wind blowing in his face, a welcome relief from the heat.

"Right now, I'm more worried about Cruise."

"You haven't left him behind yet?" Lockett folded his arms and leaned against the railing next to him, facing the other direction. "I thought you told him you weren't working for him anymore."

"I did, but Cruise has been in court this week."

"For the Zoe Taylor case?" Lockett turned around. "Because of Bates?"

"I assume so," Hennessy clenched his fist. "Bates played me from the start, and I'm sure that Cruise asked him to do that. The question is—why?"

"Don't ask me any intelligent questions. That's not my strong suit," Lockett laughed. "But if you ask me to run through a brick wall, I can do that. You just tell me what you need, boss, and I'll be straight on it."

"I need you to look into how Henry Cruise is connected to Andre Powers' murder," Hennessy said. "And I need you to work fast. The case will be wrapped up in a week, and if I'm going to save an innocent girl, I need something."

CHAPTER 45

AS HENNESSY drove home to Luca's Vineyard, he passed through the city of Columbia, the South Carolina state capital, and a few light taps on the windshield caught his attention. It had begun to drizzle again. There was darkness on the horizon. He knew the storm was coming. It'd been building for years, just over his shoulder. The grief that he'd avoided for so long, the pain that he'd pushed down, was brewing deep inside. The crisis was upon him, and the allure of the storm was a contrast to the comfort of life on the vineyard. The storm was calling out to him, tempting him to challenge it. The dark clouds were almost there, but they didn't scare him. He didn't fear them. He wasn't running. He wasn't hiding. This time, he had to face the storm head-on.

Joe made the decision to get out of Charleston for the weekend—under all that pressure, under all that stress, he had to get up to the vineyard. And he loved the drive. It gave him time to think. Damien Bates was due to take the stand on Monday, and Hennessy was sure that he would fill the court with lies. Bates claimed he stole Andre Powers' wallet before Zoe Taylor murdered him. He claimed he saw Powers sleeping in his car, and merely took advantage of the situation. He reached in the open window and took the wallet, which he claimed was sitting on the passenger seat. Hennessy didn't believe a word of the statement. He knew Bates would say anything to get out of trouble.

He stopped outside the South Carolina State House, parking off Main St., taking a break from the drive to stretch his legs. He ordered a coffee to go and began to wander the grounds around the State House. He loved this building. It represented everything that South Carolina stood for—faith, justice, and family.

"Faith, justice, and family," he whispered under his breath. Three things he used to believe in, three things that were at the center of his life, but only one had survived the years. Family. It was all he lived for. To see Wendy laugh, to watch Ellie succeed, to watch Casey grow. That was all he needed. He looked up at the building again, before he whispered, "Faith, justice, and family."

Built from the ashes of the Civil War, the South Carolina State House was a Classical Revival style building, standing proudly over the center of the city since 1865. Joe stood on the steps, gazing up at the building, and then sighed. He loved his state, he loved his country, but he knew nothing was perfect.

"Joe Hennessy?" The voice came from behind him. "Is that really you?"

Hennessy turned. He smiled. "Pastor Craig Clarkson."

They shook hands solidly, with the grip of two men that hadn't seen each other in decades.

"It's good to see you, Joe," Clarkson said, his face full of joy. He placed his hand on Hennessy's shoulder and patted it. "I haven't seen you for at least ten years."

"Twenty years. Ever since..." Joe paused. "Since I

carried Luca out the doors of your church."

"Ah," Clarkson nodded. "Of course."

Pastor Clarkson was a tall, thin man with a friendly smile. Born in South Carolina to Irish parents, he had a mix of Southern charm and Irish wit. Dressed in black trousers and a white polo shirt, he looked professional and approachable. His trimmed beard was gray, his hair was thinning, and his skin had a healthy glow.

"I'm driving up to my vineyard, out past Greenville," Joe said. "I usually only make one stop and grab some boiled peanuts down the road, but this time, I thought I'd pull into Columbia and stretch my legs. I thought the State House was as good as any spot to stop, and what a lucky stop, running into you. I was going to walk around the gardens, if you'd like to join me."

"That'd be great." Clarkson looked at his watch. "I've always got time to catch up with an old friend."

They walked slowly around the grounds of the South Carolina State House, chatting about the last twenty years of their lives. Joe spoke about the vineyard, about the wines, and about his wife and family. He told him about his return to Charleston and his return to the law profession. Clarkson spoke about his church, his faith, and his wife and sons. They laughed and wandered, calmly chatting, chuckling, and swapping memories.

"Do you have a church up in Greenville?" Clarkson turned the conversation to faith as they circled the building back towards the start of the walk.

"How could any God let that happen to my son?"

Joe whispered, staring at the ground as he walked, shaking his head. "My faith is almost non-existent these days."

"I'm sorry to hear that," Clarkson said. "You and Wendy were certainly tested, there's no doubt about that. It had an effect on all of us. Not long after you and Wendy left the church, I moved my family up here to Columbia, and we've been here ever since."

"I wouldn't even know who to pray to these days. How do you even know that yours is the right religion? There are so many religions out there, how can you be certain that you're right?"

"I can't be certain. That's why we have faith."

Joe looked around the gardens. "If there was a religion for Mother Nature, I'd be there to thank her."

"I've always said the quickest way to find God is to seek him in nature," Clarkson replied. "God is eternal in nature. Always there at the sunrise, always there at the sunset. In the winters, in the snow, in the summers, in the humidity. When the flowers bloom, and when the leaves fall. When the lambs are born, and when the old bear dies. If you're ever feeling lost, walk in nature."

Joe nodded. They finished their walk in silence until they were back at the entrance to the gardens.

"You're always welcome at my church, Joe. It'd be an honor to have you there one day."

Joe didn't respond, staring at the ground.

"Nevertheless, it's good to see you," Clarkson offered his hand. "And remember that the door to my church is always open."

"Thank you, Craig." Joe shook his hand solidly. "It's great to see you."

Craig patted him on the shoulder again before Joe turned and walked away.

CHAPTER 46

THE VINEYARD was always changing. With every season, the grounds looked different. Summers looked dry, and winters looked luscious. Fall was a vast array of colors, and spring was a luminescent green. Set on fifty-five acres, Luca's Vineyard employed ten full-time staff, with a chateau to the east of the property, which featured a café, a small store for wine sales, and a dining space for the occasional wedding. The Hennessy household was at the west edge of the property, far away from the business, but still among the vines. They were twenty-five minutes out of town, and a five-minute drive from the nearest neighbor. Joe liked it that way. He liked his privacy. He liked tucking himself away from the world, hiding in the rolling hills, surrounded by stunning landscapes.

Joe arrived home and greeted Wendy with a kiss. They shared a coffee before wandering the grounds to check on the vines. Casey wasn't home, Wendy explained, she was hanging out with friends. Joe's heart broke just a little. His youngest was growing up, sixteen now, almost an adult, and she no longer needed her father as much as she once did. She had her own life now. In his heart, he wanted her to be five forever, an innocent girl full of smiles and jokes, but he was proud of the young woman she was growing up to be.

As they walked, checking on their land, Joe could feel his lungs fill with the fresh air. He liked that feeling. The fresh air seemed to reach deeper into his lungs, filling his body full of goodness. After an hour of wandering the grounds, they walked back to their house, happy with the progress of the season. The vines were looking good. Healthy. Almost good enough for their best year. They just had to keep the bank off their backs long enough to survive.

Once back at their five-bedroom brick home, Joe set up the smoker in the yard, and began the five-hour process to make what he claimed was the best beef brisket in the state. Their house was perched on the edge of a hill, providing them with spectacular views over the lower lands nearby. Joe sat by the smoker on a picnic chair, book in hand, feeling a sense of relaxation that he hadn't felt in weeks.

Casey arrived just after 5pm, dropped off by an old white pick-up truck. When Joe saw the vehicle approaching, he stood at the end of the driveway, an intimidating figure for those who didn't know him. Casey hopped out of the truck, but the driver didn't stay to greet Joe, instead they turned back down the long dirt driveway.

"Hello Casey," Joe greeted his daughter with a hug. "Was that a boy that just dropped you off?"

"Hello Dad. Don't worry about the boys, you've scared most of them away," she smiled. "And I can have friends who are boys, you know?"

"Not boys with trucks," Joe said. "They're never just your friend. They always want something more."

"You're such an old man. We live in a modern world, Dad. The world isn't defined by gender roles anymore." Casey smiled as she walked inside. Joe followed her. She dropped her backpack on the kitchen counter and filled up a glass of water. "But I mean, you're not completely useless as an old man. You can still act as a bad example—what not to do when you're old."

"Hey, I don't know how to act my age. I've never been this old before."

"Nor has anyone else, you dinosaur."

"Ouch," Joe laughed. "I'm not that old."

"Yeah, you tell yourself that, old man," Casey laughed.

"That reminds me of a dinosaur joke. Why can't you hear a pterodactyl use the toilet?" Joe smiled. "Because the 'p' is silent."

"Come on, Dad. You told me that joke ten years ago. You need new material," Casey giggled and then sniffed the air. "What's cooking? It smells great."

"I put on a brisket when I got in. The smoker is working perfectly. Should be ready in half-an-hour."

"Yum," Casey said. "Look forward to it."

They set up dinner at the outdoor table. Wendy made a salad, while Joe attended to the brisket. Casey helped with drinks, plates, and cutlery.

They ate and they laughed, sitting outside on the back porch, overlooking the vineyard. They talked about life, about school, and about work. They talked about Charleston, and about the weather. Casey talked about her friends, and Wendy talked about the community. They talked about the grapes. They commented on the brisket, how perfectly it was cooked, and they talked about the Clemson Tigers. Casey talked about her future. Maybe NYU, she said, just like her sister. Wendy agreed, as did Joe. Or I could learn to manage the vineyard, she suggested.

Joe liked that idea, teaching his daughter how to grow grapes. A family business. He smiled. He just needed to save the vineyard from the banks first.

They called Ellie, their eldest daughter, via video call in New York, and she told them all about her week. She told them she was studying hard, but still finding time to socialize. You should party more, Wendy said, you'll never be this young again. Joe told her to forget partying and study hard. It was an evening where the family said everything, did nothing, and lived their lives. It was a night where nothing happened, but life-long memories were made.

After dinner was cleaned up, Joe returned to the back porch, looking over the valley, a glass of wine by his side. Wendy joined him after the sun had set.

"I miss the stars. You don't get to see the stars in the city." Joe looked up to the night sky. "You can see one or two, but nothing like this."

Wendy looked up as well. "It's beautiful tonight."

The stars had filled the night sky above them, covering the land like a dotted blanket. The other worlds in the universe were so close, so visible, and yet so far away. They watched the stars for a while, sipping on their wine, and talking about the vineyard.

"One of the workers is going to move to California for family reasons," Wendy said. "He'll be a loss and we'll need someone new."

Joe agreed. They looked after the workers on the vineyard, treating them like a family, allowing a sense of ownership over the wines they produced. Not one staff member had left in the last five years.

"I stopped off in Columbia today," Joe said as he saw a shooting star on the horizon. "And I saw Pastor Craig."

Wendy smiled. "And?"

"He invited me back to church." Joe sipped his wine. "But I told him I couldn't do it."

Wendy reached across and gripped his hand. "Whenever you're ready, the church will have you back. You're welcome to come with me on Sunday mornings for prayer."

Joe began to answer, to say that he wasn't ready, but his phone buzzed in his pocket. He looked at the number and answered it.

"Barry? It's 9pm on a Saturday night. Are you still working?"

"I never stop," Barry quipped. "Are you in the office?"

"No, I'm up at the vineyard. I'm about two hours and forty-five minutes' drive away."

"Well, you might want to come down to Charleston tomorrow."

"Why?"

"Because I found evidence that Andre Powers was working for Richard Longhouse."

CHAPTER 47

JOE HENNESSY raged through the Barbadoes Dining Room in the historic Mills House Hotel. The elegance of the exclusive restaurant was no foil for his rage. He'd driven down from the vineyard, and his anger was building the entire time.

The restaurant was half-filled on Sunday night, all of the patrons dressed to impress. The men wore suits, the women wore dresses, and they all wore jewelry. The ceilings were high, the atmosphere subdued, and the smell of fresh seafood filled the air. Hennessy searched for his target and spotted him at a table at the back of the room, nearest to the bar.

"Andre Powers was working for you," Hennessy charged towards him. "You did this."

Longhouse slowly raised his eyes. "Mr. Hennessy." He looked at his watch. "It's 6:05pm on a Sunday night. I didn't expect to see you here. Have you come down to join me for a drink? Perhaps you've decided to show your support for me winning the Governor's race. I'd even buy you a drink if you said that."

"You know what happened to Andre Powers." Hennessy leaned his hands on the table, ignoring the man Longhouse was having dinner with. "You know Zoe Taylor is innocent."

Longhouse looked around the bar—all the eyes were on them. The distinguished patrons weren't used to someone yelling in the restaurant. Longhouse lowered his voice. "I have no idea what you're talking about, but y'all better be careful before you make wild accusations like that." He looked towards the bar. "Go and have a drink. Calm down before you go back to court tomorrow."

"You know that Zoe Taylor is innocent, and you're not telling me the truth. What was Andre Powers doing for you? Why was he working for you?"

Longhouse stood, drink still in hand, trying to square up to the towering Hennessy. "I'm not going to warn you again, Joe. I said you'd better be careful before you make accusations like that. The best option you have is to go back to your vineyard and let the adults play in Charleston."

"What was Andre Powers doing for you?" Hennessy repeated.

"I employ all sorts of people. I've always said that the best charity is offering someone work, and I like to help those less fortunate," Longhouse smiled and looked back at his friend at the table. "I'm a helpful guy."

"I'm going to prove in court that Andre Powers was working for you. That'll be said in open court. You'll have a lot of explaining to do after that is proven."

Longhouse's mouth hung open for a moment, and then he leaned in close to Hennessy. "I have nothing to hide. And you won't be able to repeat what you did to Norris on the stand."

Hennessy squinted. "How do you know Jason Norris?"

"Who said I did?" Longhouse scoffed. "You got lucky last time in court. It was just a fluke. I don't expect that you'll do it again. I mean, you're the guy that couldn't even solve your own son's murder."

Hennessy knocked the drink out of Longhouse's hand, grabbed him by the collar, and pulled him closer to his face. The people around them gasped.

"You mention Luca again and I'll rip your throat out."

"Settle down," Longhouse grinned and opened his hands wide. "My mistake. I apologize for talking about the dead son that you couldn't save."

Hennessy pushed Longhouse back, releasing his grip from around the collar.

"Times have changed, Hennessy." Longhouse adjusted his shirt. "Go home. Recognize that you've made an error and that you're well out of your depth here. Get in your car and keep driving back to the vineyard. Leave law and justice in Charleston to the people that can handle it."

"I'm going to expose your dealings in court, and you're going to land with a lot of mud on you." Hennessy pointed at Longhouse. "And I'm going to enjoy every second of it."

Hennessy turned and faced the group of security personnel standing around him. He looked back at Longhouse, who shook his head at the men. They stepped aside, and Hennessy began to walk back out to the front of the dining room.

"Be careful," Longhouse called out as Hennessy walked towards the exit. "I wouldn't want you to accidentally fall into the river."

Hennessy stormed out of the restaurant and stopped on the sidewalk. He took out his phone.

"Barry, I need you to find Jason Norris again," he said. "He's the key to all of this."

CHAPTER 48

JASON NORRIS couldn't stand still.

He nervously shifted from one foot to the other, looking around the room, struggling to hold back his tears. He'd been down many dark roads, he'd made the wrong decision many times, and he'd lived a life he'd rather forget, but now, in front of him, he had found the light.

The First Baptist Church of Charleston was filled with history. The church was established in 1696 when a pastor and the members of his congregation immigrated from Boston to Charleston. The main home of the congregation was in a Greek Revival-style sanctuary built in the early 1800s off Church St., however, the building was under renovation. The congregation had moved to a smaller church in nearby James Island, but still, all that history, all those generations of faith, was overwhelming to Jason.

The back room behind the church was dark, with little natural light coming through the small windows. The lights hadn't been switched on. There was little ventilation. There was a musty smell, mixed with the scent of incense that hung in the air.

The building had been broken into twice over the past month. They took nothing, but the messages were received loud and clear. Longhouse and his crew wanted to find Jason Norris. They didn't like that Norris had crossed them, and they didn't like that

Norris had hung them out to dry in court. He told the police everything he knew about Roger East, but they said they didn't have enough information to charge him with any crimes.

Samuel had been approached numerous times with questions about where his brother was. Samuel didn't tell them anything, staying strong to give his brother the space he needed to heal. He knew his brother had been hiding out in Lake Marion, but he gave nothing away. When Jason called and said he wanted to come back to Charleston, Samuel was reluctant, but when his brother explained why he wanted to come back, he couldn't refuse.

Samuel stood above the small pool of water in the back room of the church, and turned to his brother. He started his speech, the same one he gave to every person who was in his situation.

"Faith is trust," he said. "But it's not trust in me, it's not a trust in the church, and it's not trusting what is written in an old book. No, faith is the trust that you must have in yourself. Not in a powerful, motivational way, but in a calm inner knowledge that you know the truth. You know the truth about the world, you know the truth about nature, and you know the truth about God. Faith is having trust that what you feel is real. Faith is having trust in your inner knowledge. Faith is having trust in yourself."

Samuel walked into the small pool. The water was waist deep.

"Are you sure you want to do this, Jason?" Samuel asked. "This is a big commitment for your future. This isn't something that you should take lightly. This is it. This has to be the moment when you recognize you cannot run anymore. This has to be the moment when you realize that your new life begins now. You have to face your past, face your demons, and tell the truth."

"I understand," Jason said. "I'm ready."

Samuel held out his hand, and his older brother approached him. He stepped into the water. It was cold. He continued until the water was up to his waist. He stood next to his brother.

"Jason, is this a time in your life when you accept the Lord Jesus as your savior?" Samuel asked, holding out his hand.

"Yes," Jason replied.

"Will you obey and serve Him as your King for the rest of your life?"

"Yes."

Jason held onto his brother's wrist.

"Because you've professed your faith in the Lord Jesus," Samuel said. "I now baptize you in the name of the Father, Son, and Holy Ghost."

Jason leaned back, holding onto his brother's wrist, dunking his body fully underwater. Samuel held him there for a moment, and then raised him up.

Jason wiped the water from his face and smiled. Not a small smile, not a polite smile, but an unrestrained smile full of emotion.

This was it. This was the moment he wanted, the moment he'd longed for. The decades of hurt, the years of pain, washed away under the spell of his baptism.

He hugged his brother tightly, gripping him with all the emotion that was flooding out of him.

The brothers laughed as they hugged.

They'd taken different paths in life, chosen different careers, chosen different professions, but they'd ended up at the same destination.

Jason couldn't wipe the smile off his face as he stepped out of the small pool. He grabbed a white towel off the chair nearby, and Samuel did the same.

"Thank you," Jason fought back the tears that were threatening his smile. "You don't know how much this means to me."

"It was my pleasure," Samuel grabbed his brother on the shoulder. "I'm proud to call you my brother."

"Now it's time to face my sins." Jason ran the towel over his hair. "I've got to right the wrongs of my past."

"And you can start with the trial of Zoe Taylor." A voice called out from the entrance of the room behind them. The brothers both swung around.

"And how can we help you?" Samuel stepped forward. He stepped between his brother and the man, protecting Jason. "This is a place of worship, not of violence. Please don't bring any trouble through these doors."

"I haven't come to cause any trouble," Barry Lockett held his hands up. "But Mr. Norris—you and I need to talk again."

CHAPTER 49

DAMIEN BATES had started the morning like he did most mornings—two Advil for the hangover, with two extra in his pocket, a hot shower for the body odor, and two coffees for his mind. Early on Monday morning, the eyes of the judge, jury, and lawyers were going to be squarely on him. He hated that thought. All those judging eyes, all that scoffing and smirking, all that goodness. He hated lawyers, with all their smart words and tricky questions. He'd been to court many times in the past, and each time, he was made to feel dumb. He was laughed at by the lawyers, just like the teachers had done when he was in elementary school.

He walked through the courtroom doors once called, settling into the witness chair. He was wearing his best suit, but it was too tight around the waist. He left the button on his trousers undone, with just his belt holding them up. He'd made a deal with the prosecution to suspend his conviction for possession of the stolen wallets, but he had to sit on the stand to fulfill his end of the deal.

Once he was sworn in, he turned to the prosecutor, staring at her, waiting for the lawyer to try and outwit him, but he had a plan of his own.

"Can you state your name for the court?" Robinson stood, ready to question the witness.

"Damien Bates." Bates leaned forward to the

microphone. "That's my name."

"And can you inform the court how you know Mr. Powers?"

"I don't, or I mean, I didn't."

"Then can you please explain how you were arrested with Mr. Powers' wallet in your car?"

"No."

"I'm sorry?" Robinson raised her eyebrows.

Bates didn't answer.

"Mr. Bates, I understand that you've signed a deal with the Circuit Solicitor's Office to testify today," Robinson held a piece of paper in her hands. "If you fail to testify, then any deal you signed will not hold up."

"The deal I signed said that I had to come here. It didn't say anything about talking. That's what my lawyer said," Bates pointed to a portly older man sitting in the front row. "That's my lawyer there. Mr. Henman. He said that the deal says I only have to show up. I don't have to say anything that will incriminate me."

Robinson stood with her mouth open, staring at the witness. She turned to the lawyer seated behind her, but Henman just smiled. She turned to her assistant, who shrugged his shoulders, before she turned to Judge Whitworth. "Permission to treat the witness as hostile, Your Honor."

"He's your witness, Miss Robinson."

"And he's withholding information that's important to this case."

Judge Whitworth considered her response for a moment, before she turned to look at the defense. Hennessy shook his head, showing he had no objections. "Then permission is granted."

295

Robinson took a moment, gathering her thoughts before she walked to the lectern at the side of the room. "Mr. Bates, can you please tell the court why you were in possession of Mr. Powers' wallet?"

"No." He shook his head, and then looked up at the judge. "There's the fifth amendment."

"You're indicating that you don't wish to answer the question for fear of self-incrimination?" Judge Whitworth leaned forward.

"Yeah. That's it," Bates rolled his tongue around his mouth. "I don't want to answer the question because of the fifth amendment. That's what my lawyer told me to say."

"Mr. Bates," Robinson drew a breath in an attempt to calm herself down. "Is it true that you signed a deal to come to court today in exchange for a reduced sentence on being in possession of a stolen item?"

"That's right."

"Ok. I'm going to ask you some questions that you can answer," Robinson nodded slowly. "Did you see Mr. Powers in his Chevy sedan on the 15th of March?"

"Yeah, I did."

"Was he alive?"

"Yeah." He chewed on his lip and then pointed to Zoe Taylor. "As I was leaving, I saw that woman. She was running away from the car. I saw a knife in her hand too."

"Can you explain exactly what you saw that morning?"

"Nope."

"Why is that, Mr. Bates?"

"The fifth amendment. My lawyer told me that all I had to do today was come to court and say that I saw that woman running away from the car with a knife in her hand. My lawyer said not to answer any other questions."

Robinson considered her next move. Bates was supposed to be the witness that tied the facts all together, the witness that cemented their case against Zoe Taylor, but he'd turned into a disaster for the prosecution team. He looked unreliable, he seemed dodgy, and his refusal to answer questions changed the make-up of their entire case.

Robinson decided to cut her losses. "No further questions."

"Good," Bates stood, ready to exit the witness stand. "I'm out."

"Not so fast, Mr. Bates," Judge Whitworth called out. The bailiff moved to the area in front of Bates. "The defense has the opportunity to question you first."

"Nobody said anything about that," he looked up at the judge. "The deal I signed said I just had to come here, sit in the witness stand, plead the fifth amendment, and then I got a suspended sentence for stealing a guy's wallet."

"Not quite," Judge Whitworth said. "You're required to answer questions from the defense lawyer, otherwise I'm sure that any deal you signed would not be fulfilled."

Bates looked at his lawyer seated in the front row. The lawyer nodded.

Bates groaned and sat back down. "Alright. But I'm not saying anything."

"You will answer the questions," Judge Whitworth stated, "unless they will incriminate you, at which point you may claim protection under the fifth amendment."

"Whatever," Bates muttered under his breath. "As long as I get off that charge, I don't care."

Hennessy stood and moved to the lectern. The witness was going from bad to worse for the prosecution.

"Mr. Bates, were you arrested for being in possession of Mr. Powers' wallet, along with other wallets?"

Bates looked up at the judge. "Yes, you can answer that question," she said.

"Yeah. That's right."

"And did the prosecution offer you a suspended sentence on that charge if you came to court today to testify?"

"Yeah."

"How did you come into contact with Mr. Powers' wallet?"

Bates sat still in the witness box, not opening his mouth.

"Mr. Bates?" Judge Whitworth leaned across. "Can you please answer the question?"

"No. It's the fifth amendment thing again."

"Are you saying that you don't wish to answer the question because explaining how you came into contact with the wallet will incriminate you in Mr. Powers' murder?" Hennessy pressed.

"Objection." Robinson quickly rose to her feet. "Asked and answered."

"Sustained," Judge Whitworth said. "Be careful where you tread, Mr. Hennessy. The witness has claimed the fifth amendment. Mr. Bates, if you do not wish to answer a question, you can simply state that you plead the fifth amendment. You don't need to elaborate further than that."

"Mr. Bates," Hennessy continued, "Can you please tell the court where you were on the morning of the 15th of March?"

Bates looked at his lawyer in the front row, who held up five fingers. "I plead the fifth."

"Mr. Bates," Hennessy's voice began to rise. "Can you please tell the court if you were inside Mr. Powers' car at any point on the 15th of March?"

"I plead the fifth."

"Mr. Bates," Hennessy's voice was firm. "Can you please tell the court if you interacted with Mr. Powers on the 15th of March?"

"I plead the fifth."

"Mr. Bates, can you please tell the court if you stabbed Mr. Powers?"

"I plead the fifth."

There was a gasp in the jury box. Bates looked stunned at the reaction, but he drew a breath and calmed himself. He ran his hands along his thighs, rocking back and forth slightly.

Hennessy turned to Jacinta, who was seated in the front row of the courtroom, with an empty seat next to her. He gave her a nod. She stood and hurried out of the courtroom doors.

"Mr. Hennessy?" Judge Whitworth called. "Do you care to continue questioning the witness?"

"Yes, Your Honor," Hennessy said. He rested his hand on the lectern, leaning closer to the jury, and then looked to the courtroom doors, making sure that Bates' eyes followed his.

"Mr. Hennessy?" Judge Whitworth called out again.

"Mr. Bates," Hennessy drew a breath, "why were

you outside Mr. Powers' apartment building on the morning of the 15th of March?"

"Who says I was there?" Bates snapped back.

The courtroom doors opened, and the eyes of the court turned to look at the two people walking in. Jacinta led a man to the front row of the court.

"Mr. Bates, why were you outside Mr. Powers' apartment building on the morning of the 15th of March?" Hennessy asked, but Bates' eyes remained on the man who had just sat next to Jacinta.

Jason Norris.

"Mr. Bates?" Hennessy tried to capture Bates' attention again. "Can you please tell the court why you were at Mr. Powers' apartment building on the morning of the 15th of March?"

Bates' mouth hung open. "I'm not going down for this. Not like this."

Hennessy turned to Norris, who shifted in his seat. Norris kept his gaze locked on Bates.

"I want to do a deal," Bates called out to the prosecutor. He was running scenarios through his head, trying to figure out the best way to save his skin. "I'll tell you everything, but I need a deal. Whatever that guy told you isn't true," he indicated towards Norris. "I want to do a deal before he tells you his lies."

"Mr. Bates, this isn't an interview room," Judge Whitworth cautioned him. "This isn't the place where you can just call out for a deal. Mr. Hennessy has asked you a question, and I expect that you will answer it."

"I didn't kill him, alright?" Bates began to sweat. He couldn't sit still. "I didn't kill him. I'm not going down for it."

"Kill who?" Hennessy asked.

"Andre. Alright? It wasn't me. It was Jason Norris. Look, I was there, ok?" Bates' eyes darted all over the room. "I was there, but it wasn't me. I can tell you everything, but I need protection. I need a deal."

"There's no more running, Bates," Hennessy's voice rose. "There's no more hiding. It's time to admit the truth. You killed Mr. Powers, didn't you?"

"Objection!" Robinson called out. "Argumentative!"

"Sustained."

"It's over, Bates," Hennessy's voice grew loud. "You stabbed him, didn't you?!"

"Objection! Badgering the witness! Your Honor!"

"Bates, answer the question!"

"Mr. Hennessy!" Judge Whitworth shouted. "You're well out of line. The objection is sustained!"

"We know the truth, Bates. The truth is coming out whether you like it or not!" Hennessy slammed his fist into the lectern. "You killed Andre, didn't you?!"

"Mr. Hennessy!" Judge Whitworth warned him. "The objection is sustained!"

"Bates!"

"Alright! Alright! I was there!" Bates shouted. "But it was Norris who stabbed him! It was him—sitting over there. I'll testify against him for a deal. I was there. We met Andre because he set up Cruise with the paintings, and we had to sort him out."

"Andre set him up for the paintings?" Hennessy's mouth hung open.

"Yeah, I bet you didn't know that, did ya, smart guy?" Bates spat the words out with venom. "You think you're so smart, but you didn't even realize that we had to get revenge for what he did! You're stupid, lawyer man."

Bates scoffed before he realized the eyes of the court were focused on him. Bates looked at his lawyer, who had his head in his hands, avoiding any sort of eye contact. The pieces of the puzzle fell into place for Hennessy.

"Andre Powers planted the paintings in the gallery, and you exacted revenge for Cruise?" Hennessy whispered.

"I didn't mean to say that."

"Andre Powers was working for Richard Longhouse. Andre Powers set up Henry Cruise." Hennessy's tone was soft. "That's why you had to get revenge on him."

"It was self-defense," Bates tried to save himself. "It was self-defense, alright!"

"What happened?"

"He tried to attack me, and I defended myself. I didn't know what else to do next. I couldn't call the police. They're so corrupt. They would've arrested me on the spot. They're all corrupt. I couldn't trust them. It was self-defense, alright!"

"Damien Bates, the time for lies is over. You stabbed Andre Powers because Cruise paid you to do it, and then you had Jason Norris set up Zoe Taylor." Hennessy stared at the man on the witness stand. "That's not self-defense. That's cold-blooded murder."

Hennessy had a killer. He had a conman. A fraudster.

But he didn't have Cruise.

Not yet.

CHAPTER 50

JOE HENNESSY, Barry Lockett, and Jacinta Templeton sat on one side of the conference room just off the foyer in the courthouse. Zoe Taylor sat on the other side of the table while her father, Frank Taylor, paced the perimeter of the room. The room was cool, as was the atmosphere. The air conditioner pumped in cold air, rattling above their heads, providing at least some distraction from the stress. The long wooden table that took up most of the space was spotless and recently cleaned. The chairs were leather, without so much as a scratch on them, and the walls were pristine white, with framed old photos of Charleston hanging up. No one was looking at the pictures.

"What's taking so long? It's been two hours since Judge Whitworth called the recess." Frank's brow was deeply furrowed. "What are they even doing? How long does this process take?"

"The detectives are re-interviewing Damien Bates," Hennessy was calm. "We should allow them to take all the time they need to get to the truth. Let's not rush them."

Frank continued to pace the small room. He punched the wall gently. He repeated the action a number of times before he started to tap his forehead against the drywall. "I can't believe it. That investigator, Bates, murdered Andre Powers?"

"Andre Powers set up Henry Cruise. He was the one that planted the art inside Cruise's gallery. And Cruise needed to get revenge on Andre."

"And he was killed for it," Zoe whispered, fighting back tears. "That scum wanted revenge, and he killed my Andre for it."

"And Jason Norris set you up," Lockett added.

"So what happens to Henry Cruise?"

"That depends on how much evidence they have to connect him to the murder," Hennessy said. "If Bates rolls over and tells the truth in a statement, Cruise will be gone for good."

A knock on the door made them all jump. Hennessy stood and opened the door.

Two detectives entered the room, followed by prosecutor Nadine Robinson, carrying her laptop. They didn't make eye contact. They sat on the chairs at the end of the meeting room, not saying anything until they were all seated. Frank leaned against the wall at the far side of the room, arms folded across his chest, head leaning against the wall.

"The prosecution is moving to drop all charges against you, Zoe," Robinson began. "We've re-interviewed Damien Bates, and he's changed his statement. He's admitted that he stabbed Mr. Powers and was employed by Mr. Cruise to do so. His confession means that we are no longer proceeding with the charges against you."

"He can do that?" Frank became breathless. "He can just change it like that?"

"Our job is to find the truth," Robinson said. "We're not out to get people, and we're not out to just put wins on the board. Our job is to find out what really happened when this crime was committed.

And in this case, the truth has presented itself at a later time than we would've liked. However, we have the truth now. Damien Bates has signed a confession stating that he stabbed Andre Powers."

"So that's it? I'm free?" Zoe's eyes filled with tears. "This nightmare is now all over?"

"Yes, it is," Robinson responded. "All the charges have been dropped. You're a free woman."

Zoe's head fell into her hands, resting on the table.

"And murder charges against Henry Cruise?" Hennessy asked.

"Bates has agreed, in principle, to testify against Cruise for a reduced sentence on this charge. He's told us that Cruise paid him to conduct criminal activity, but we'll have to gather more evidence. At this point, we've put out a warrant for his arrest," Robinson explained. "Zoe, I'm sincerely sorry this happened to you."

The detectives stood, as did Robinson. None of them had a smile to offer. Jacinta thanked them and opened the door for them to leave.

Once Jacinta closed the door behind them, Zoe Taylor let the tears flow out.

CHAPTER 51

ECSTASY FILLED the room in Poogan's Porch restaurant.

The restaurant was an institution in Charleston, and it was where Hennessy used to go to celebrate every special occasion. Housed inside a charming Victorian townhouse, the iconic establishment had been serving Southern-style seafood since the 70s, delighting locals and tourists alike with locally sourced specials. The knotted heart pine floors, the dual staircases, and the first and second-story porches all reflected the grand history of the beautiful city.

On that day, Zoe Taylor was celebrating a piece of history for herself.

They had spent the rest of the day at the courthouse, filling in form after form, ending the ordeal, and finalizing the case. Once it was all done, Hennessy took Frank, Zoe, and his team to the restaurant to celebrate.

Wendy had made the trip down from the vineyard when she heard the news. She always felt that it was important to celebrate the wins, and after hearing Joe talk about the case for the last two months, she felt as personally involved as her husband.

Jacinta laughed most of the time as she ate her seafood, unable to control her joy. Barry Lockett dropped past for a drink, although he couldn't stay. He shared a few jokes, and everyone laughed, and then he left for dinner with his family.

Satisfaction was the strongest feeling for Hennessy—satisfaction that he had kept Zoe out of prison, satisfaction that Bates was arrested, and satisfaction that the house of justice, the house he had faith in, still stood strong.

"We cannot thank you enough." Frank wrapped his arm around Hennessy's shoulders again. It was the fifth time in the past hour. "What you did for us was amazing. We have our lives back. Zoe's free. She can live her life again."

"Thank you, Mr. Hennessy," Zoe smiled, reaching across to rub his arm. "Thank you so, so much. I can't even begin to thank you enough. I can move on. Finally, I can start to think about the future again."

Hennessy's phone buzzed in his pocket, but he ignored it, not even looking at the number. This was not a time to field work calls.

"So what happens now?" Frank finished another glass of red wine. "Apart from more celebrating, of course!"

He clinked his glass with Wendy's, smiles beaming across the room. They were unable to contain their happiness, unable to hold it in any longer. The drops of wine spilled onto the red tablecloth, but it didn't matter. For the people at the table, this was no time to think about the little things.

"The murder charge against you has been dropped. There's no record of this on any of your files, and you can move on." Hennessy's phone buzzed in his pocket again. He ignored it a second time. "This case is now just a memory."

"And Cruise?" Frank asked. "Tell me he'll be joining Bates behind bars."

"The police have put out a warrant for his arrest. They haven't been able to locate him yet, but they will. Now that Bates has provided a statement, Cruise will be going away for a very long time, and most likely, he'll live out his last days behind bars."

"Yay!" Zoe clapped her hands together. "It won't bring Andre back, but it's worth celebrating."

Over the course of the dinner, they laughed, they smiled, and even sang together. The buzz of winning a case, the joy of claiming victory against the odds, was a moment Hennessy enjoyed immensely.

Joe could hear Wendy's phone buzz next to him as he finished his beautifully cooked braised lamb. Wendy hated phones at the dinner table. She was strong on that rule. Joe felt his phone buzz again in his pocket. Despite Wendy's glare, he took out his phone and had a look at the number.

It was Casey. He answered the call.

"Dad," she whispered. "Someone is sneaking around the vineyard."

CHAPTER 52

JOE AND Wendy raced to the vineyard. The two-hour and forty-five minute drive disappeared in one and a half. Wendy kept Casey on the phone the entire time, telling her to hide in the basement of the vineyard until their neighbor, Jack Allen, arrived.

Jack had raced to the vineyard the second Hennessy called him. An older man with grown children, he was as much a part of the land as the vines themselves. He'd arrived at the vineyard within five minutes, followed by his adult son, then another neighbor, gun-loaded and ready to shoot on sight. The police arrived within fifteen minutes of Hennessy calling them and searched the grounds as the sun set. They found no one.

Hennessy roared the car into the vineyard's front yard, skidding to a halt at the front of the homestead.

The neighbors were waiting outside, sitting on the back of one of the trucks, rifles leaning on their shoulders, waiting for anyone to dare and be brave enough to approach Casey.

"Thank you for staying, Jack," Hennessy shook his neighbor's hand. "I really appreciate it. You too, Tom. Thank you for getting here so quickly."

"Anytime, Joe. What are neighbors for if we can't protect our daughters?" Jack tucked his shotgun under his arm and nodded. "She's inside. She's a bit shaken up, but she's ok. We didn't see anyone, but we found a fresh footprint in the mud. Looked like a city-man's shoe, not a boot. Could've been a guy working today, or it could've been someone sneaking around."

"Could've been a werewolf," Tom joked. "It's a full moon tonight."

They laughed a little, and talked a little while longer, before Jack and his son got into their trucks and drove away. They offered to stay and protect Casey, but Hennessy assured them that he could take it from there.

Casey was shaken. She explained that while she was alone at home, as the sun was setting behind the hills, she saw a man sneak past the kitchen window. She was sure it was a man. She heard someone try to open the front door, but it was locked. Wendy calmed her, while Hennessy took a rifle and flashlight to search the grounds.

The mountains loomed in the background under the moonlight, standing strong like they were guarding the area. As he searched the grounds, he heard a branch snap in the distance. He approached the sound, but found nothing. He figured it was an animal, perhaps even the elusive mountain lion.

After sweeping the grounds, he stepped back inside the home. It was after 11pm, and the full moon was shining brightly.

"Anyone there?" Wendy asked. "Any sign of anybody?"

"I couldn't see anything. I'll be able to see more in the daylight," Hennessy said. "But that doesn't mean there wasn't anyone out there."

"Casey is sure that she saw someone right outside the kitchen. She said that he was staring in the window. She's pretty shaken up."

"She knows where the guns are, doesn't she?"

"Joe, she's sixteen. She doesn't want to walk around the house with a gun."

Hennessy drew a long breath, his fists clenched tight.

"Who do you think it is?" Wendy asked. "We're too far out of town for some lost person to be wandering around."

"I don't even want to think about it," Joe said, leaning the rifle against his shoulder. "We'll lock the house up and see if he's still around in the morning."

He walked into the living room, placed the gun by the couch, and sat down.

"Joe," Wendy whispered from the hallway. "Joe."

Hennessy stood and approached her. "What is it?"

"The man," Wendy said. "I just saw him walk past the window."

CHAPTER 53

HENNESSY PICKED up the rifle and stood in the hallway while Wendy went to retrieve another weapon. She took it from the locked cupboard.

"Wait until I call the cops," Wendy pleaded when she returned. Casey was a step behind. "They'll be here soon. They'll be less than fifteen minutes away."

"And then what? The man will be gone, just like before. And where does that leave us? We'll be worried for days." He checked the rifle. "No, this person wants something. That's the only reason they're here, and if we don't deal with it now, they'll keep coming back."

Wendy reached up and kissed him on the cheek, followed by a hug from Casey. He nodded, and then moved to the side door of the house. "Lock the door behind me."

Quietly, cautiously, he stepped out the door, into the darkness. He heard Wendy click the door lock.

He scanned the fields. The moonlight was bright, and shapes were visible in the distance. He stepped forward, under the cover of a nearby tree, staying out of sight of any potential assailant. He walked to the edge of the vines closest to the house. He heard a noise to his left, near the largest oak tree on the property.

He studied the shadows under the tree.

Hennessy caught the reflection of something in

the darkness. He crouched down. It was the shadow of a man. Hennessy moved towards the tree, circling around the back.

He took his time to move closer. He stopped a hundred yards away.

As his eyes focused, the silhouette of a man became clearer.

The man was crouching on one knee in the shadow of the tree, watching the lights in the house.

Hennessy circled around him, careful not to make a sound.

Seventy-five yards.

He aimed the rifle, setting his sights on the shadow.

He crept forward. The man stayed crouched on one knee.

Fifty yards.

Still the man watched the front door.

Hennessy stepped forward.

Twenty-five yards.

He set the rifle sight on the man.

Fifteen yards.

"Put the gun down," Hennessy called out. "And no sudden movements."

The man stood slowly, his handgun gripped in both hands, and turned around.

"Cruise," Hennessy grunted. "I knew it was you."

"I didn't expect you to sneak up on me like that, Joe. I didn't think you were the type of guy to take a cheap shot."

"Put the gun down."

"I won't do that," Cruise kept the gun in front of him, holding it at hip height, pointed towards the ground. "This isn't going to end well for you, Joe."

"Why are you here?" Hennessy kept the rifle trained on Cruise. "This is my home."

"You should've known I would come for you, Joe," Cruise stepped forward, coming out from the shadows into the moonlight. "I was never going to let you get away with what you did to me."

"So you threaten my family?"

"Is that why you think I came here? To threaten them? No, Joe. I came for you," Cruise said. "You think I would just let you try to take me down without getting my revenge? I've lived my life destroying people that have crossed me, and now I'll destroy you."

Hennessy kept his rifle trained on Cruise.

Cruise kept his handgun in front of him.

"Did you hire Bates to track me?"

"Of course," Cruise laughed. "Bates was supposed to make sure that you never found out that it was him who stabbed Andre. That was the deal." Cruise kept the gun steady in his hands. "We heard that Andre planted the paintings in my gallery. I had to exact revenge on him. I had to make an example of him, to show that I'm not a man that people can mess with. Just like I'm going to make an example of you. That's how I survived my whole life, and that's how I'm going to keep surviving."

"Why didn't you tell me before the trial that Andre was the one who planted the paintings?"

"Because we had no evidence. All we had was the word of a drug addict that Andre said he did it. And I knew that you'd get me off."

"And Longhouse? What happens to him?"

Cruise lowered his gun, just a little. "I'm surprised that you and he are still talking."

"Why?"

"He knew."

"He knew what?"

"About Luca. All those years ago, Richard Longhouse knew what happened to your son."

Hennessy struggled to hold in his rage. He gripped his gun tighter.

"You didn't know that, did you?" Cruise shook his head. He took another step closer to Hennessy. "You still don't know what happened to Luca, do you? You don't know why it happened?"

Hennessy didn't respond. Cruise was enjoying tormenting his foe. Cruise smiled, waited a moment, and then raised his weapon a little.

They stared at each other, both waiting for any sudden movements.

The faint hum of sirens echoed in the distance. Cruise looked to the valley and saw the swirl of red and blue lights.

"You called the cops?" Cruise said. "Come on, Joe. We had to sort this out—man to man. You and me. I'm disappointed that you called the boys in blue."

Hennessy didn't budge. The weapon remained trained on Cruise's torso.

"Now what?" Hennessy looked down the barrel of the rifle.

"Now we get to test if you're a man or not," Cruise said. "And I'm betting that you're not. You see, there's something about shooting another man that tests a soul. And I don't think you've got it in you."

Hennessy gripped the rifle tighter, keeping it focused on Cruise.

Cruise paused for a long moment before he quickly lifted his handgun.

And then a shot rang through the air.

CHAPTER 54

"LET HIM in," Hennessy grunted as he placed the phone down.

He sat in his office and waited for Richard Longhouse to enter. Longhouse walked in and stood behind the chair in front of Hennessy's desk. He was dressed in a black and white suit. His hair was combed, and he was clean-shaven.

"You really killed Cruise? You really took it that far?" Longhouse's face was furrowed. "I'm going to his funeral now, but I thought I'd come past here first and see if you'd like to come with me. But I guess you're not coming. I suppose that's understandable, considering that you put a bullet in the old man's chest."

Hennessy didn't respond.

He'd spent five days at the vineyard after the shooting. The cops took him in, questioned him, but cleared him of any wrongdoing, noting the Castle Doctrine, and that Hennessy had acted in self-defense.

"The case is over, Joe. You can relax. Henry Cruise is about to be put six feet under," Longhouse said. "And I suppose we have you to thank for getting rid of the old criminal. I tried my best to get rid of him, but you blocked that. There were a lot of people that weren't happy when you got Cruise off."

Hennessy narrowed his eyes and leaned forward.

He rested his elbows on his desk.

"But justice has a funny way of being served sometimes, doesn't it?" Longhouse continued. "All these degrees on your wall, all that fighting in court, but in the end, a bullet to the chest does the job just as well."

Hennessy let the words fall to the ground.

"Don't get me wrong," Longhouse continued. "Like I said, I'm grateful. Justice was done. The old fool got what he deserved. But tell me, what evidence did you have in court when you held up that old folder?"

"It was a bluff."

"Of course," Longhouse scoffed. "I should've known. The great Joe Hennessy was just out there using every trick in the book. You fooled me with that one." He shook his head. "And what happened to Jason Norris?"

"I spoke to him yesterday. He's found God, and he's going to spend some time away from Charleston."

"Where is he?"

"I'm not going to tell you that," Hennessy shook his head. "Between Norris, Bates, and Cruise's old records, the police know everything. They know you paid Andre Powers to plant those paintings in the Five Corners. They know you wanted to take down Cruise, but unfortunately, the police don't have enough evidence to charge you."

"Ah," Longhouse waved his finger in the air. "I was wondering about that. I was wondering if they were going to come for me, but that answers my question. I get to fight another day, don't I?"

"My only question is, why did you put those three

Stephen Scully paintings in the gallery?"

"Who says they were mine?" He opened his arms wide and shrugged. "But hypothetically, I guess the owner of those paintings would need to get rid of them. There was about to be a lot of attention thrown on those paintings, and a lot of questions would've been asked by the police. Plus, they were about to become worthless. No artist in history was going to survive the allegations that were about to be aired. The artist spent decades doing horrendous things to young boys. Now, if I was Mr. Mailings in New York, I would pay someone to steal them, then take the insurance payout before the paintings were devalued. If I was Mr. Mailings, I would use someone that I know, someone with the skill set to make it happen. Then the person who helped him would take a substantial cut of the insurance payout as well." He paused and smiled. "But of course, that's all hypothetical."

"Your reputation will take a hit."

"I've survived worse."

Hennessy slowly rose to his feet, his towering frame casting a shadow across the room. He walked to the area next to Longhouse and stared him down.

"Cruise said that you know what happened to Luca." It was a statement, not a question.

"Did he?" A flash of panic spread across Longhouse's face. He paused for a little while before he turned and walked to the door. Halfway out the door, he turned back to Hennessy and whispered, "Joe, I don't know what he's talking about. I had nothing to do with it."

CHAPTER 55

HENNESSY WALKED around the vineyard, checking on the grapes, wandering through the land. He drove the tractor over to the sheds and talked to the workers for a while. They were happy with the season and how well the grapes were growing. But we need a new fence on the west corner, one said. And one of the tractors isn't starting, another said. Joe smiled. He had some time to tinker with the tractor, and he liked getting under the engine.

He thanked them and went to the main shed. He spent an hour under the tractor, twisting and turning, clanging and banging, and after a while, sure enough, the beautiful old John Deere started up first time.

He spent the rest of the day working with the team, moving equipment and fixing irrigation lines. He loved the land. He loved working on it, he loved working with it, and he loved producing something for others to enjoy.

The law had been his passion in his younger years, driven by a desire for justice. That notion, that magical ideal, was smashed after his son was murdered. In the year after Luca's death, he questioned everything and he questioned everyone, until he turned his back on his passion. He couldn't take it anymore. His grief was too much, and he needed to hide it away, tucked under a layer of stoicism.

He spent the day on the land before he returned home to eat dinner with Casey and Wendy, a beautiful homemade thick crust pizza. He then poured a glass of Merlot before moving back to the porch to watch the sunset.

After a while, Wendy sat next to him, just as the sun started to drift behind the mountains.

The evening sky was mostly clear, except for a few clouds gathered on the horizon. A cloud drifted across the sun, casting a shadow across the land, and the sky became covered in a soft pink glow.

"You know, yesterday I saw a guy drop his Scrabble letters on the road," Wendy said as she sat next to Joe. "So I asked him, 'What's the word on the street?'"

Joe smiled.

"And a guy from over yonder came past this week. He asked me if I could help round up nine cows, so I said, 'Yep, that's ten cows,'" Wendy giggled at the joke as she looked out to the sunset.

As the horizon put on a show worthy of a spot on Broadway, Joe looked to Wendy. She looked back at him and reached across, holding his hand. She gripped it tightly. She knew what he was thinking. It was the same thought he always had when he watched the sunset. 'Luca would've enjoyed this,' they often said in those first years. After a number of years, those words fell away, replaced by only a look. They both knew it. They both could feel it. He was up there, looking down, beaming with that innocent smile.

But this time, it felt different. There was something building inside Joe, something that would soon become unstoppable. He wanted to move away from the grief, away from the pain, but he knew it was time to confront it. He could no longer hide from it. He could no longer run.

The sunset had turned from a light pink to a deep red, and the sun's rays were streaming upwards through the gaps in the clouds. The sky looked like a dome above their heads, a cover over the world. The land stretched out before them, the wind gently rustling the trees. As the sun moved behind the mountains, darkness was descending upon the land.

How beautiful the sunset was, Joe thought. How beautiful, and bright, and powerful, and calm, and serene, and fierce. He wished there was one word, just one word, that could describe the beauty of the vast sunset, as no words he knew could do it justice. He could see a hundred miles to the mountains, a hundred miles of rolling landscape, but the land was nothing compared to the sky. So he simply sat and watched. He watched until the sun disappeared behind the hills, until the day turned to night, until his grief began to morph into something else.

"Joe," Wendy whispered. "What are you thinking about?"

"Justice," he said.

"For Luca?"

He nodded. "That's something I need. I know that now."

THE END

JOE AND WENDY WILL RETURN IN 2022

ALSO BY PETER O'MAHONEY

In the Tex Hunter series:

POWER AND JUSTICE
FAITH AND JUSTICE
CORRUPT JUSTICE
DEADLY JUSTICE
SAVING JUSTICE
NATURAL JUSTICE
FREEDOM AND JUSTICE
LOSING JUSTICE

*****

In the Jack Valentine Series:

GATES OF POWER
THE HOSTAGE
THE SHOOTER
THE THIEF
THE WITNESS

Printed in Poland
by Amazon Fulfillment
Poland Sp. z o.o., Wrocław
09 December 2022

5677e938-9d2f-40d5-b01e-dcfb92093688R01